Dance Steps

By

Don Harris

W & B Publishers
USA

W & B Publishers
For information:
W & B Publishers
9001 Ridge Hill Street
Kernersville, NC 27284

www.a-argusbooks.com

ISBN:9781635543780

Book Cover designed by Dubya

Printed in the United States of America

Prologue

Donald Emmerson was just an average Southern kid growing up in the '60s. He was smart, but not real smart. Donald, known as Donno to a few people, wasn't a bad looking boy, but his looks weren't anything special either. Although tall and slender with a runner's build, he didn't play any sports, not even little league baseball. Donno was just an average kid with only three things going for him — he could dance a little, was a pretty good artist, and had a pest neighbor girl who pushed him to be more than the low expectations his father had for him.

Chapter 1

They glided across the floor like they were on ice skates—small, smooth steps and their feet never left the floor. Almost always connected between his left hand and her right, he spun, she twirled, she smiled and he winked a sexy wink. He took her in his arms and spun her around two or three times, never missing the beat of the music and then returned to holding her right hand with his left.

The dancers' moves were in perfect unison with the music and they looked like they had been dancing together forever. The rest of us standing around the pavilion walls had never seen dancing like that before. If we danced at all, it was an awkward attempt at the "Twist" or the "Stroll." Even the older kids nodded at the couple in appreciation.

One of the local girls proudly announced that the guy was her cousin from Walterboro, South Carolina and the girl was his college sweetheart from Columbia. The dance they were doing was called the shag. They had come to our town in the mountains because a tropical storm was headed to Myrtle Beach and closed the country club where they were working as life guards.

To my tortured, 14-year-old, insecure psyche, the guy was a god and his partner was his goddess queen. He wore a short sleeve yellow knit shirt with an alligator on the front, starched khakis, shiny penny loafers and no socks. She wore her own penny loafers, tan Bermuda shorts, and a sleeveless yellow blouse with a lady bug on the front rather than an alligator like her boyfriend's. There, in front of us on the pavilion dance floor, they were in living color, more real than the couples we watched do the "Twist" or "Watusi" every week in black and white on American Bandstand. Their dance reminded me a little of the old black and white movies from the 1940s I had seen on TV of people doing a dance called the jitter bug, except it wasn't jerky and fast. It was slower and way smoother. The god and goddess were tanned, blonde, graceful and self-assured. They awed all of us at the Milton Hills Community Pool upstairs snack bar and pavilion.

Our little town of West Ashton was actually part of the much larger city of Ashton. However, West Ashton was pretty much a stand-alone community, separated from the big city by a river and economics. Ashton proper was where the bankers, lawyers, doctors, shoe store owners and country club members lived. West Ashton was where the one chair barber shop owners lived along with welders, mechanics, school teachers and paper mill workers who lived with their non-purebred dogs, always tired wives and about a million kids born between 1946 and 1962.

West Ashton was once an independent incorporated town with its own mayor, city hall, police force and fire department. Then the Great Depression forced the town to merge with the folks across the river. In addition to the community pool, West Ashton had a two mile long main street, two movie theatres, a church on every street corner and a drug store with a soda fountain on every block. There were a bunch of mom and pop stores and an A&P on one end of Main Street and a Winn-Dixie on the other. Both closed on Sundays. We had two elementary schools and one junior high. By the time we were in the seventh grade, every teenager in West Ashton knew each other. We really didn't think we were from the wrong side of the river. West Ashton was a safe, mostly white, mostly lower middle class, small town. It was a perfectly okay home town, because we really didn't know any better.

Although we sometimes went across the river with our parents to eat dinner at a place named The Crystal Cafeteria or buy school clothes at one of the big chain department stores, we kids didn't really need to cross the river until we enrolled in the tenth grade at the only senior high in the whole city. It was located in Ashton proper.

Once West Ashton kids reached 16, could drive and figured out that the kids their age from Ashton weren't all that different except for the size of their houses and the age of their cars, they spent a lot more time across the river. That's because Ashton was where the drive-ins and most popular cruising drags were located. There was even a drive-in hamburger and pizza joint that boasted a broadcast studio for the only rock and roll radio station in the county. *Big WASH AM – 1300 on your radio dial* broadcast from the *Rockin' Tower of Rhythm* from six o'clock until ten o'clock Monday through Saturday nights. On Sundays, the station switched to classical music from nine until one and then to country music until ten.

For me, growing up in West Ashton was a little like the lives led by the kids on *Father Knows Best, Leave It to Beaver*, and *My Three Sons* except that for most of us, our fathers didn't come home in suits and ties like the dads on the TV shows. They certainly didn't resemble Ozzie Nelson on *The Adventures of Ozzie and Harriet*. Ozzie was always at home with no visible means of support but was always well dressed in a cardigan sweater and golf shirt. *The Adventures of Ozzie and Harriet* was a favorite among the West Ashton girls because of Ricky Nelson, the youngest boy in the family and a real heart-throb for any girl under 16.

Unlike the TV dads, our fathers came home in sweaty work shirts and steel-toe boots from their jobs at the paper mill just outside of town. They always smelled of rotten eggs from the sulfur used in the paper manufacturing process. Our fathers were privates and sergeants in the war and they drove used Chevys and Fords, or International or GM pick-ups like my daddy's and not new Buicks or Chryslers. The primary mode of transportation for kids under 16 was a bicycle — usually a J.C. Higgins single-speed from Sears that was handed down from an older sibling.

The social life in West Ashton for teenagers who were too young to drive consisted of either going to the movies on Saturdays at one of the two theatres, playing in or watching the youth baseball games on the field behind one of the elementary schools or harassing the soda fountain boys at one of the drugstores. We went to junior-high sock hops even though most of the younger kids didn't dance. Sock hops really were "sock hops." The coaches didn't want street shoes messing up the gym floor so everybody had pull off their shoes and pile them up at the door. White was the preferable color for socks for both boys and girls, but a few fashion leaders wore pink, yellow, or blue to match the color of their shirts.

Every other Saturday night during the school year, chaperones played 45 RPM records by Chubby Checker, Sam Cooke, Little Eva, The Contours and Mary Wells at the teen center below the fire station on Main Street.. I doubt any of us ever saw the irony in the fact that much of the music we liked was sung by black people, but we never saw a Black face at the teen center, the swimming pool or at school. At the teen center, just like at the sock-hops and at the pool, a few brave kids danced but mostly we stood around the wall and watched. The girls stood on one side and the boys on the other. The girls talked to each other and acted like they couldn't care less that the boys were looking over at them. The boys, between rounds of running combs through their Brylcreem-plastered hair and mock-boxing bouts, checked out the girls to see if they were looking their way. The non-dancing dance lasted until about eight o'clock. At 7:50, the chaperones played one last song that was usually a slow one — something like "Theme From A Summer Place," "Moon River," or "Wonderland by Night." A couple of boys, ones who had been building up their courage all night, finally asked a girl to dance. Slow dancing was a whole lot less threatening than fast dancing because you could stand in one place and rock back and forth to the rhythm of the music without actually moving your feet.

Sometimes you could act like you really weren't serious about dancing by just standing there talking to your partner while rocking back and forth. If the girl happened to put her head on the boy's shoulder, he was obligated to be a bit more active while keeping his eyes closed. If the boy and girl both kept their eyes closed, they immediately became an item for all of the wall-standing girls to gossip about and for the wall-standing boys to make plans to kid their buddy about "going steady with a girl" on the way home.

Chapter 2

During the hot days of summer, the Milton Hills Community Pool and upstairs pavilion was Mecca for every white kid in West Ashton from age eight to eighteen. No one's house was air-conditioned back then, so going to the pool was a respite from the heat. However, the water in the pool was unheated and always ice cold. In just a few minutes, it turned everyone blue who was brave enough to swim. After a quick splash, we either tried to warm back up by sitting in the sun beside the pool or we went upstairs. The pavilion was on the second floor of the bath house and open around the sides with no windows. You could sit on the brick wall and watch people down in the pool. There was a snack shop that served Cheerwine, RC Cola, Pepsi, burgers, hotdogs, crinkle fries and Moon Pies. You could also get something called a Twinkie Bar. It was vanilla ice cream on a stick with bits of peanuts imbedded in the chocolate coating. Because of the heat, you had to eat Twinkie Bars in a hurry. Often, puddles of melted Twinkie Bars spotted the dance floor.

Mrs. Bronson ran the snack shop and was sort of the chaperone for the pavilion. The kids knew that she would call their parents if they got too rowdy and parents trusted Mrs. Bronson to keep the kids in line. The pool and pavilion were great babysitters for the West Ashton mothers. Except for the 12-year-old boys who spent their time ogling fully developed 17- year-old girls in two piece bathing suits, the main attraction for everyone else was the jukebox. Songs cost a nickel for one and a quarter for six. The records were updated every few weeks so we could hear some of the latest tunes without having to buy the record ourselves or wait to hear them on the radio. There were also some really old songs that seldom got played, yet were never changed. The juke box was never silent for very long. The younger kids stood around the edges and watched the older kids dance.

It was on the last day of August of 1962 at the Milton Hills Community Pool upstairs pavilion when my outlook on life and my future changed. As I watched a god and goddess do a dance called the shag, I also saw envy in the eyes of the local boys and admiration in the eyes of the local girls. I decided if I could learn to do the shag, it would be my ticket to popularity and adoring girlfriends. I was anything but self-assured. I was not a particularly good student and I had failed to make the football or square dance teams, both of which were prerequisites for being allowed into the popular group in junior high. I was also a complete bumbling fool when it came to girls. My arm pits started leaking, I stuttered and I always worried that my zipper was down when I was around one, especially if they were a ninth grader or a cheerleader. I thought it would look cool and debonair if I could be as smooth and as self-assured as the South Carolina boy with the shiny loafers. Boys would envy me, and girls would smile at me in the cafeteria line and invite me to sit at their table. I would also have my choice of dance partners without having to ask. The arm pit sweats and zipper worries would surely end. The shag could be my ticket to the top of the social structure.

At the time, the only girl who ever expressed any interest in me was goofy little Sarah Jane Allison, my pest of a next door neighbor. Sarah Jane and I were born four days apart and always had to celebrate our birthdays at the same time. She was about four and a half feet tall with skinny legs, a bunch of freckles, thick glasses and bright red hair usually tied up in a haphazard ponytail. She looked like she was 10-years old instead of 14. Worst of all was the fact that Sarah Jane's mother and my mother were best friends and the two of them were determined that Sarah Jane and I should be boyfriend and girlfriend. Sarah Jane thought so too.

Sarah Jane and her mother moved in with her grandmother next door to us when Sarah Jane was three or four. Her daddy was killed in Korea. Turns out he had been in the Army during World War II and was called back up when the Korean War started. My daddy was in the Marines during World War II. He didn't talk about it much and I might not have ever known about it if it weren't for the black and white picture on the mantle of a younger him in uniform with his arm around a much younger version of my mother. Daddy wasn't called up to go to Korea. When that war started, he already had two kids and was too old to fight again. I figured that's why my mother and father sort of looked after Sarah Jane and her mother. Sarah Jane's daddy went to Korea instead of my daddy. Being next door neighbors and our mothers being close friends meant Sarah Jane and I were always around each other. When we were real little, we shared baby sitters, and in school through the sixth grade, we were always in the same class. By the time I turned 12, Sarah Jane was a nuisance and I tried to avoid being seen with her when I could.

Chapter 3

The only two things I had going for me was a pretty good sense of rhythm and a little art talent. I could do simple dances like the "Twist and Jerk" in front of my mirror at home without looking like a complete klutz. Both dances were perfect for klutzy kids because you could get by with just standing in one place and not moving your feet. Moving feet, arms and hips all at the same time was tough on klutzes. I was probably in the upper half of the boys at the pavilion when it came to the "Twist" just because I could keep time with the beat of the music.

I could also draw pictures of hot rods and sports cars. Drawing cool cars won me approval from other nerdy kids like me. A couple of the ninth graders who had a failed a grade or two and were almost old enough to drive actually paid me a quarter each to draw a hot rod driven by a sexy looking girl with long flowing hair on their notebooks or the brown paper book covers people made out of grocery bags. My drawing ability did land me a spot on the school newspaper and yearbook staffs. Both publications featured my drawings of '57 Chevys, old '32 Fords and a bad rendition of a Runnin' Rebel, our school mascot.

On that fateful day in August, Sarah Jane was standing next to me and I was so mesmerized by the shag dancers that I almost missed that she was just as mesmerized as me. She was moving her feet in the same steps as the dancers out on the floor. I could hear her counting "one and two, three and four, five six" as she shuffled her bare feet back and forth. She even held out her right hand as if her phantom partner was holding it. Sarah Jane was teaching herself the shag standing right there wrapped in a towel with pool water still dripping off of her wild red ponytail. When she looked up at me and smiled, I knew she was planning something. She was always planning something that involved me.

"Donno, we are going to learn to do this. Wouldn't that be just super cool?"

My parents had stuck me with the name Donald Oskar Emmerson after my Swedish great-grandfather. My big sister Becky pinned Donno on me as a nickname when I was a baby. It was okay until the third grade. After that, I hated it. I got kidded a lot and kids started calling me "Don't Know Emmerson." I preferred just plain Don like Don Everly of the Everly Brothers, but I would answer to Donnie too. Almost everyone had dropped Donno by the time I got to junior high except my family and Sarah Jane. I was certain she did it to irritate me. "Whada you mean *we*, Sarah Jane? What makes you think I would ever want to dance with you?" In the back of my mind, I knew that if I were to ever achieve my goal of being the smooth talking, smooth dancing shagger I envisioned, I would eventually have to learn with a real live girl instead of the make believe one with a refrigerator handle or bed post substituting for a hand. "Hey, and I've told you not to call me Donno in front of other people." I looked around to see if anyone noticed. They were all too interested in the show the dancers were putting on. Even Sarah Jane had gone back to mimicking their steps.

None of us had ever heard the song the couple was dancing to. We had no idea it was even on the juke box. It must have been buried far away from "The Twist," "Johnny Angel," and "The Peppermint Twist" that were played the most that summer. The lyrics to "Sixty Minute Man" meant nothing to us until we heard it three or four times over the next couple of days. Mrs. Bronson never realized the lyrics were dirty. She thought that the dance the nice young couple from South Carolina was doing was preferable to some of the rear-end shaking that the Twistproduced or the "too close" slow dance some of the older kids did to Ray Charles and "I Can't Stop Loving You." Of course, Mrs. Bronson favored Pat Boone, Connie Francis and Tennessee Ernie

Ford songs. There was a rumor going around that she kept a pocket full of quarters so she could keep the jukebox playing songs she thought were appropriate instead of what we wanted to hear. We overcame that by pooling our quarters and playing 12 songs in a row when we got the chance. Another rumor said that she didn't like to hear us play any songs by "colored" singers. Her greatest fear was that playing Black music would somehow bring Black kids to the pool and her pavilion. She just couldn't have that. I guess her hearing wasn't good enough to tell the difference between a Black voice and a white one. More than half the songs on the jukebox were sung by Black people.

Big WASH 1300 on your radio dial was the only rock and roll station I could get on my little transistor radio, but I never heard it play any music that sounded like the "Sixty Minute Man" that the South Carolina god and goddess had used. There were two other radio stations in our county besides WASH. There was a religious one that was owned by some evangelist. It broadcast his sermons from 9:00 a.m. until 7:00 p.m.. That was my grandmother's favorite. She was my mother's mother and she lived with us. Another station was mostly news and weather reports. We had to listen to that one in the winter to know when the schools were closed due to snow. My father liked that one because there was a show that came on around 8:00 p.m. that talked about how Communists were infiltrating the labor unions. Daddy had transferred his hatred of the Japanese he fought in the war to Communists, especially Russian Communists.

Big WASH broadcast from Buster's Burgers drive-in restaurant across the river. Kids drove under the *Rockin' Tower of Rhythm* and honked their horn. The DJ lowered a bucket and the kids wrote a song request on a pad. The DJ pulled the bucket back up and would play the requested song sometime during the night. The requests usually sounded something like this: "That was "Peppermint Twist" by Joey Dee and the Starlighters sent out by Tommy Hawkins in his hot Rambler American to that special someone in Mrs. Blankenship's home room."

Big WASH also took requests over the phone. We only had one phone and it was down stairs in the front hall. Around 8:30 on the Friday evening after I was so impressed with the shaggers at the pavilion, I snuck downstairs to use the phone and saw that Daddy and Mama were watching *The Flintstones*. We got three stations but only one clearly unless Daddy got on the roof and adjusted the antennae. The clear station is what we watched all the time and *The Flintstones* came on at 8:30 on Fridays. I dialed the *Big Wash* request line and the DJ answered on the second ring.

"Yo! This is Swingin' Bobby bringin' you the *Big WASH* Friday night dance party sponsored by Buster's Burgers. What's your pleasure, my fine radio listener?"

"Please play "Sixty Minute Man" and dedicate it to the dancers from South Carolina. Dedicated by Don from the west side."

"Whoa! That's an oldie-moldy and I'm not sure the boss in charge will let me play it on the air. It's kind of, uh rowdy if you know what I mean. Hey, but Swingin' Bobby will do his best for ya, Donnie my man."

Wondering what was rowdy about "Sixty Minute Man," I was halfway back up the stairs on the way to turn my radio back on (you can't leave them on too long if you're not listening because the batteries die) when Daddy yelled, "Donno, you comin' down to watch *The Flintstones*? It's the one where Barney drops a bowling ball on Fred's foot."

In the summer time, even *The Flintstones* were reruns. "Uh, no, Pops. I uh, I'm uh, working on something. Be down later."

"Well, okay, but we're not saving you any popcorn." Eating popcorn during TV shows was a ritual for our family and it was my father's job to pop it. He poured oil and corn kernels into a metal basket that had a wire screen top and long handle. He then shook the basket over one of the glowing red eyes of our stove until the corn popped and filled the basket. With a victory shout of "There's a good batch!." he would divide the contents of the basket into bowls that were assigned to the different members of the family who happened to be around. It was up to the owners of each bowl to determine how much salt and the melted butter that had been simmering on another eye would be added to their bowl. Each bowl lasted about the same amount of time as the length of the program we were watching. My favorite part was licking the melted butter off my fingers once I finished my bowl.

I listened to three other songs before DJ Swingin' Bobby got to my request. "My man Don from across the river on the west side requested an oldie called "Sixty Minute Man" for some dancers from South Carolina. I'm guessin' those dancers are doin' a thing called the shag. Sorry, Donnie boy, can't put that one on the airways, but try this one on for size. It's got a little of that shag beat you're lookin' for. It's new from a cat named Gene Chandler. Give a listen to "Duke of Earl."

The DJ was right. The song had sort of the same beat as "Sixty Minute Man". Or at least it did when I awkwardly tried to remember the shag steps I had seen. With my left hand on my bed post, I tried to move with the same silky smoothness I had admired by the dancers at the pavilion. I soon realized that rubber soled tennis shoes were not made for shagging. Before I could take them off, Swingin' Bobby interrupted, "Duke of Earl with another request—"Hope you shaggers out there did your thing to West Side Don's request. Now, all you love birds parking up on Mistletoe Overlook get close and personal to "Can't Help Falling in Love" by the king himself, Mr. Elvis Pressley. It is requested by Carolyn D. for her soldier boy Herbert W. who is on his way to basic training at Fort Jackson."

Chapter 4

The next day was Saturday and I had to cut the grass — one of my regular chores that my father said gave me a sense of responsibility. He also said that the old manual push mower gave me character and built up my endurance. I doubted both of those things after it took me two hours to finish the yard when a gas-powered mower would have done the job in half that time.

After a quick bath and a peanut butter sandwich, I rode my bike to the pool. I didn't even bring my bathing suit because instead of swimming I wanted to go directly up stairs to see if the god and goddess dancers were back. When I got near the top of the steps, I heard the unmistakable sound of Pat Boone singing "Moody River." I figured Mrs. Bronson must have played that one. I knew the shaggers wouldn't be dancing to that, but thank goodness, they were there, leaning against the half-wall and drinking Pepsis out of the bottles with straws. The way they were dressed was even more impressive than the day before. They wore different, but color coordinated Madras shirts, khaki Bermuda shorts and penny loafers with no socks. How much cooler could they possibly get?

I came to watch them dance again and hopefully absorb some of their coolness just by being near them. I also wanted to see them dance to "Duke of Earl" like I had tried to do in my bedroom the night before. My weekly allowance was seventy five cents, which I received on Saturdays after I finished my chores. I was willing to invest two of my three quarters that Saturday morning — one for a Pepsi and a Baby Ruth Bar and the other for songs on the juke box to which the god and goddess dancers would shag.

I was searching through the song selections as Pat Boone finished singing a peppy ballad about his unfaithful girlfriend jumping into a muddy river. I never could figure out why Mrs. Bronson liked that song so much. Finally, I found "Duke of Earl" and had already dropped my quarter into the slot and was about to push J55 when goofy Sarah Jane suddenly appeared beside me.

"You know they don't like " Duke of Earl."

"What?"

"Chad and Ginger, the shaggers, they don't like "Duke of Earl"."

With my finger still poised over J55, I asked "Wait, how do you know that and how do you know their names?"

"Well, do do Donno, I heard your request on the radio last night. And so, I got here early and waited to see if they came back today. I asked them if they liked " Duke of Earl."

I looked over at the dancers, now with the god and goddess names of Chad and Ginger, wondering if I had offended them by dedicating a song to them that they didn't like. "Boy, Sarah Jane, you are a real pain. You know that?" That was the only thing I could think to say after she destroyed my hopes of watching the shaggers dance to a song with a beat I could almost follow.

"Well, they said they like it okay, but it's not beach music."

"Beach music? What do you mean beach music?"

Sarah Jane flashed her know-it-all smirk. "Oh, you are such a dumb dumb. You know the dance they do? The shag? That's where it all started, down around Myrtle Beach."

I still couldn't figure out the connection between the dance I wanted to learn and a South Carolina beach. I had never even seen the ocean and wondered how it could inspire a dance. I thought about that for a second until I looked around. The other kids were beginning to stare at me because the juke box had been silent for more than a minute and I was next in line to play some tunes. I had already dropped my quarter in the machine, so I had to play something. "Okay, smarty farty, what do they like?"

"I asked them that too. Punch L42, 'It Will Stand' by the Showmen, C22 'Hey Baby' by Bruce Channel, A26 'Stubborn Kind of Fellow, by Marvin Gaye, and R15 'Sixty Minute Man' by the Dominoes." Chad and Ginger say those are about the only good shag songs on this juke box. You can pick whatever you want for your other two." With that, Sarah Jane strutted over to her new best friends, Chad and Ginger.

I did as I was told and punched in the numbers for the four songs Sarah Jane said would bring the dancers to the floor. Just to spite her, I punched in "Duke of Earl" two times to finish my six selections.

Sure enough, as soon as the first notes of "It Will Stand" came out of the juke box speakers, Chad gave me the thumbs up sign and grabbed Ginger's hand. Just like the day before and just like Moses and the parting of the sea, the other kids moved to open up the dance floor. A shaft of sunlight suddenly illuminated a spot on the dance floor where the god and goddess stood arm in arm, preparing to take their first dance steps. Chad held Ginger close for a moment and then with the grace and coolness possessed only by those special few who have a direct connection to Mount Olympus, he twirled her away from him twice. At the end of the second spin, he caught her right hand in his left and brought her back into a close hold. I joined all of the other kids with appreciative "oohs and ahs."

When "It Will Stand" ended, Ginger and Chad actually took a bow to a smattering of applause. In a minute, "Hey! Baby" came on with the couple still standing in the middle of the dance floor surrounded by 20 or so other kids. The song was faster but so were the dance steps. There were more spins, twirls, fancy footwork and sexy expressions, especially by Chad. The applause was louder.

When "Stubborn Kind of Fellow" came up, Ginger waved her hand and told Chad she needed to cool off. Then, to my dismay, Chad turned to Sarah Jane and asked her to dance. I couldn't help myself and shouted out loud, "Oh no! Please no! She will never stop bragging about this!" My only hope was for her to make a fool of herself. Maybe she would fall down or throw up on his loafers or something. Of course, she was nowhere near Ginger's level and made some awkward steps, but she could actually keep in step with the rhythm of the song and managed to smile at Chad when he twirled her one last time. He bowed to her and she curtsied to him. I turned away so I didn't have to see her stick her tongue out at me. When "Sixty Minute Man" came up, I looked up to see Sarah Jane walking toward me.

"Come on Donno, let's give it a try." With that, she grabbed my hand and drug me toward the middle of the floor. I was so dumbstruck, that I didn't resist. She said "Remember, it's one and two, three and four, five six."

Sarah Jane was still holding my left hand and I actually tried to remember what she had said about the dance steps and started moving my feet. Suddenly, I came to my senses and saw that all other activity had stopped in the pavilion. Every kid had turned to look at us with their mouths open and their Twinkie Bars melting. I jerked my hand away and slinked back to the wall in hopes that the god and goddess hadn't witnessed any of it.

No one danced to either of my two plays of "Duke of Earl." In a few minutes, Chad and Ginger left the pavilion — the sun stopped shining, the sky grew dark and the birds stopped singing. The god and goddess were gone, but the memory of their glory and the way the other kids were in awe of them stayed with me. I was determined to learn to shag so I could enjoy such awe and payback Sarah Jane for embarrassing me in front of my idols.

Chapter 5

The god and goddess left us mortals on Saturday. The next day was Sunday and there was no dancing or wearing of bathing suits on the Sabbath so the pool and pavilion were closed. The fine folks at the Baptist churches insisted on that. Monday was Labor Day which was the last day the pool and pavilion would be open before school started. Mrs. Bronson went all out for that last day. There were banners and balloons hanging all around and except for hotdogs and hamburgers, the food and drinks were free. I figured that any candy and canned drinks not consumed on Labor Day would reappear next Memorial Day, a little stale. Best of all, Mrs. Bronson fixed the juke box so every song was free.

The dance floor was packed with all ages of dancers. There were the 17 and 18-year-old rising high school juniors and seniors who were the best dancers. Then there were the 16-year-old rising sophomores who were trying to act like they were 17 or 18 and their dancing was more chaotic and uncoordinated. As usual, not many of us rising ninth graders, or any of the junior high age kids danced. Mostly we just stood around, tapping our feet, nodding our heads and acting like we were too cool to dance or had something really important to talk about with the other non-dancers. Then there were the little kids — first grade up to fifth. They didn't worry about being cool or what anyone else thought about their dancing. They just danced for fun, mostly trying to do the twist, no matter what song was playing.

I got my free Milky Way and Pepsi and parked myself along the half wall right at the edge of a group of other rising ninth graders who were all part of the popular crowd. I really wasn't part of the group and wasn't included in their conversations, although I laughed when they laughed without knowing about what. I just didn't want to be seen standing all alone.

Because the juke box was free, there was a crowd gathered around it choosing songs. Most of the buttons pushed was some variety of tune for doing the twist, locomotion, Watusi or mashed potato, all of which were popular because of seeing them on *American Bandstand.* Only a few could do the dances anything like those superstars we watched dance on TV. Of course, *Bandstand* was broadcast from Philadelphia, Pennsylvania. We never saw them doing a dance that originated in the South.

After hearing "Let's Twist Again" by Chubby Checker, "Do You Love Me" by the Contours and "Peppermint Twist" by Joey Dee and the Starliters about ten times in a row, I sort of blocked out the music and tried to move closer to the bunch of popular kids so I could hear what they were saying and so I could laugh or nod at the appropriate times. All of a sudden, the music changed and the dancers stopped twisting. Someone had punched the number for "Sixty Minute Man." Sarah Jane was at it again.

I guess she knew I would make another scene if she tried to get me to shag with her. Instead, she grabbed another rising ninth grader, Ricky Stillman, by the hand and pulled him out on the floor. I had nothing against Ricky. He lived one block from me and once he and I blew up model cars together with fire crackers. Ricky was also a tuba player in the West Ashton Junior High School Marching Band. That meant that he was big and strong enough for bullies not to pick on him too much, but it also meant no one much cared if he got picked on or not. In the social pecking order, junior high tuba players ranked just above kids with thick glasses, braces and pocket protectors.

Ricky was at least six inches taller than Sarah Jane and outweighed her by 50 pounds. Yet, she had no trouble pulling him out to the dance floor and pushing him around so he was facing her with his left hand stuck out in front of him. She took his hand and started to count "one and two, three and four, five six." At first Ricky didn't respond. He just stood there looking confused in his Bermuda shorts, Chuck Taylor high-top sneakers and a too small t-shirt that had *I've been to Rock City* printed in big red letters across the back.

Sarah Jane nearly jerked Ricky's arm out of the socket and scolded him in a spooky threatening voice just like Bette Davis in *What Ever Happened To Baby Jane?.* My mother let me see the movie with my sister only because she thought it sounded like a cute film about baby dolls. I had nightmares for a long time.

"Come on, Ricky. Pay attention! Just move your big fat feet. It's one and two, three and four, five six. Do it now! One and two, three and four, five six." Sarah Jane was brutal.

With fear in his eyes, Ricky looked down at his feet and started to move while whispering "One and two, three and four, five six. One and two, three and four, five six."

Sarah Jane beamed with pride while moving her own feet in rhythm to the song. "That's it Ricky! You're doing the shag."

I guess playing a tuba while trying to walk in a straight line on a football field must have prepared Ricky a little for the ordeal. He actually kept in step with Sarah Jane and "Sixty Minute Man." She even forced him to twirl her once or twice. Sarah Jane smiled, but Ricky had a look on his face like someone who was going to the dentist when they know they have a cavity.

When the song ended, Ricky ran away and didn't notice Sarah Jane making a face at me or hear the popular kids I was standing near laugh out loud at the whole thing.

Chapter 6

School started the Wednesday after Labor Day and I was finally an upper classman — a big ninth grader, the top of the world at West Ashton Junior High. Being ninth graders brought about several transitions from childhood to adulthood. First of all, we could and were expected to harass the incoming seventh graders and still neophyte eighth graders. I didn't carry much weight with other ninth graders but at least most seventh graders thought I was a big shot. Secondly, ninth graders actually changed classes between periods like high school students. That gave us time to go to our lockers and parade up and down the ninth grade wing hallway. Being ninth graders, we were also able to choose from a few "elective" courses in addition to our required math, English, health and history courses. With my mother's encouragement and to my father's dismay, I chose art. Daddy said I should start learning a useful trade and thought wood shop would be more appropriate. He never said much about my drawings and paintings, even when my mother proudly displayed them on the refrigerator. I was sure that when I got to high school, he would insist that I take motor shop or welding as an elective rather than "pansy artsy fartsy" classes. My father was a good man and I'm sure he had my best interests at heart, but his whole view of life for himself and his family was colored by growing up poor during the Depression and the fact that everything he had accomplished in life was because of his ability to fix mechanical things with his hands. He gave credit to the Marines for that because they put him in a tank that always needed fixing.

The first grading period ended in early October and my report card was a topic of family conversations for several days. The Ds in algebra and health were not balanced by the Bs in English and history. My father reminded me that my sister was a whiz in math and that I would need it if I was to ever amount to anything. Neither my mother nor father had much to say about the A in Art. He didn't want to encourage me artistically and she didn't want to rile Daddy. My sister, now a senior at the high school just told me to cry a little and act like I was sorry for everything I did wrong. That would make Mama try to help me even more and would make Daddy think I was working on doing better. I knew algebra was a lost cause. I just couldn't figure out all of the Xs and Ys instead of numbers. I would be lucky to pass it. Because it was required to move on to the tenth grade, I wondered how long they would let me stay in the ninth grade.

I liked English and history and if I tried harder, I could probably make As in them. In health, I figured it would eventually get around to something interesting like sex and stuff and I would be interested. But art, that was different. Even though my art teacher, Mr. Fontain, was a cocky young man who favored the girls, drove a red sports car and disciplined the boys by smacking them over the knuckles with paint brush handles, I looked forward to the class every day. In art, I was expected to be creative. I could experiment with different colors and shapes. There was always a blank piece of paper or canvas ready to use. Best of all, I was pretty good at it — good enough to make the teacher yell at me when I got a little lazy and was good enough for him to use my work as an example for the other students. Though he scared me, Mr. Fontain obviously cared about me and wanted me to take art seriously. He demanded it and I loved that class.

My sister turned 18 in September and for her birthday got a real stereo system with a turn table and separate speakers. She could still play the little 45s she had collected for years but could also play 33 speed, long playing, 20 song albums which she started buying weekly with money she earned as baby sitter and part-time after school checker at the

Winn-Dixie. The money she spent on records was supposed to be saved for dental hygienist school. That was something between her and Daddy to figure out. For me, her new stereo meant that I got her old RCA Victor portable record player she had since she was 14. It came in a pink suitcase sort of thing and only played 45s. That was okay with me. On my allowance, I was certain I couldn't afford to buy albums anyway.

In addition to a big Sears store, there was also an actual standalone record store across the river in downtown Ashton, but that required a long bus ride or talking my father or sister into taking me to either of them. Lucky for me, McMurray's Furniture and Bedding on our little main street in West Ashton had a section in the back corner of the store that sold record players and TVs. It also had a limited selection of 45s and 33s and that made it a resource for West Ashton kids like me who couldn't get to the stores downtown. A few days after I inherited my sister's record player, with three dollars' worth of allowance money in my pocket, I rode my bike to McMurray's, intent on buying some 45s. Because I never had a way to play them in the past, I never looked through what McMurray's record department had to offer. As I thumbed through the 45s, I saw recent releases by Elvis, Connie Francis, Burl Ives, Neil Sedaka, Dion and a lot of the other singers I heard on the radio. That was okay, but I realized that they were all white. There was not a single song by a Black singer or group in the whole bunch.

Mr. McMurray's daughter Britney was standing behind the counter reading a magazine. Britney was a couple of years older than my sister and came back to West Ashton after dropping out of a fancy girls' college down in Raleigh. We didn't have any doctors, lawyers or factory managers in West Ashton, so owners of furniture stores and hardware stores were sort of top of the social pecking order. Mr. McMurray was probably the richest man on our side of the river and he doted on his only daughter. She had a 57 Thunderbird in high school and bought her clothes in Greenville,

SC. When Britney left college, Mr. McMurray put her in charge of the record department at his store until she could get back into college somewhere. She had been leader of the popular group in junior high and that had continued at the high school where she was a majorette and homecoming queen. Everybody in West Ashton followed the comings and goings of the McMurray family and thought of Britney almost as a movie star.

Mama said that Britney had "gotten in trouble" and had to leave college. I didn't know what "in trouble" meant. Grandma said Britney acted like some of the girls in *Peyton Place* I asked Becky what *Peyton Place* was. She told me that it was a book and a movie about some teenagers in a small town up north. She said she would loan me her copy of the book when I got old enough.

My earliest memory of recognizing the differences between boys and girls was when I was about eight-years-old and saw a then 14-year-old Britney in a two piece bathing suit. It was at the pavilion and she was surrounded by at least five or six drooling teenage boys.

Britney looked perturbed when I asked her about the absence of Black music. "Uh, excuse me, Britney, I was sort of looking for uh, uh "The Twist" by Chubby Checker. Don't you have that?" I used Chubby Checker as an example only because I was absolutely sure he was Black because I had seen him on American Band Stand. I wasn't sure of other singers. I didn't necessarily want "The Twist" because my sister had it. But, I figured the shag music I was looking for was mainly recorded by Black singers and if the store had "The Twist," it might also have others.

Britney shook her head and looked at me like I was some sort of foolish child. "Of course we have 'The Twist', dummy. That and 'Peppermint Twist' is what all of you little kids want to hear."

"Uh, oh, well, why isn't it here in the racks?" I got another look of bored disgust.

"Well, you know my Daddy. He doesn't like Nig...I mean, he doesn't like Black music out where his white customers can see it. He calls it race music. I told him he was losing money if he didn't have some Black music. Daddy can't stand to lose money." With that, Britney pulled a big cardboard box from beneath the counter and sat it on top. "Look through these and see if you want any of them." She went back to reading her magazine.

There they were: "Unchain My Heart" by Ray Charles, "Do You Love Me" by the Contours, "Twisten the Night Away" by Sam Cooke, "The Wa-Watusi" by the Orions, "Shout" by the Isley Brothers, and of course, "The Twist" by Chubby Checker. I picked it because that's what I told Britney I wanted and also chose "Do You Love Me." Most of them either had an Atlantic Records or Motown label on them. I had seen the Motown label on a lot of the records on the pavilion juke box. They were good songs, but I really wanted a shag song or two so I could practice. "Uh, excuse me, Britney. I don't want to bother you again. I was also looking for something called 'beach music.' Do you have anything like that?"

Britney looked up and asked "You mean beach, as in South Carolina beach? Like shag music?"

"Uh, yeah. Like 'Sixty Minute Man' or 'Stubborn Kind of Fellow?'" Those were the only two songs I knew for sure were shag tunes.

Britney smiled. "Well what do you know? Somebody in this little hillbilly town knows about the shag." As it turns out, the fancy girls' college where Britney went was one of the places where the shag got started back in the '50s and it was her favorite dance. "Because nobody knows about the shag, I don't even mix them in with other Black music. I have a few 45s you can see." She went to another counter and pulled out another box. "Look at these." Britney's attitude toward me improved dramatically.

Immediately I saw "Stubborn Kind of Fellow" and "Sixty Minute Man" and pulled them out. But there were another 20 or 30 records in the box. Britney came and looked over my shoulder. "Bet you've never heard any of these, have you?"

"I've heard these two and another one called 'Hey! Baby.' They're on the juke box at the pavilion. Nobody ever played them until some college kids from South Carolina showed up and danced. That's what got me interested in it. I want to learn how to shag."

"'Hey! Baby' is in there. It's by Bruce Channel. He's a white guy, but he can sing." Britney pulled out two or three more records. "Shag rhythm songs go way back, back into the early 1950s probably. Here are two by The Drifters: 'Drip Drop' and 'Dance With Me'. Ever heard of Drifters?"

"Uh, no. I've never heard of any of these groups. Never paid much attention to who sings songs anyway. I just listen to *WASH* on my radio or play stuff at the pavilion."

Britney took one of the records out of its paper sleeve and walked over to a record player near the counter. "I've seen The Drifters a couple of times at Black clubs in Raleigh and on a road trip down to Ocean Drive near Myrtle Beach. There's a little club called The Shack. It started out as a hole-in the wall that sold beer, hot dogs, and had a juke box. College kids in the late 40s and early 50s found it and it became the most popular place on the beach. They added a dance floor and a stage for live bands. The best shaggers in the world dance there now. It's sort of the home of beach music and the shag, you know. I saw The Drifters there too. They had a lead singer named Ben E. King. He's a great singer and cute too." Britney fit a record on the spindle and pushed play. This one is 'Dance With Me.' It's one of my favorites."

I was still trying to absorb the notion that Britney thought a Black man was cute when the 45 dropped down on the turn table and the music began to play. The rhythm was different than any of the other shag songs I had heard but I could still feel the beat and I silently counted the steps: *one and two, three and four, five six...one and two, three and four, five six...*

Suddenly, without warning, Britney took my left hand in her right hand. “That’s right, just feel the music — feel the beat. Do the basic steps with me. Count it out, one and two, three and four, five six. One and two, three and four, five six. Now you’ve got it! You’re shagging, little guy.”

In shock and with my mouth open wide and eyes bugging out, I did what she said. Right there in the McMurray’s Furniture and Bedding record department, I was actually dancing with THE Britney McMurray. Together, we sounded out the steps, “One and two, three and four, five six.”

“There you are, little guy. With some practice, you can be a pretty good dancer. Hey, what’s your name, anyway?”

It took me a second or two to remember my name. “Uh, Donald, uh uh Don. Don Emmerson.

“Are you Becky Emmerson’s little brother?”

“Uh huh.”

“I remember her. She was a sophomore when I was a senior. I think she was sweet. I’ll tell you what, Mr. Donald Emmerson, you go home and practice with these records, maybe with your sister or one of your little girl friends. Then come back here and I’ll give you another lesson. I’ve got to get the shag started here in good ole West Ashton. And, tell me, how old are you, Donald?”

I started to lie and say 16, but then I figured she would see my sister somewhere and find out. “I’ll be 15 in a few months.” I guessed that 10 months qualified as a few.

Still in shock, I paid for my four records and started for the door when Britney laughingly said “Remember, come back for a lesson after you have practiced. And uh, you probably shouldn’t let your parents hear you play ‘Sixty Minute Man’. It’s not exactly a Ricky Nelson or Connie Francis tune.”

I rode my bike home, still floating on air with the memory of holding Britney McMurray’s hand and her telling me that I could be a pretty good dancer. It didn't even bother me that she had twice called me "little guy." The promise of going back and dancing again with her reinforced my determination to practice and become a real shagger.

Chapter 7

Over the next couple of weeks, I almost wore away the grooves on all three of the shag records I bought, but my favorite was "Dance With Me." To me, it sounded as if the singer was in love with a girl who hardly knew he was alive — he hoped they would be friends when the music played. He was begging her to dance with him. In my 14-year-old state of mind, the lyrics described me and my relationship with any girl. They were most meaningful because of my crush on Britney McMurray. I had to practice so she would dance with me again.

To practice, I closed my bedroom door, pulled back the rug down to the wooden floor and took off my shoes. I discovered that the steps were easier if your feet could slide. Socks slid better than tennis shoes on a wooden floor.

Once, when I left my door open, my sister Becky stuck her head in and asked, "How many times in a row are you going to play that song?" Then she saw me holding my bedpost. "What in the heck are you doin' anyway, Donno?"

"Oh, leave me alone, Becky. I'm not botherin' you."

Becky paid me no attention and walked on into my room. "No really, what are you doin'?"

"Can't you see? I'm trying to learn how to dance."

She laughed out loud. "With a bedpost? What kind of dance are you tryin' to learn, a sleep walking waltz?" She laughed again.

For a big sister, Becky was actually okay. She didn't pick on me too much and gave me tips on how to manage Mama and Daddy. I decided to let her into my plan. "Well, Miss Nosey, if you really gotta know, I want to learn how to shag."

"Shag? Nobody around here does it. I've barely even heard of it. What brought that on?"

I told her about the god and goddess shaggers at the pavilion and how they seemed to glide through the air and how everybody stopped what they were doing just to watch them dance. I sheepishly told her that I thought that if I could learn to dance like that, girls would like me and bullies would leave me alone at the high school. Then I told her about buying the records at McMurray's and how Britney told me that I might be a good dancer if I practice. "Oh, and Britney said she remembered you and that you were sweet and that you should practice dancing with me."

"Britney McMurray said I was sweet? Hm, what do you think about that? I wouldn't have thought she even knew I existed."

"Mama says Britney left college because she got in trouble."

"I heard that too. Do you know what that means?"

"Not really."

"That's what I figured." With that, Becky walked over to my record player and picked a couple of 45s. "Okay, Mr. Shagger. Show me what you have learned, but let's not hear that record you've been playing night and day. Play this one. It's called uh, 'Sixty Minute Man'".

Becky put the needle down on the record and as it started to play, she grabbed my left hand with her right. "Okay, show me, little brother."

"All I have learned are the basic steps. Watch me and count one and two, three and four, five six. Start with your left foot and move it forward a little bit on *one*. On the *and two*, you move both feet a little in place. On *three and four*, you move them a little bit again. On *five six* bring your left foot back and put your right foot down."

Becky looked at me and shook her head. "You say that is basic? I think the Twistis a whole lot simpler. Show me again."

I put "Sixty Minute Man" back on and grabbed my bedpost again. Awkwardly, I counted out "one and two, three and four, five six" as I moved forward and back almost in rhythm to the music. "I think it really adds up to eight steps if you count the little shuffle step on the *ands*."

Becky stopped me. "Okay, let's try it together. But first, have you listened to the lyrics of that song?"

"Yes."

"Do you know what they are talking about?"

"Uh, sort of."

She shook her head. "I guess you are growing up, aren't you? Okay, okay. Let's try this."

I put the record back on and took Becky's right hand in my left. She nodded and I nodded, and together we counted out the steps while moving our feet back and forth. "One and two, three and four, five six."

Becky, who was very graceful and athletic, got it immediately. "One and two, three and four, five six." Then she twirled me around and counted again, "one and two, three and four, five six."

"Okay, let me twirl you around this time. Let's count. One and two, three and four, five six." On *two*, I lifted my left hand, Becky ducked under it without missing a step and without turning loose of my hand. "Wow, we did it!"

Becky grinned and agreed. "Yep, I think we did."

"Thanks, Beck. You think maybe you can practice with me again some, uh so I won't be such a dummy when I practice with Britney?"

"Well, I guess, a couple of times, but remember it's not too cool for a big sister to spend too much time with her little brother. Maybe you ought to practice with someone your own age. That's who you will be dancing with for real. Maybe Sarah Jane would like to learn to shag too." Becky laughed when I faked a wretch at the mention of dancing with Sarah Jane.

Chapter 8

Stanton Junior High, named for some Confederate general and located in downtown Ashton, was West Ashton Junior High School's fiercest and most hated rival. Stanton was bigger, newer and wealthier than West Ashton Junior High and usually beat us in the annual showdown football game in October. However, West Ashton always used the game, which usually drew as many as 2,000 fans, as a way to motivate and excite the students with a pep rally and parade before the game on Friday, and a sock hop on the Saturday after the game. The 1962 game was scheduled for Friday, October 19th and it was a home game for West Ashton.

About two weeks before the game, Sarah Jane called me and announced that she had been appointed as chairman of the Spirit Committee. I suspected it was a self-appointment and nobody had the courage to argue with her. Sarah Jane had a way of getting involved in something and before anyone knew it, she was in charge and giving orders. Sometimes it back-fired on her and she ended up doing all the work. This time it involved me.

"Donno, guess what. You get to help me make a banner for the pep rally that the team will also run through at the beginning of the game and another one for the sock hop. Isn't that exciting?"

"Uh, what?"

"Well, you are the best artist I know and I promised the head cheerleader that you would be glad to help me."

I doubted that the head cheerleader even knew my name much less that I could draw. I started to hang up, but then thought, maybe, just maybe, some of the popular crowd will know that I did the banners and might allow me to sit with them at the cool table at lunch sometime or hang out with them while waiting for the bus after school. "You said I would be glad to help?"

"Well, I just know you are. I've already got some big sheets of paper and some tempera paint. I thought something like 'Stomp Stanton! Go Runnin Rebels!' would be great for the pep rally and for the team to run through at the game. For decorations for the sock hop, I think a theme of 'Wonderland by Night', like the song, you know. Maybe with a big moon and stars. Won't that be great?"

"Uh, who else is on this spirit committee?"

"Besides you and me, Ricky Stillman said he would help unless he has asthma one day or an orthodontist appointment to adjust his braces. He says his mouth always hurts after an orthodontist appointment. Loraine Biggerstaff said she will check in with us to approve of everything."

Loraine Biggerstaff was the head cheerleader and vice-president of the student council. I figured that head cheerleader sort of out ranked even the chairman of the spirit committee. Knowing Loraine was going to see my artwork swayed my decision to participate. That had to earn me some points with her crowd. "Uh, where are we supposed to do the painting? My basement is flooded again and Mama won't let me do and any kind of art in the living room because of the sofa."

"That's okay. Mr. Fontain said we can stay after school and work in the art room. He even said we can use the school's paint brushes. He did say that we would have to leave the door open so a teacher or janitor can check on us. I guess they can't trust you and me together all alone." She snickered and I did my fake retching thing again.

"You're sure Loraine Biggerstaff is going to know I'm doing this?"

"Sure I'm sure. Would a student council vice president lie about something like that?"

She was probably right. "Okay. I'll do it. When do we start?"

"Tomorrow. Meet me at the art room right after the last bell. And uh, why don't you do a few sketches to make sure you are following my ideas?"

As usual, Sarah Jane was in charge. "Well, I guess I'll do it. Uh, uh, unless something else comes up." Of course I knew nothing else would come up. But I didn't know America was close to a nuclear war with the Soviet Union either.

The next day, Sarah Jane made a few changes to my sketches, but basically she approved of my drawings. After her approval, I painted a football player with the ball and in our blue and white school colors running toward goal posts after stepping on another player in Stanton's red and yellow school colors. There was a big smile on the Runnin' Rebel's face and a look of anguish and pain on the face of the Stanton Stallion player. You could see the expressions because junior high teams had yet to get face masks. Across the top of the banner, I painted STOMP STANTON in big block letters with a bright green snake intertwined among the letters. Snakes had absolutely nothing to do with the football game, but I thought it made the sign more dramatic. I was surprised that Sarah Jane agreed.

For the sock hop "Wonderland by Night" banner, in addition to the words in a gold script, I painted a bunch of stars and a big yellow moon on a dark blue background with the Man In the Moon wearing sun glasses. I told Sarah Jane I got the idea from watching Bobby Darin singing "Mack The Knife" on *The Ed Sullivan Show* a couple of years before. She bought that too.

It took about a week and a half to finish the two banners because we could only work for an hour or so after school before the janitors and teachers wanted to leave. When I draw or paint, I kind of go into a twilight zone and don't really pay much attention to anything else going on around me. Sometimes I also hum and sing while I draw without realizing I'm doing it. I guess because I had listened to it so many times, I sang "Dance With Me" over and over as I worked. After the third day, Sarah Jane finally stopped me.

"Donno, stop that! What are you singing? It is driving me crazy!"

I hardly even knew she was there because all she was doing was sitting and watching me paint. It was my chance to dig at her a little. "Oh, you don't know that song? It's by The Drifters and it's a great shag song. Britney McMurray recommended it. She said she has heard them live a couple of times." Sarah Jane didn't seem as impressed as I had hoped, so I went on. "And you know what? Britney actually gave me a shag lesson and said if I practice, I could be a really good dancer."

Sarah Jane smiled the smile she uses when she thought she's gotten something over on me. "Really? That's wonderful. I've been practicing too. Maybe we can dance together at the sock hop. Why don't you bring that record to play?"

I turned back to the painting without saying a word. In my mind, I thought, *Darn it, how do I let her do this to me every time?*

On the day of the pep rally, Ricky Stillman did show up to help pin the "Stomp Stanton" banner to the curtain on the back of the stage of the auditorium. Of course the only thing he could do was hold the ladder while I struggled to attach the banner and while Sarah Jane fussed at me to move it higher. Ricky said heights gave him nose bleeds.

Loraine Biggerstaff, dressed in her short blue and white cheerleader uniform, did come up on stage and I eagerly waited for her appraisal of my artwork.

She said, "Really, a snake? Oh well, who cares?"

Not many of the students got to see the banner. The football team came up on stage and blocked it before the rest of the school filed into the auditorium.

That night at the game, it started to rain just before the team was to run through the banner. My "Stomp Stanton" artwork and snake turned into nothing but green, blue and red drips, runs and smudges. We lost the game 13 to 6.

No one got to see my "Wonderland By Night" banner either. The sock hop was canceled. While I was worrying about beautiful cheerleaders, banners, ball games and being forced to dance with my pest of a next door neighbor, the rest of the world was on the brink of annihilation. All big events were canceled and people were ordered to stay home. Somebody higher up must have known what was going on and canceled our sock hop.

We didn't get an explanation until Monday when President Kennedy came on the TV. We hadn't known it, but a bunch of guys sponsored by the US failed when they tried to take Cuba back from another bunch of guys led by Fidel Castro. The Russians were friends with Castro and started building places to launch nuclear missiles at America. President Kennedy found it out when a spy plane flew over Cuba and saw the building going on and some missiles already in place. Mr. Kennedy told Mr. Khrushchev, the Russian leader, that he couldn't send missiles to Cuba and the ones already there had to leave. Mr. Khrushchev said he was going to keep missiles in Cuba anyway and sent ships loaded with more missiles toward Cuba. Mr. Kennedy sent some of our Navy ships to stop them. On TV, Mr. Kennedy said if a missile was fired from Cuba toward America, the US would consider it caused by the Russians and would fire missiles at them. It sounded to me like the whole world could be shooting at each other soon. My father yelled at the TV, "Go ahead Mr. President, go ahead and nuke the commies! Then you should invade Cuba with our Marines and hang that bastard Castro!" Even my mother couldn't calm him down. Daddy hated communists, among other groups..

Back in September, right after school started up again, Mr. Kennedy made a speech and said we would send a man to the moon in 10 years and we were all excited about that. But for the next few days, nobody knew if the world would still exist the next day or not, much less last for 10 years. I asked Daddy if we could hide in our basement even though it was still flooded because of the leaky water heater. He said not to worry about it. I didn't know if he meant there was nothing to worry about or if he meant that when nuclear war broke out, we shouldn't worry about hiding in the basement because it wouldn't make any difference.

We went to school the rest of the week, but we practiced "duck and cover" under our school desks. On a signal from the principal over the intercom, we would stop what we were doing and dive under our desks and cover our heads with our hands. I wondered how much good being under my desk would do if a Russian missile landed nearby. Earlier that year, the Supreme Court said that schools couldn't require students to pray at school anymore. That didn't stop my teachers. We prayed the Lord's Prayer from under our desks.

As soon as school was out each day, we were supposed to rush home without stopping anywhere. I usually rode my bike, but Sarah Jane asked me to walk with her, so I just pushed my bike and walked. We didn't say much on the way home except when Sarah Jane said she liked my snake on the pep rally banner and that I was her best friend in the world. I didn't know what to say, so I told her I was glad she liked the snake drawing. We walked home together like that for until the weather started getting cold.

Finally in November, Mr. Kennedy and Mr. Khrushchev must have talked on the phone because Mr. Kennedy promised not to try to take Cuba away from Mr. Castro and to take our missiles out the country of Turkey. Mr. Khrushchev promised to take all of the missiles out of Cuba and never send any more there again. I guess both men realized that nobody could win a war with nuclear missiles and a tie would mean everybody in both countries, along with a lot of other people, would die.

Before the Cuban missile thing happened, none of us even talked about the big argument Mr. Kennedy got into with the governor of Mississippi. A Black man named Meredith or something wanted to go to college and the governor didn't think Black people should go to school with white people. Mr. Kennedy said they should and he sent Army soldiers to Mississippi to help Mr. Meredith go to college. I couldn't figure out why someone would want to go to school so badly that they would go through all of that. I guess Mr. Meredith and Mr. Kennedy thought it was pretty important. Mr. Kennedy had to deal with a lot of stuff in 1962.

Chapter 9

Nothing much happened the rest of November. I kept practicing the shag in my room with Becky helping a couple of times. At school, math was still a total disaster. In art class, Mr. Fontain let me work on a painting of a red bird using real oil paints on real canvas. I loved it. Art class only met three times a week so it took me two weeks to finish the painting. As always, Mr. Fontain said I could do better, but he also said he thought I ought to enter it in an art contest put on by all of the schools in our county. That made me feel good.

On Thanksgiving, Sarah Jane, her mother and her grandmother came to our house for lunch. Daddy's brother Al also came. He didn't have any family of his own. During lunch, Al talked about how the son of one of his fishing buddies was killed in a place called Vietnam. Al said the boy had just turned 20 and there had only been 50 or so American soldiers killed there in 1962. Sarah Jane's mother got up and left the table for a while. I guess it was because Sarah Jane's daddy was killed in a war and she didn't want to hear about somebody else dying in one. Sarah Jane stayed at the table, but didn't say anything. She looked at me and just shook her head.

After lunch, Daddy, Al and I went in the living room while all the women cleaned up in the kitchen. I asked Daddy where Vietnam was located and he said it was sort of near China and Korea. Then I asked him why Americans were fighting there. He pounded his fist on the arm of his recliner and almost shouted at me. "American boys are over there because the God damned Communists are trying to take over that country just like they're trying to take over every country in the world, including this one. They're worse than the

God damned Nazis and Japs!" Daddy didn't cuss like that very often. Maybe he did it because he and Uncle Al drank some beer before lunch. Mama fussed at him when he cussed or drank too much beer. She also fussed at Daddy and Uncle Al for smoking in the house. Daddy only did it when Uncle Al came to visit. He smoked outside and in the car the rest of the time. They both said they learned to smoke in the Marines. They said they almost had to smoke because there were little packs of Chesterfield and Lucky Strike cigarettes in their food boxes the Marines gave them. They called the boxes C-Rations.

I looked, but I couldn't find Vietnam on my globe. I found a place called French Indochina. My globe was pretty old. The boy that Al talked about getting killed was only a little more than five years older than me. For some weird reason, I pictured Ricky Stillman, the tuba player, as the soldier.

Mama and Sarah Jane's mother insisted that Sarah Jane and I exchange gifts at Christmas. I think it was part of the long range plan to make us be boyfriend and girlfriend. To make sure I would buy a gift, Mama always gave me money to do it. Around the first week or so of December, I got a bright idea. I would buy Sarah Jane a record from McMurray's. That would give me an excuse to see Britney and maybe dance with her again. On the next Saturday morning, I practiced up in my room to "Dance With Me" for an hour before I took the four dollars Mama gave me for Sarah Jane's gift and rode to the store. Mama didn't know that 45s only cost a dollar. That meant that I could get Sarah Jane a record or two and still get two for me. Remembering what Britney had said about how you needed to slide your feet to dance the shag and how hard that was to do in sneakers, I wore my lace up black Sunday shoes with thick soles. I figured they would slide better than my old Converse High Tops on the linoleum floors at McMurray's. My Sunday shoes didn't look so good with jeans, so I put on a pair of dress pants that were part of my only suit. The dress pants didn't look good with a knit shirt and sweater, so I put on a white long sleeve shirt instead. It was cold outside so I needed to wear a jacket. I decided that I should wear the suit coat that matched the dress pants. Then I thought wearing a suit without a tie didn't seem right. I didn't know how to tie one so the only tie I had was a black and red clip-on.

Luckily, Mama was at the grocery store and didn't see me because she didn't like me wearing my Sunday clothes except on Sundays and to funerals. Becky did come down the steps as I was heading out the door. "Hey, uh Donno. Where are you headed all dressed up? You getting married or something?"

"Yeah. Real funny, Becky. I'm going Christmas shopping."

"Yeah, where?"

As soon as I said McMurray's, I knew it was a mistake.

"Oh, McMurray's. Does it have anything to do with Britney McMurray? Do you think she will like you better in your good clothes?"

I didn't answer, but I wondered if Becky was right. Would Britney think I was dopey wearing a suit to a record store? I thought about changing, but decided to stick with the plan for the Sunday shoes rather than sneakers.

I got some stares from people on Main Street as I rode by them with my suit coat and clip-on-tie flapping in the breeze. I got the same kind of look from the lady at the front desk of McMurray's. But when I walked into the record department, Britney just smiled and said "Well, look at you. Why are you all dressed up? Is there a special occasion this afternoon?"

If I had been smooth and sophisticated like I hoped to be someday, I would have come back with a quick answer like *coming to see you is a special occasion* or *You make every day a special occasion*. The best I could come up with was "Uh, I wore my good shoes because my jeans are too short." Before Britney could react to that, I blurted out "I need to buy a present and, and I've uh, uh been practicing a lot."

"So, what do you want to do first, show me your new and improved dance steps or shop for a present?"

"Uh, Can we dance? I mean, will you uh show me some more, please."

Britney's beautiful face broke into a smile. "Well sure, I promised, but I'll bet you have improved so much, you can teach me some things now." I blushed and Britney walked over to the record player on the counter. She picked up a record and read from the label, "This is one by The Marvelettes. They're a Black girls group. You ever heard of them?"

"Uh, no, don't think so."

"They're really good and I think this song is a good shag tune. It's called 'Playboy'. And because you are dressed like a playboy, let's dance to that."

I blushed again.

The record started and I tentatively took Britney's right hand in my left. Britney said "Let's go" and we both started the count out loud, "One and two, three and four, five six. One and two, three and four, five six." As we started to count the steps the third time, I lifted my left arm and stepped to the side. Staying in step and as if we had done it a thousand times, Britney ducked under my arm and ended up facing me from the other direction still holding my hand. Without missing a beat, Britney smiled and started singing along with the record, I decided that would be a good time to twirl her again and then add a spin after that — big mistake. I hadn't noticed that the lace on my left Sunday shoe had come untied. In my attempt to spin around, I stepped on the lace with my right foot and nearly fell. Britney had to catch me.

"Whoa there, playboy. The shag isn't supposed to be dangerous. You don't want to break a leg before you get to show your stuff with your best girl friend."

In my head, I wanted to say *I don't have a girlfriend, but you could take the job if you you'd like.* Of course I knew that would be just as dumb as me asking the goddess at the pavilion to dance that first day I saw her and her boyfriend. Instead I said, "I guess I will have to practice a lot more, especially spinning around like that."

"Well, I think you're doing fine. Remember, some of the really good shaggers have been doing it for a long time. It's a lot harder than something like the Twistor the Swim. You really have to have a lot of rhythm, plus you are doing lots of things with your hands while moving your feet." She smiled.

Her smile was like sunshine. "Thank you for uh helping me. I thought you would be really stuck…uh really busy and stuff." I almost said what everybody I knew said about Britney McMurray — that she was so stuck on herself that nobody in West Ashton stood a chance with her.

"You know, Donald, your shoes are a problem. I mean they are nice shoes and all, but they are not for dancing."

I looked down at my Sunday shoes and realized that one of them was still untied.

"The really cool dancers down at The Shack at Ocean Drive wear penny loafers and no socks when they dance. They call them Weejuns. They have leather soles that slide really well on a dance floor. Plus they are cool looking."

"Oh yeah, I think that's what the guy at the pavilion was wearing when I decided that I want to learn to shag."

"Weejuns are almost required to shag." She laughed and tossed back her long blonde hair. "Well, almost required. The Ye Olde Shoppe down town sells them. Maybe you can get a pair someday."

Weejuns immediately went on my Christmas wish list. I had also hoped to get an easel and oil paint set. Wasn't sure which I wanted more. I decided I would just go for both.

"Uh, I need to do some things, so maybe you ought to go ahead and pick out that gift you mentioned."

I had almost forgotten the other reason I had come to the McMurray's. "Yeah, I have to buy a gift for my dopey next door neighbor, Sarah Jane Allison."

"Is she a little tiny thing with a red pony tail and glasses?'

"Yeah, that's her. Do you know her?"

"She was in the store a couple of days ago. I was surprised when she wanted to see some shag records too. I thought you were the only person in West Ashton who had even heard of the shag. She bought a couple of records. In fact she bought my other copy of "Dance With Me" by The Drifters. Maybe you two should get together and dance."

Oh shoot, I thought. *What is Sarah Jane up to*? I bought "Playboy" by The Marvelettes and "Hey Baby" by Bruce Channel for me. I bought "Theme From Doctor Kildare" by Richard Chamberlain for Sarah Jane. I wasn't about to buy her a dance record.

"Britney, may I come back again after Christmas and maybe you can show me some more steps or something. Maybe I will have a new pair of shoes by then."

"Of course, especially because there are two shaggers in town now. But you had better make it right after Christmas because I am getting married the tenth of January. I'm marrying a guy I met at The Shack this summer. He's a very good dancer and we are going to live at the beach. Isn't that cool?"

I rode home numb and depressed. First, Sarah Jane now had a copy of my favorite song. Did she do that on purpose? What was she planning? Secondly, and equally disturbing, Britney was getting married. I guess I should have known that would happen sometime. But somehow, I thought…well, I don't know what I thought. Did I believe the beautiful Britney McMurray could care a lick about a goofy, dumb, love sick 14-and-a half-year-old? She was getting married to a really good dancer and moving away, that's all I knew.

Chapter 10

Nothing about Christmas relieved my depression. I didn't get a pair of Weejuns. Mama told me $12.99 was too much to pay for any kind of shoes much less ones with no laces and thin leather soles. I also didn't get oil paints and an easel. The only artist material I got was a sketch pad and a box of colored pencils. Becky gave me those and Daddy just sort of shook his head when I opened the package. Other than socks, underwear and a pretty neat yellow sweater, my big present from my parents was a clock radio. Even though I would have rather had the Weejuns and art stuff, I was glad to get the plug-in radio because the batteries in my little transistor kept dying.

Just like every other Christmas I could remember, Sarah Jane, her mother and grandmother came to our house after breakfast to exchange gifts. Sarah Jane's mother gave our family a loaf of homemade bread and an apple pie and my mother gave Sarah Jane's family a big round fruit cake in a metal tin and three jars of homemade apple butter.

Sarah Jane and I were the only ones who exchanged individual gifts. We both knew that the other one was giving a 45 record just by the way it was wrapped. My record was "Stay" by Maurice Williams and the Zodiacs. I had heard it at one of the teen center nights and liked it.

When I looked up at Sarah Jane, I expected to see her wondering why I had given her a song about a doctor's show and maybe even mad that I haven't given her a dance record. Instead the expression on her face was—I don't know—goofy. She was looking at me with her head cocked and with a silly little smile rather than her irritating smirk. She mouthed the words "Thank you, Donno. Thank you."

I didn't know what caused Sarah Jane's weird actions until Becky stopped by my room later.

"Hey, Donno boy, I thought you and Sarah Jane weren't exactly getting along these days."

"We're not. She can really be a pest sometimes, you know. She's always doin' something to make me like her but then does somethin' else to make me mad."

Becky shook her head and held her hands out wide. "Then why did you give her that record?"

"'The Doctor Kildare' thing? Why not? It just talks about doctor stuff. I didn't want to give her any ideas by giving her a dance record. She might think I want to dance with her."

"Have you listened to the lyrics, dummy? It's a love song! Come in my room. I've got it on an album with other Richard Chamberlain songs."

The song talked about young lovers dreaming about getting together and stars in the sky. With Richard Chamberlain's handsome face smiling up at me from Becky's album cover, it finally hit me that I had given Sarah Jane a reason to keep pestering me. Now she probably thought I wanted her to do it. "Oh no! What have I done?"

"Yep, Donno. You basically sent little Miss Sarah Jane a love letter. Get ready, little brother." Becky picked up the album and kissed Chamberlain's picture. "Um, um, but you couldn't have picked a better person to deliver the letter for you. Isn't he luscious?" Becky laughed as I slumped out of her room and retreated to mine.

In a couple of days, things went from bad to worse. With school still being out for the holidays, I decided that it would be a good time to go back to McMurray's and see Britney for the last time. I thought about taking her a gift or something, but what could it be? What could I possibly give the most beautiful girl in the world? I was depressed, but I wanted to see her and wanted to dance with her again. I wasn't going to wear my Sunday clothes. The new yellow sweater and a blue shirt looked good with freshly washed and ironed jeans. I also polished an old pair of school shoes with soles that were worn down nearly smooth. I figured they would slide better than my good shoes.

The temperature was below freezing and the bike ride down Main Street was brutal. It made my eyes water and my nose run. As I walked back into the record department, wiping my nose on my last Kleenex tissue, I stopped short — Sarah Jane was there, dancing with Britney. I stood and watched for a minute before they realized I was there. To my horror, Sarah Jane was actually dancing well. She and Britney were still counting out loud, "One and two, three and four, five six," but they were smooth together with no bouncing and stumbling. I was jealous and hated that they were dancing to "Dance With Me," my favorite song.

I was about to turn and leave when Britney saw me. "Hey, look who's here. It's the playboy."

Sarah Jane frowned and pointed to her nose. My nose was dripping down my chin and Sarah Jane saw it. All I could do to stop it was wipe it on the left sleeve of my new yellow sweater. *Oh brother,* I thought. *Could this get any worse?* It could and did.

I don't know if Britney actually saw the nose wipe action, but I assumed that she did and it destroyed my plans of acting smooth and confident when we danced together.

Britney turned away and lifted the needle off the record. Without looking back at me, she said, "Well now, with the only two junior shaggers in West Ashton here, let me see the two of you dance together." She put the needle back down on "Dance With Me."

While I tried to decide if I would dance or bolt and run, Sarah Jane reached out and grabbed my left hand. She scrunched up her nose and shook her head — I guess because she thought my nose wipe had contaminated my hand — she started to count "one and two, three and four, five six. One and two, three and four, five six."

I was so befuddled by my drippy nose, by Sarah Jane being there and by Britney insisting that I dance with Sarah

Jane rather than her, I didn't start moving my feet at the right time and was completely out of step to the music. Sarah Jane, always trying to take control of every situation, jerked my hand toward her and almost pulled me down. Even though Britney had told me that it was usually the boy who initiated spins and twirls, Sarah Jane wasn't going to wait for me. As I was stumbling forward, she raised my arm as high as she could and spun underneath while still holding my hand. That threw me completely off balance and I bumped into Sarah Jane, knocking her into the counter and making the record skip. Sarah Jane screamed at me. "Come on, Donno sweetheart! Pay attention! Move your feet to the music. We have to learn to dance together sometime."

Britney snickered and said, "I think you two love birds need to practice together. And, Don, Sarah Jane can help you. She has the basic steps down pat."

That was it. I couldn't take any more. Sarah Jane called me "sweetheart," I made a fool out of myself in front of Britney and I didn't get the chance to dance with her for the last time. I said something dumb and silly to Britney about her getting married and then I left. I rode home, hating Sarah Jane all the way. This time, tears mixed with the output of my runny nose and ran down my chin.

On New Year's Eve, I made another stupid mistake. As usual, there was no big celebration at our house. Becky did go out with some of her friends and Daddy even let her take Mama's '62 Chevy II station wagon as long as she was back by 10:00. I was stuck up in my room listening to the requests on *Big WASH Radio*. Most of them were wishing some girl or some boy a happy New Year with songs like "Good Luck Charm" by Elvis, "Johnny Angel" by Shelley Fabares and "Love Letters" by Kettey Lester. None of the songs were even close to a shag tune. That gave me what I thought was a great idea. I would request a song for Britney, something for her to remember me by. It took me a while to come up with the words, but I finally settled on "This is for the prettiest girl in West Ashton and my favorite dance partner. From her special Playboy." I requested "Dance With Me" by The Drifters. Surely Britney would hear that and know it was me. She called me playboy and knew that my favorite dance song was "Dance With Me."

When I called it in, the disc jockey promised he would get it on before he left the air at midnight. He said it would be his New Years' gift to the good people of West Ashton. I was just about to fall asleep around 11:45 when I heard my request. I was proud of myself for about five minutes and hoped Britney would be pleased. Then it hit me...Britney probably wasn't listening to the radio near midnight on New Years' Eve. But guess who certainly would be listening and who might even think the song was dedicated to her...oh no! Sarah Jane would think I was calling her the prettiest girl in West Ashton and my favorite dance partner. Oh no!

Nobody I knew got invited to Britney's wedding, yet it was still the talk of West Ashton. Her picture and description of the wedding and reception filled half a page in the little *West Ashton Weekly Courier* and a quarter page in the big daily *Ashton News and Record.* Even in black and white, she looked like an angel. The article in the paper said hundreds of people attended the wedding at the big Baptist church down town and the reception at the fancy Oak Grove Inn. There weren't any pictures of the groom, but said his name was Russell Chambers and that he was an assistant golf professional at a country club near Myrtle Beach, South Carolina where the couple would live. I imagined that the groom was the spitting image of the shagger god at the pavilion except taller and with a dark tan. The story said a band called The Royals provided the entertainment and dancing lasted late into the night. I also imagined Britney and Russell putting on a show to shag songs. After Mama finished reading the article, I snuck and cut Britney's picture out of the paper and put it in my sketch pad that I had also turned into a combination diary and scrapbook.

Chapter 11

School started back up after the holidays and I spent the entire month of January trying to avoid Sarah Jane. I wasn't very successful. We didn't have any classes together (she was in the smart kid classes and I wasn't), but she managed to be in the same hallway with me at least three times a day. Every time I saw her, she would whisper something like "Hey Playboy" or "Dance With Me". I vowed never to request a song on the radio ever again.

The school year went about as I expected. I was still a math dummy and knew I was destined to rely totally on simple addition and subtraction to make my way through life. History was boring but I made good grades because I drew illustrations of Americans shooting at British soldiers and Indians throwing tea off a sail boat.

Before Christmas, phys-ed was all about climbing ropes, tumbling on mats and running. I hated being sweaty the rest of the day. After Christmas, phys-ed switched over to square dancing and that was pretty good. Because I had a little rhythm, I didn't draw the attention of the teacher and didn't fall over my feet when dancing with a partner. Girls did not turn up their noses at me either. Luckily, Sarah Jane was not in that class.

English wasn't bad once we started doing some creative writing assignments. It wasn't hard for me to use words to describe what I imagined in my head. It was a lot like seeing a drawing or painting in my mind before actually putting it on paper or canvas. I got an A on a story about getting lost in the woods and having to spend the night there. The teacher told me I was a fine writer and should keep it up.

Art was still my favorite. It still only met three times a week for only 45 minutes at a time. I spent a lot of time in other classes thinking about what I was going to do in art. Math was my class right before art and often there were more sketches of trees, cars, and animals on my math work sheet than equations.

It was in art class in early February that one of the two big events of my ninth grade year happened. I was busy working with modeling clay to sculpt a puppy when Principal Phillips came in the room. In the same booming voice he used making morning announcements on the PA, he said, "Alright young artists, I am pleased to tell you that one of our very own has won the district wide art contest. Congratulations to Mr. Donald Emmerson. His painting of a red bird has been judged best overall among 37 entries, including six from that other junior high across the river and 11 from the high school." My mouth dropped open and didn't close until after the class finished applauding and Mr. Phillips and Mr. Fontain shook my hand. Mr. Phillips told me that there would be an award ceremony complete with a picture in the newspaper and that my painting would hang in the school district office until the next year. Later that school day, Mr. Phillips announced the award to the whole school. When I left my last class and walked down the hall to my locker, I sort of expected to get some nods and acknowledgement. It only happened once and it was Sarah Jane who rushed up to me said how proud she was of her "Playboy."

I waited until dinner before telling my family about the award. Mama shouted and hugged me. Becky shouted and kissed me on the cheek. Daddy poured himself another glass of tea and said, "Well that's fine, son. Just fine." That was it from Daddy.

When I told Mama about the award ceremony and the newspaper picture, she asked if the family was invited. "Yes, ma'am and there is supposed to be a lunch too. Mr. Fontain said the school district really makes a big deal about the art contest and there would be two or three winners from each of the schools in town." Mama shook her head and said, "And my Donno is the overall winner. Well, I suppose we ought to get you something nice to wear, like those khaki pants you've been wanting, and maybe a new pair of shoes. Didn't you say that those Weejuns penny loafers were nice?"

I loved my mama.

I have to say my painting looked pretty darn good compared to all of those other winners. Mama was proud when Mr. Fontain said I had a lot of talent and would it be alright if he got a picture together with me. He said, "Who knows? Donald here might wind up in a fancy New York gallery someday." Mama beamed. Daddy didn't come to the award celebration. He said he couldn't get off from work, although I did see him reading the article in the paper when it came out later that week.

The other big thing that happened to me during my ninth grade year was an emergency appendectomy about ten days before school was out. It happened in art class too. I was sitting at a table with another kid working on a pencil drawing of a bowl of oranges. All of a sudden, I started feeling sick to my stomach. It was like I felt when I ate a chilidog and drank a Pepsi too fast, except the pain didn't go away when I burped. I started to get up to ask Mr. Fontain if I could go to the restroom, but instead, I threw up all over my bowl of oranges. That's the last thing I remember until I woke up in a hospital room with a nun standing beside me. That was a shock. I thought I was dead and gone to heaven. Except when I tried to sit up, the pain in my side convinced me I was still alive. "Uh, ma'am, uh sister, uh what happened? What am I doing here?"

"Well, young man, you have been very sick. I suppose you could say you almost died. Your appendix ruptured and they rushed you here to Saint Mary's for an operation. The good Lord was truly looking after you."

"Almost died" didn't register with me for a while. I was more concerned about all the people who watched me being wheeled out of art class and down the hall at school on a stretcher. I figured that couldn't have been good for my social status. "Uh, excuse me, uh ma'am, but what day is it?"

"Oh it's Saturday morning. You've been asleep for a good long while. Your family and your sweet little neighbor girl just left to get some breakfast. They will be back soon."

"You mean a girl with red hair in a ponytail?"

"Why yes. Your mother said she is your best girl friend."

"Oh brother," I thought. *Sarah Jane was here watching me while I was out cold. What did I do? What did I say? What could I do?*

As it turned out, back in 1963, an appendectomy was considered a pretty serious operation, especially if the appendix ruptured. I had to spend five days in the hospital and four days at home before going back to school. That was okay with me. It gave people time to forget about my dramatic exit in an ambulance. The thing I hated most about getting sick was messing up Becky's high school graduation on the Monday after my operation. I was still in the hospital. Of course, Mama and Daddy went to the ceremony and gave Becky a nice necklace and some money as a graduation gift, but there was no big family celebration and Becky didn't go on a trip or anything. Becky was cool about it, but I felt bad.

Mr. Fontain came to visit me in the hospital and told me I could start over on the bowl of oranges painting when I got back. Our year books were handed out while I was out of school and Sarah Jane volunteered to pick mine up and get people to sign it. Of course Ricky Stillman, Sarah Jane and some seventh grader I didn't know were the only kids who signed it. Sarah Jane covered a whole page with a bunch of stuff about us being best of friends for all of our lives and how she was looking forward to going to high school with me. She drew little hearts around the words "Dance With Me" above her name. Mr. Fontain and my English teacher signed it under their pictures. The picture of me was terrible — taken the day after a really bad haircut. The only good thing about the year book for me was my drawing of a rocket ship on the cover being launched from in front of the school building with the words "Blasting off for the future" spelled out in the flames from the rocket's tail. I hid my initials in the billowing smoke, but I don't think anyone noticed.

There were a few things that weren't so bad about having an appendectomy. Mama kind of babied me a little and Daddy didn't expect me to do chores for a while. At school, I wasn't allowed to carry any books. I guess they thought lifting them would pop my stitches or something. So, my homeroom teacher assigned another kid that had the same schedule as me to carry my books. He and I got hall passes that let us leave class a few minutes early to beat the crowds in the halls. That lasted the whole week before school was out even though I felt pretty good.

The end of the year ninth grade dance was scheduled for the second Friday after my operation. At our school, the ninth grade dance was a pretty big deal. The eighth graders put it on for the ninth graders and we were supposed to dress up in our nicest clothes. It was held in the cafeteria rather than the gym so it wasn't a sock hop and we could actually wear shoes.

Being a ninth grader, Sarah Jane couldn't be in charge of planning the dance. That was supposed to be done by eighth graders. However, she still figured out a way to be on the decoration committee. Because the fall sock hop was canceled due to the US almost going to war with the Russians, my "Wonderland By Night" banner was never used. Sarah Jane had taken it home and resurrected it for the Ninth Grade Dance. She bullied the eighth graders into using it. She also got them to use dark blue table cloths with little cut out moons scattered all over them. I was surprised when Principal Phillips let her turn the lights down pretty low. That made for some dark corners where a few couples went and the chaperones couldn't see.

My mother gave me two strict orders as she dropped me off at the school. First, it was okay for me to wear my new Weejuns, but I couldn't take them off or go outside and scuff them up. I agreed. Secondly, I was not to dance at all, not even slow dancing. I agreed to that too. Because most of the dancing would be the "The Twist" by Chubby Checker, I didn't want to take a chance of popping something loose inside. That would have meant another dramatic exit and I couldn't stand another one of those. So, I just sat at a table sipping on some sort of pink punch and nibbled on Chex Mix. I turned my chair enough so my feet and freshly starched and pressed khakis were visible. I wanted everyone to see my Weejuns.

There were other people sitting at my table and I listened to what they were saying to each other although I was not included in their conversations. If someone told a joke, I laughed. If someone said something that needed affirmation, I nodded in agreement even though my vote didn't count. If someone commented on the way a couple was dancing or what a particular girl was wearing, I waited until I saw how the rest of the group reacted and then I agreed. I don't think it mattered much.

I was right about the kinds of dances everybody was doing and except for slow dances, they all would have popped my remaining stitches. The music was from records brought in by the kids and then played by a teacher. Every other song was a "Twist" record. We heard Chubby Checker sing "The Twist," "Let's Twist Again," Twistin' USA," " Slow Twistin," "Teach Me to Twist" and "Twist it Up". Occasionally, there was a break from the "Twist" songs like the "Watusi" by The Orions and "Loco-motion" by Little Eva. Most everybody tried to twist to those as well. Some kids even tried to twist to some new songs we had never heard by a new group called The Beach Boys and one called "Wipe Out" by another new group called The Surfaris. I figured both groups were from California and would never make it big in the South.

I mostly just sat and tapped my foot to the rhythm of whatever was playing. Every now and then, someone would walk by and give me a nod. If it was a kid, they nodded more at my shoes than at me. Teachers mostly told me how glad they were that I was feeling better.

Finally, listening to 10 different versions of "The Twist" and after four or five cups of punch, it was time to go to the bathroom. I stayed there longer than I should have trying to decide if I was going to leave and walk home or wait for my mother to pick me up at nine. I decided to stick it out.

I came back in the cafeteria just as a song was ending and the dance floor was still crowded. I waited by the door for a chance to walk back to my table. Suddenly, a non-"Twist" song began to play. It was "Dance With Me" and the dance floor emptied. Only one person could have requested that and only two people in the room could possibly dance to it. Sarah Jane met me halfway across the floor. "Come on Donno, let's show these guys something different. Let's shag. You know you want to because you wore your dancing shoes."

I was tempted. I had just spent an hour being completely ignored. If I allowed Sarah Jane to take my hand and begin to dance all alone on that empty dance floor, people would certainly notice me then. Would they say "Hey, that dufus kid can kind of dance"? Or would they say "Look at them, they're pretty good for dorks?" However, as I thought about it, I knew the memory of me throwing up in art class and being wheeled out under a white sheet was still fresh in a lot of their minds. My self-confidence, always fragile, just couldn't take another humiliation, even though I was certain that the "Shag" was the coolest dance and would put the "Twist" to shame.

I lowered my head and mumbled, "I can't do it, Sarah Jane. Mama told me not to dance because it might do something crazy to my operation." Of course I was lying. I sort of slithered away, leaving Sarah Jane to endure the stares while standing alone in the middle of the dance floor as the record ended.

I should have known that Mama had volunteered to pick up Sarah Jane and me after the dance. We didn't speak to each other and only nodded when Mama asked if we had a good time.

Chapter 12

I suppose the summer of 1963 pretty much started out the same as all of the summers I could remember. It was hot. Mrs. Bronson still ruled the pavilion. The water in the pool was still freezing cold and all the girls over 14 hung around the life guards, unless they were upstairs in the pavilion putting nickels and quarters in the juke box.

About the middle of June and several weeks short of my 15th birthday, I started noticing some weird things. First of all, every time I started to talk, my voice cracked. It would start out like I had been breathing helium gas — real high pitched — then change to something like I was talking in a cave — low and gravely. Secondly, even though I felt fine and was fully recovered from my appendectomy, I didn't have much of an appetite. I stopped stuffing myself with ice cream and peanut butter, mayonnaise and potato chip sandwiches and started liking things like green beans and salad. At the same time, it seemed like almost overnight, I lost weight and grew about three inches. Suddenly, nothing fit. Bathing suits, jeans, church clothes, and underwear had to be replaced. My feet stayed about the same I guess, because I could still wear my Weejuns, even though they were a little tight. Mama said I was a late bloomer and losing my baby fat. Becky said I was turning into a "hunk." Daddy just said I was expensive and needed a job.

The music on the juke box at the pavilion had changed some too. There were still some "Twist" beat songs like "The Monkey Time" by Major Lance and "Heat Wave" by Martha and the Vandellas. There were also some strange, new sounding songs too. As far as I knew, nobody in West Ashton had ever been surfing in California, but songs with twangy guitars and fast beats by The Beach Boys, The

Surfaris, and Jan and Dean got played a lot. I did like the drum solo in "Wipe Out." Mostly kids tried to twist to those songs too. Then there were some songs that were not even close to being dance tunes. Somebody said they were folk songs and all you did was stand around and sing along with them. My favorites were "Blowin' in the Wind" by Bob Dylan and "Puff the Magic Dragon" by Peter Paul and Mary. Both of them were kind of sad. Becky said that "Puff the Magic Dragon" was really about drugs called LSD and marijuana. I thought it was about a kid that lost his best friend. Other folk songs that got played a bunch that summer were "If I had a Hammer" by Trini Lopez and "Walk Right In" by The Rooftop Singers.

Of course the god and goddess shaggers didn't come back that summer and the only new songs that sounded like you could shag to them were "Ruby Baby" by Dion and the Belmonts and "Pride and Joy" by Marvin Gaye. I played both of them a few times, but nobody danced to them other than once when Sarah Jane tried to teach an eighth grade girl to shag.

Watching Sarah Jane and the eighth grader counting out "One and two, three and four, five-six," I realized something else had changed dramatically. It was Sarah Jane. She had uh, developed hips and a bosom. A few weeks earlier she was still the skinny kid with thick glasses and wild red hair. I guess I hadn't noticed the changes until I saw her in her two piece bathing suit. Without really meaning to, I stared at her and thought about Britney at the same time. Suddenly, our eyes met and we looked at each other for a second or two until she gave me a weird smile — not her usual smart-alecky smirk, but something different.

"Donno, do you want to dance and show her how good we are together?"

That broke my spell. "Uh, you know I don't want to dance with you, Sarah Jane." My voice cracked as I tried to sound put-out and angry. "You keep asking and I keep saying no. Just stop!" I turned and walked away, but the rest of the day I found myself sneaking peeks at her. That lasted all summer long and she caught me looking several times.

For our combined birthdays, Mama thought we should do something different than the usual family dinner and cake with Sarah Jane's family. Mama decided Sarah Jane, her mom, Becky, and Mama and I would drive across the river, have dinner at the Crystal Cafeteria and then go to a movie at one of the big up-town theaters. When Mama said we all had to wear our good clothes, Daddy and both grand-mothers backed out. That was okay with me. If they had come, all three would have snored during the movie.

When Sarah Jane and her mom came to our front door so we could all ride together, I almost didn't recognize Sarah Jane. She was wearing a bright yellow and orange dress with big sunflowers on the skirt that made her summer tan darker. For the first time I could remember, her hair was combed and not balled up in a ragged ponytail. And, how had I missed that her teeth were no longer covered with strips of metal? Her braces were gone.

Before we left for dinner, we opened gifts. Mama gave me a neat short sleeve knit shirt with a guy riding a horse on the front. Becky said it was a Polo shirt, what all the cool guys were wearing. Daddy pulled out his wallet and gave me a five dollar bill. He said I should pay for my own dinner with it and I didn't have to bring him any change. Sarah Jane's gift was last. It was a book about Vincent van Gogh with a lot of color pictures of his paintings. Mr. Fontain talked a lot about van Gogh in art class and said nobody ever heard of him until after he died, yet he became one of the most famous painters who ever lived. I quickly thumbed through the book and saw that there were several pages with paintings of sun flowers. I looked up at Sarah Jane. The sun flowers on her dress were brighter and yellower than any in the book. Did she wear the dress just because of the book? Did she think that would make me change my attitude toward her? It didn't matter. I loved the book and planned to spend hours looking at the paintings and reading about van Gogh. "Uh, thanks Sarah Jane. This is pretty neat." I paused and without thinking of the repercussions I added, "And I like your dress with all the flowers." She smiled that strange smile again.

I had given her a pink diary book with a picture of Elvis on the cover. Mama picked it out.

Even though it was a cafeteria, The Crystal was one of the fanciest places in the whole county to eat. It had crystal chandeliers, fancy wallpaper, real paintings on the walls and potted plants everywhere.

You stood in line until you picked up a tray and looked at the menu. There were several boards with black fabric and white letters that told you about specials, about what kind of meats were available, what vegetables you could choose and a board with nothing but desserts described. You could order as many different items as you wanted, but each one cost, even rolls and butter.

As you went down the line, nice Black ladies in green and white starched uniforms would ask you what wanted. Meat came first, then vegetables, then salad and then dessert. You just followed your plate down the line until you got to the checkout lady at the end. Mama paid for Becky, Sarah Jane and her mom. I paid for my dinner with Daddy's five dollars. Because I got roast beef, green beans and a salad plus dessert, my bill was highest. Dinner cost me $2.35.

After we paid the check-out lady, some other Black ladies in starched uniforms carried our trays to a table that was up some stairs to a balcony. Mama called it a mezzanine. The Black ladies put all of our plates on the table and took away the trays. Mama gave each of them a quarter tip.

Before I sat down, I decided it would be best if I went to the bathroom. Mama said there was one upstairs. When I went in, there was a Black man wearing a vest and bow tie sitting on a stool near the door. He said "Good evening, sir." When I finished and washed my hands, the Black man came up behind me and handed me a warm towel. I thanked him and headed for the door — then I remembered Mama giving the Black ladies a quarter tip. I fished in my pocket and found the 50 cent piece that was part of my change and handed it to the Black man. He said "Why, thank you young man. I hope you have a wonderful evening."

From our table on the mezzanine, we could look out over the entire restaurant main floor. I could probably see 40 or 50 tables below me. All of them were filled. It took me a while to realize it, but all of the people sitting at the tables were white and all of the people moving around in a hurry — carrying trays, clearing tables, pushing carts with dirty dishes — were all wearing starched uniforms and were Black. I wondered how many quarter tips they made a day.

The dinner was fun and we all laughed a lot, especially when I couldn't figure out how to cut a Brussels sprout that came as part of my "vegetable medley." I didn't know what it was or in what country the city of Brussels was located. I didn't really mind the laughing and kidding, even from Sarah Jane.

Mama had said we were going to a movie about birds. I was looking forward to seeing the scary Alfred Hitchcock movie, *The Birds.* Seeing seagulls and crows ganging up and attacking people looked pretty cool to me. I had misunderstood Mama. She meant we were going to see *Bye Bye Birdie* at the other big downtown theatre. Even though we had just eaten a big dinner, we got bags of popcorn, boxes of Raisnettes, Goobers, Milk Duds and big cups of Cheerwine with crushed ice. Mama and Becky made sure I sat next to Sarah Jane so we could share my popcorn.

The movie was a musical set in 1958 and told the story of a rock and roll singer like Elvis getting drafted into the Army. Before he was to report to the Army, Conrad Birdie was supposed to kiss his greatest fan as part of a promotional stunt. The fan turned out to be Ann-Margret. By the way, I fell in love with Ann-Margret, especially after she wore a tight pink outfit with a short top. It was all sort of goofy, but I enjoyed it and laughed a lot. I thought it would make a good high school drama play.

Mama, Becky, Mrs. Allison and Sarah Jane must have had the best memories in the world. After the movie, walking back to the car, they sang every song, especially the theme song “Bye Bye Birdie.” They must have sung it three times before we got to the car. Becky, Sarah Jane and I squeezed into the back seat. Sarah Jane sat in the middle and pushed up against me the whole way. I think she had more room than that. Just as we started to cross the bridge over to West Ashton, they started singing again. But this time, they sang “One Boy.” It was what Ann-Margret sang to Bobby Rydell, her boyfriend. He was afraid she would quit liking him after she kissed Conrad Birdie. In the song, she promised that he was her one and only boyfriend. Sarah Jane sang particularly loud and smiled up at me. Could she have planned all of that? Could Mama and Mrs. Allison have planned it? Who knows? All in all, it was a pretty cool birthday.

Chapter 13

A week or so after my birthday, Daddy came home from work one day and gave us all a shock. "Alright, family, listen up. Given that Becky will be startin' at the community college and Donno will be goin' to the big high school soon, I think we need a little vacation before all of these big changes happen. We're going to the beach!"

I don't think I had ever seen my father so happy or so proud. As it turned out, there was a contest at his job asking for suggestions on how to solve a problem they were having with the way water was used in the paper making process. I still don't understand it, but Daddy did and his suggestion won. The prize was three nights and four days at a motel near Myrtle Beach, SC. Mama, Becky and I danced around the kitchen together, acting silly and Daddy beamed with pride. Even Grandma was impressed although she said she "hadn't lost anything at the beach" and would just stay home so she could watch her stories on TV.

As a family, we had only gone on one other vacation. It was to Uncle Al's travel trailer at a lake in Tennessee. I was four or five and the only things I remember were lots of buzzing mosquitoes and Daddy trying to teach me how to put a worm on a hook.

Our vacation motel wasn't exactly luxurious and wasn't exactly on the beach. It was up near the main highway between Myrtle Beach and Ocean Drive Beach. Daddy's prize was only for one room, so he had to spring for another one. Becky got it and I slept in the same room with my parents. It was a little weird, but we all shared one bathroom back home so we handled it. I figured it had to be better than Uncle Al's trailer.

The motel was five or six blocks from the ocean which made it too far to carry folding chairs, umbrellas, fishing rods, air mattresses and giant bottles of sun tan lotion. We found that out the first day when we tried to walk with all that stuff. We were about halfway there when Daddy got mad and sent Becky back to the motel to get the car. Mama said we probably looked like Gypsies sitting there on the side of the road with all of our stuff piled around us.

Daddy stayed in a bad mood until we finally found a parking spot near the public beach access. From the parking lot, you had to walk down a long path and over a sand dune before you saw the ocean. I could hear the waves breaking as I got close to the top of the dune — then there it was! Of course I had seen pictures of the ocean and movies with ocean scenes in them, but it was still more than I had imagined. I stood there in awe, looking out toward the horizon and realizing that there was nothing between me and Africa or England or someplace over there except ocean. I stood there with my mouth open until Daddy yelled at me to get out of the way. I was blocking the path down to the beach.

Even though it was Thursday morning, the beach was crowded. It took us a while to stake out a few square feet of sand where we could assemble all of our stuff. When Daddy finally stretched out on a huge towel with a picture of a sailing ship on it and Mama settled into a folding chair with her big floppy hat and oversized sunglasses, I headed to the water. Instead of slowly easing my way into it a little at a time, I ran full speed down the wet sand, through the shallows and dove head-first into an incoming wave. The first thing I realized was that the water was warm and not cold like I expected. The second thing I realized was that it was not a good idea to dive into an oncoming wave with your mouth open. I came out sputtering and coughing seawater. Sure enough, it really was salty. I staggered back to the beach where Becky slapped me on the back and laughed.

It didn't take long for me to get over my first seawater experience. Soon, I was body surfing, wave jumping and generally having a ball. There were probably 50 other people of all ages doing the same thing right next to me. It was fun. Daddy even got in the water and splashed around a little. Mama only got her feet wet. Within an hour or so, Daddy and I were sunburned, Becky had a dark tan and Mama was still wrapped up in a long cover-up thing. She said she wasn't going to get cooked and that Daddy and I should've covered up because of our pale Scandinavian skin.

Becky got in the water some, but not above her waist and didn't get her hair wet. I guess I never thought of my sister as a pretty girl until I saw the attention she got from every college age guy who walked by. Sitting there with her hair up, summer tan and her cute little bathing suit, she reminded me of Ann-Margret without the red hair. Most of the guys on the beach just stared while a few of them did speak to Becky. One guy sat down on the sand beside her and they laughed a lot. Eventually they got up, spoke to Mama and then walked down the beach together.

We hung around the beach most of the day and I spent almost all of the time in the water. Once, I needed to go to the bathroom and started toward the public restrooms near the parking lot. When I told Daddy where I was going, he sort of nodded toward the ocean. That saved me a long trip across hot asphalt. I guessed Mama and Becky couldn't do the same thing and made the trip across the asphalt a couple of times.

Just as Becky returned from her walk with her beach boy, Daddy announced that we needed to leave and go back and get ready for supper. Mama complained that it was only 3:30. Daddy reminder her that when we checked into the motel, they gave us a bunch of discount coupons for restaurants, amusement parks and movie theatres. The coupon for the seafood restaurant where he wanted to eat said it had to be used before 5:30 p.m. Daddy wasn't going to miss out on a ten percent discount on the "all you can eat fried shrimp" and complimentary bowl of clam chowder.

I was ready to go, I had a great time, but all the hot sun, fighting the surf and swimming wore me out. When we got back to the motel, I fell asleep on the bed. Luckily, Mama woke me up in time to take a shower and change clothes. We got to the restaurant just in time. Obviously a lot of people got discount coupons just like us. The place was packed. We got a table and saw that you could order from the menu or go through a buffet line. The buffet line was the where you could get the "all you can eat shrimp" plus stuff like French fries, fried clams and hush puppies. Daddy said that was for us. It took a while for us to finally get to the shrimp so we loaded up. That made the people behind us in line kind of mad. I could only handle one helping, but Daddy went back twice. Becky laughed and said it looked like a feeding frenzy every time they brought out more fried shrimp to the buffet. People rushed from every direction, kind of like the pigeons up on Main Street when you dropped popcorn. I decided that I liked clams better than shrimp, but hush puppies were my favorite.

After dinner, we were driving down the main drag toward Myrtle Beach when we saw the glow from thousands of lights in the distance. When we got close we saw the glow was coming from the roller coaster at the Myrtle Beach Pavilion. Mama said she bet they had cotton candy there and Daddy agreed. It didn't take much begging from Becky to go in.

Daddy and Mama got their cotton candy and I found out that it was not a good idea to ride the "Scrambler" after a big meal of clams and hush puppies. I survived it, barely, and decided that the side-by-double Ferris wheel was safer. Mama and Daddy got in the car just below Becky and me. We looked down and saw Daddy put his arm around Mama and give her a kiss. It was the first time I had ever seen him being affectionate with her or anyone else in the family. Becky and I smiled at each other. Our first day of our first real family vacation was pretty good.

The first day of our vacation was so good, Daddy thought we ought to relive it. The next day, we used one of our coupons to go to a pancake house for breakfast. We had to be there by 7:30 a.m., which didn't make Becky and Mama happy. That didn't matter, we saved ten percent off of our "All You Can Eat" blueberry pancakes — they had to be blueberry — with free refills on coffee and orange juice.

We went back to the beach and found a spot near where we were the day before and set up camp. Like the day before, Daddy stretched out on a towel, Mama bundled up in a folding chair, pretty Becky attracted attention just by sitting and I splashed around in the surf like a hooked flounder. After the beach, guess what — we went back to the same seafood restaurant because we had another coupon and as Daddy often said, "Hey, if somethin's good, why risk goin' some place that ain't so good?" Figuring that we might be going back to the pavilion with all of the rides, I stayed away from the clams and only ate one helping of hush puppies. I did taste part of Daddy's complimentary clam chowder and a bite of his pecan pie.

I was right. Daddy drove straight to the pavilion. He and Mama went to the carousel and sat down in a side-by-side swan. They were happy. I went to the "Round Up" which would have caused a catastrophe if I hadn't laid off the clams at dinner. It twirled and tossed me up and down and it was great. I rode it two or three times. Becky wandered over to the arcade games and had guys try to win her a stuffed animal by knocking over milk bottles with baseballs and shooting basketballs through hoops that were almost too small for the ball. She brought two stuffed seagulls and a stuffed octopus back to the motel. Although pretty much a repeat of our first, the second day of vacation was pretty good.

Saturday, our third and last full day at the beach, started out like the first two. We ate more blueberry pancakes and then hauled all of our junk to the beach. I swam, Mama read a book in a folding chair, Daddy stretched out and Becky took a walk down the beach. About 3:00, Mama stood up and announced that she had had enough heat, sand and sun. She wanted to spend time some place cool. She wanted to go to the movies, so we packed up all of our beach stuff and headed back to our room to change clothes. The guy behind the desk at the motel had a newspaper and looked up what movies were playing and where. There were three theatres pretty close to the motel. *The Great Escape* with Steve McQueen was playing at one. Daddy and I liked that one. *Cleopatra* with Elizabeth Taylor and Richard Burton was playing at another. Becky liked that one. The *Courtship* of *Eddie's Father* with Glenn Ford, Shirley Jones and Opie from the "Andy Griffith Show" was at the third. Mama liked that one. Mama won, but Becky had a different plan.

"Mama, why don't you and Daddy have a nice date night in an air-conditioned theatre? The newspaper said the movie started at seven. That gives us time for the early bird shrimp special again. After dinner, Donno and I will drop you off at the theatre and we will drive up to Ocean Drive and check out the pavilion up there. We will pick you up in front of the theatre at nine. How about that, Pops?"

I didn't know what Becky had in mind, but I went with it, especially after she winked at me.

Mama looked at Daddy and said, "You know, Frankie," that's what she called Daddy, "I really don't want to go to any more amusement parks. Let's let the kids go exploring and you and I go where it is cool and dark." Mama didn't often express her feelings about things. She usually went along with what Daddy wanted. But when she did come right out and say what she wanted, Daddy usually listened.

Daddy looked at Mama. Then looked at Becky and then looked back at Mama. "Ruthie, baby, if that's what you want, that's what we're gonna do. After all, the Emmersons are on vacation." Things were weird. I had never seen Daddy put his arm around Mama and now he was calling her baby. I figured it either had to be the sun or all that shrimp getting to him.

It was only 3:30, so we all had a chance to go in and take a shower and take a nap. Before we went into our rooms, Becky pulled me aside. "Okay little brother, wear your Weejuns and your new Polo. Uh, and no socks. After dinner, we're goin' dancing."

At the restaurant, I was too excited to eat much. I only had a piece of pecan pie, an order of onion rings and a couple of glasses of sweet tea. Daddy had barely finished his last helping of shrimp when Becky stood up and announced that we needed to go. "Okay you two. Let's get moving. You don't want to miss the coming attractions and the news reel stuff, do you? Besides, you need to get there a little early to get a good seat. Don't you know there are a lot of people who want to see *The Courtship of Eddie's Father* on a Saturday night at the beach?" I laughed out loud at that one.

We pulled up in front of the theatre at 6:30 and there actually was a line waiting to get in. Daddy handed Becky the keys and gave her his best fatherly warning. "Alright now, listen up. No fast drivin', nobody else in the car and no booze. You got me?"

"Oh, Daddy, remember me? I'm the good kid. We're are just going up to Ocean Drive to check out the pavilion up there. We will pick you up here around 9:15."

"Well, be good and don't be late."

I wondered if Mama noticed what I was wearing when I got out of the back seat and got into the front. If she did, she didn't say anything. She had told me not to wear my new shirt and Weejuns.

As Becky pulled away from the curb, I asked, "Are we really going to a dance place or to an amusement park?"

"Don't be silly. You want to hear some beach music and see some shagging, don't you?"

That really got me excited. "You know I do!"

"Do you remember Eric, the boy I walked with the first day here? Well, he's a DJ at a place called The Shack and says it is the best shag club at the beach. And, he says there is a live Black band called The Soul Brigade there to-night. Isn't that cool?"

"The Shack, where have I heard that name before?" Then it hit me. Britney had talked about The Shack and said it was where all the best dancers went. Then something else hit me. Britney and her new husband lived near Myrtle Beach. Maybe she would be at The Shack. She said that's where they met.

Becky turned right off of the main road and drove down a short street that ended at the road that was close to the beach. She turned right again and all of a sudden, there seemed to be thousands of teenagers and college age kids in the road, on the sidewalk, in the doorways of all of the shops and hanging off the balconies of the two story motels along the street.

"Alright! There it is. See the sign for The Shack? It's right beside the one for Fat Harold's. I wonder if it is a dance club or restaurant. Let's see if we can find a place to park." We had to drive another few blocks before we saw some-body pulling out of a parking spot. When we walked back down the sidewalk toward The Shack, Becky, with her dark tan, blonde hair, short shorts and yellow alligator shirt, must have gotten a dozen whistles and "Hey babies."

The closer we got to the door, the bigger the crowd, the louder the music and the longer the line to get in. Becky snuck up and whispered something to the big guy guarding the door. He disappeared for a minute. When he got back, Becky's friend Eric was with him.

"Hey there mountain girl. You showed up. Come on in."

"I have my brother with me. Can he come in? I can't leave him outside."

Eric frowned. "How old are you little brother?"

I gulped and mumbled, "Almost 16" I lied, but it didn't matter anyway because you're supposed to be 18 to get in a place like The Shack.

Eric inspected me up and down. "Well you look pretty old. Just don't try to buy a beer. You understand?"

"Uh, uh, sure. No beer for me." The rest of the people in line weren't happy when we went in ahead of them.

Just as I walked in and before I could adjust my eyes to the spot lights on the band and darkness everywhere else, one of the guys in the band walked up to the microphone and announced to the crowd standing in front of the stage, "Now, we're going to do one that gets requested a lot, especially down here in Shag Land. Get out on the floor and dance to "Cry to Me" originally recorded by Mr. Solomon Burke in 1961."

The crowd screamed and when the music began, most of them started dancing. Just like the god and goddess I saw at our pool back home, the dancers glided across the floor, spinning and twirling, hand in hand and moving perfectly to the music. Although some were doing different moves at different times, they all seemed to be on the same beat — and I counted it out…one and two, three and four, five six…one and two, three and four, five six. As I watched them, I realized the dancers were all dressed pretty much like the god and goddess – khaki shorts, pastel colored shirts and loafers with no socks. It was exactly how I was dressed. I truly was in shag heaven. I had heard of people going on religious pilgrimages. This place had to be like that. It must be the place where all shaggers dreamed of coming sometime in their lives.

As the music ended and the dancers moved back to their spots in front of the stage, Becky tapped me on the shoulder. "What do you think, little brother? Pretty cool, huh?"

Before I could answer, trumpets and saxophones blasted out a note and a female singer, a Black girl, started singing lyrics I recognized immediately. It was "Playboy" by The Marvellettes, the song Britney played for me and I dedicated to her. The crowd screamed again and moved to the dance floor. Becky grabbed me by the hand and pulled me out on the floor. "Come on, Donno, let's show 'em what mountain shaggers can do."

The crowd was loud and the band was louder, so nobody noticed me counting the steps out loud. When I finally got the rhythm, I realized that Becky and I were actually doing pretty well. I could tell she had been practicing. She surprised me by spinning twice in front of me as the song ended.

"You see. These people don't have anything on us, do they? Becky had to shout because the guy with the microphone announced "Ta Ta, (Like a Baby)" by Clyde McPhatter. Immediately the horns started blasting away. Becky was trying to tell me something else when Eric grabbed her and drug her out on the dance floor. Watching them dance and laugh, I saw that he was just as good as all the other dancers and Becky was keeping up.

I was standing at the edge of the dance floor with my hands in my pockets watching Becky and Eric dance when a girl came up beside me and put her arm through mine. She sort of slurred, "Hi guy. You wanna dance?"

When I first turned to look at her, for a second, I thought it was Britney. I had been looking for her on the dance floor ever since we got there. But no, it wasn't Britney. It was another pretty girl. I'd never been around drunk people other than Uncle Al, but I was pretty sure she was a very drunk girl.

"That's uh, kind of, like my favorite song. So come on and dance with me."

Before I could respond, the girl pulled me out on the dance floor, put her arms around my neck and asked, "You know how to do the belly roll, don't you?"

I didn't have a clue what she was talking about and just stood there. With her arms still around my neck, she put her face right in mine and then swayed back and forth. I still didn't move. She turned loose of my neck and spun around twice in front of me. I finally thought I ought to do something so I started moving my feet and counting "One and two, three and four, five six." I guess the spins were too much for her and she nearly fell down.

As I grabbed her to keep her from falling, she hung on to me and announced, "Whoopsy daisy! Belly roll was a bad idea. Maybe you ought to help me over to the bar." I just about had to drag her over to the bar where luckily there was an empty stool. I started to walk away when she grabbed my arm. "You know, you're a really good dancer. My name is Mary Chapman. I go to college in Greensboro. Where do you go to school?" She stuck out her hand for a hand shake and nearly fell off the stool.

I took her hand and pushed her back onto the stool. "Uh, I did go to West Ash…" I stopped mid-sentence. I didn't want this college girl, even if she was drunk, to know I had just gotten out of the ninth grade. "Uh, I go to uh, West Point, starting next month."

Mary clumsily saluted and tried to stand up.

Just then, Becky walked up. "Hey there, Donno. Who's your friend?"

Still trying to get her balance, Mary said, "I'm Mary and your boyfriend here can really shag. How long has he been in the Army? But hey now, I've gotta go to the little girls' room." With that, Mary staggered off toward the back of the building as the guy with the microphone announced they were going to play an oldie-moldy from 1959 called "So Fine" by The Fiestas. Becky and I silently watched Mary disappear among the crowd that was rushing back to the dance floor.

Becky looked at me with a quizzical look on her face. All I could do was shrug. As we turned to listen to the band, Eric walked up and handed Becky a bottle.

"Here you go, Mountain Girl, a cold PBR just like you ordered."

It was my turn for the quizzical look. Becky responded with a finger to her lips and then said, "I'll talk to you later."

We stayed at The Shack for another half hour. Becky and I danced once and I watched her and Eric dance a couple of more times. She really was getting good. After Becky gave Eric a big kiss and a promise to call him sometime, we walked out the door, and the ocean air felt nice and cool after the body heat generated by the crowd of dancers inside. I turned back and looked at the crowd waiting to get in The Shack. I decided that even if I never came back to the place, at least I could say I had been to holy ground, the temple of shag. I would remember going there forever. It was also something I could hold over Sarah Jane's head. About a block from the car, I heard the band play "Dance With Me."

On the way back to the theater, Becky finally broke the silence. "You want a Tic Tac? I need one to hide the beer smell on my breath." She looked at me and smiled. "You know, Donno. I'm 19 and it's legal for me to drink beer. But, I would just as soon not let Mama and Pops know about it for a while. Is that cool with you?"

I really didn't have to think about my answer very long. There was no way I was going to rat on Becky for a lot of reasons, especially because she had covered for me in the past and probably would in the future. "Yeah, I'm cool with it." Then I added what I thought was a very responsible and adult thought. "As long as you don't drink and drive or something dumb like that."

"Okay. Agreed." She paused for a minute and then went on. "There's something else I need to confess and ask you not to tell the folks. On some of the nights I was supposed to be going to the library to study or over to a friend's house for a sleepover, we've actually been going out to the Maple Lodge to dance."

The Maple Lodge was an old resort inn south of town that had been converted to a night club. I had heard that it was a pretty rough place but that a lot of top bands played there.

Becky didn't wait for me to respond. "You know I have always loved rock and roll and when you started in on this shag thing, I sort of fell in love with it too. That's the kind of music they play out there. You probably thought I had been practicing a lot. Well, in a way, I have, but it has been at the Maple Lodge every weekend and sometimes during the week. I think I'm getting pretty good. Don't you?"

All I could say was "Yep, you're really getting good and I'm jealous."

"So you're not going to tell the folks about all of this?"

I looked at my sister and realized that we were no longer older sister and baby brother. We had become almost equals. Now that she had confided her secrets in me, she could tell me anything and I could do the same. "No, I won't tell them, as long as you promise to take me to the Maple Lodge sometime."

She laughed out loud. "I promise, except I don't think they will be as lenient as the guys at The Shack. We might have to wait until you really turn 16 or you grow a beard."

We drove around the block a couple of times before we spotted Mama and Daddy waiting for us on the curb in front of the theatre. I was surprised when they climbed in the back seat. I was even more surprised when Daddy put his arm around Mama and she snuggled up close to him. I would say the last night of our beach vacation was pretty darn good for the whole Emmerson family.

I went to the pool a couple of times after we got back home. When she asked how our beach trip had gone, I couldn't help but brag to Sarah Jane about seeing some great shaggers at The Shack and how I actually danced to a real Black band with real singers. "It's a really cool place, Sarah Jane. The band is so loud you can barely hear yourself talk, but you can feel the beat of the music in your stomach. I hope I can go back there some day and dance again."

Sarah Jane didn't seem to mind that I was bragging. She acted like she was glad I had a chance to hear some live beach music. "Oh, that sounds so great. I want to go sometime too. Why don't you play a shag song on the juke box and show me how you danced there."

Uh oh. I thought, *I set myself up for that. How was I going to get out of dancing with her in front of all the other kids?* Then I looked down at my shoes. I was wearing my beat up, old Keds black and white high tops. "Can't dance in these shoes."

Chapter 14

A week or so before school started up the first of September, I got something in the mail from the high school. As a sophomore, I had to take plain geometry, English, U.S. History and phys-ed. I didn't have a choice. However, they did give me a choice of electives. I could choose between home economics, wood shop, auto shop, band or art. We had a big argument at the dinner table when I made the mistake of showing the choices to my family. Daddy immediately said I should take auto shop as my first choice and wood shop as my second. He said I needed to start thinking of a way to make a living in what he called "the real world". Of course, I wanted to take art. Mama just tried to keep the discussion peaceful and Becky smiled and shook her head. She was becoming less and less involved in family discussions.

Because I finally gave up and quit arguing, I guess Daddy thought I would choose the elective he wanted when I went for orientation two days before classes started. For the first time in my life, I defied my father and also lied about it. I signed up for art.

We were back at the dinner table again when I admitted what I had done. I knew Daddy would be mad so I tried to come up with an excuse to calm him down. "But Daddy, by the time I got there, auto shop and wood shop were full. The only things left were home economics, band or art. You know I can't play an instrument and do you want me to learn how to sew and bake cookies?"

Daddy pounded the table and made the plates rattle. "Hells bells, boy. Baking cookies makes more sense than drawing little pictures that nobody will ever buy or even see. At least you can eat cookies instead being a freakin' starvin' artist."

I realized then that I would probably spend the rest of my life trying to make my father understand that being an artist meant much more to me than just earning a living. Even as a 15 year-old I saw that being creative had to be what my life was about.

After the argument with Daddy, I was in my room listening to "Dance With Me" wondering how I would ever find my way around in the big high school. Becky knocked on my door and asked if she could come in.

"You know, Donno. He's only trying to prepare you for the future and it's the only way he knows how."

"I guess so. But why won't he ever just listen to my side for once? Why won't he ever say he is proud of me or that I might be just a little bit talented?" The record ended and I put on "Stubborn Kind of Fellow."

Becky plopped down on my bed before she answered. "I don't know. Maybe he's jealous. Maybe he wishes he had some kind of talent like that. Maybe he's afraid of the future. But, I'm sure of one thing. If you let him or anybody else talk you out of doing something you love and are good at, I bet you will always wonder what you missed. You know, I really don't want to be a dental hygienist. I let Daddy convince me that it was more practical than what I really want to do."

I was shocked. All I could remember hearing was how Becky was going to live at home and to go to the community college for a couple of years and then step right into a good paying job and probably marry a dentist. She was going to start at the community college a couple of days after I start at the high school. "I uh, I never heard you talk about anything else. What would you rather do?"

"Do you know what a computer is? I read about some guys out west who are working on machines that can almost think. You know, I have always been good at math. Numbers just make sense to me. I want to go to college and study higher math and learn more about the thinking machines." Becky punched at my pillow with both hands. "I started thinking about going to college to study math and computers when President Kennedy talked about sending people to the moon before 1970. That means computers are going to be important. Just think about being part of that. But, our daddy thinks it's all a hoax. Says there's no future at all in computers, especially for girls. I let him talk me out of my dream." Becky stood up and took my hand. "Come on, let's dance. Count it out with me. One and two, three and four, five six" My sister and I danced in our sock feet on my bedroom floor to Marvin Gaye singing "Stubborn Kind of Fellow." She gave me a hug before she left my room.

The fall semester went pretty well. As it turned out, I was pretty good at geometry. I guess it was because it was all about shapes and lines. I understood circles, squares and triangles because I could see them. I made A's and B's. Algebra had been nothing but X's, O's and theory that was a mystery and I made D's.

Of course, art was my favorite class. The teacher was Miss Walincourt, a kind of chubby middle-aged lady who wore bright colored clothes with wild designs and beads and things. In class, she wore a smock or apron kind of thing that had paint stains all over. I thought she was cool. Miss Walincourt was a friend of Mr. Fontain, my junior high art teacher and he had told her about me. She had also seen my painting of the red bird that won the district art contest. On the first day of class, she pulled me aside and said "Mr. Emmerson, I expect a great deal from you this year. You have raw talent and a creative eye. Do not let me down." She scared me a little, but made me feel pretty good about myself at the same time. I loved art.

Toward the end of September, Sarah Jane had not only gotten herself put on the school spirit committee, but was also going to run for sophomore class secretary. Of course, that meant I was drafted to do banners for the football team and posters for her campaign. I had given up saying no to her on things like that. Secretly, I was proud that somebody liked my art and the chance it gave me to show off to others.

On a Sunday afternoon, Sarah Jane showed up with about 10 pieces of poster paper and an eight foot long canvas banner. She also brought brushes and a bunch of poster paints in little jars. Sarah Jane and I grew up together, so it was no big deal for Mama when we went up to my room. Although, I insisted we leave the door open.

Sarah Jane's idea for the football banner was kind of lame. The Ashton High School mascot was a black panther. I always thought that was sort of strange because there were only two Black faces in the school and they were our janitors, Mr. Washington and Mr. Roosevelt. The kids called them "The Presidents." On the football banner, Sarah Jane wanted the picture of a snarling black panther and "Beware! Panthers Have Sharp Teeth!" Easy enough — I could knock that out in a couple of hours if she didn't hang around and bug me. Her campaign posters were another story. She wanted her face and the words "Red Heads Rock and Can Spell Too!" The words would be easy, but she didn't want the drawing of her face to be a cartoon. She wanted it to look like her. She wanted a portrait.

"Sarah Jane, I can draw faces, but I've never drawn one that that really looks like someone, especially 10 times. You want it on 10 posters. Why don't you take a picture with a camera and get 10 copies made at the drug store? That would be a heck of a lot easier."

Using the little pouting look she used sometimes, she started to beg. "Oh come on, Donno. The drug store charges 50 cents for every enlargement and Mama doesn't have five dollars for that. Besides, the copies would only be 5x7 and I want it bigger than that. I know you really want to do it. You really can draw and you like a challenge — and it doesn't have to be another Mona Lisa."

I was proud of myself for knowing about Mona Lisa. Mr. Fontain said it was the most famous portrait ever painted and was worth millions of dollars. To me, the lady looked like her feet were being tickled and she was about to break out laughing. I hated to admit it, but Sarah Jane was right. I really wanted to see if I could do it. "Oh, good grief, Sarah Jane, you're really a pain, you know it?" She started to pout again and I gave in. "Okay, I will try one but only one and it won't be in color. It will have to be in charcoal." I pulled out one of my sketch pads and piece of dark brown charcoal. "Okay, sit there on my chair and look up at me."

I had never done a serious drawing of a real person before, but I knew that I should start with the basic shape of her face and hair and then position a faint line for where I wanted her eyes to be, then her nose and finally her mouth. After I was satisfied with that, I started adding details. I constantly looked at her then back to the paper, without really noticing the progress I was making. I added shadows beside her nose and highlights to her hair. I rubbed out one side of her lips and made it a little higher. I really struggled with her eyes and I had to rub them out and start over several times. Finally, I lightly added to her eyebrows and gently rubbed out a little the of charcoal to add highlight to the pupils of her eyes. I decided I had done as much as I could do and looked up at Sarah Jane and then back down at the drawing. It was her, really her and I suddenly realized how pretty she was and how open and kind her face could be. I was shocked. Why had I not noticed it before? Sure, she could be a pain in the rear and was way too bossy, but I now understood that the girl in the picture, and sitting across from me, was probably my best friend in the entire world.

"Come on, Donno. Let me see. Did you give me buck teeth and big zits? Did you make my nose real big?"

I handed Sarah Jane the sketch book and the normal cocky, smart-alecky smile faded from her face and was replaced by the sweet grin I had captured in the drawing. She looked at the drawing for a while before speaking. "Donno, this is beautiful. Do you really think I look like this?"

"Well, I can add some zits if you want."

She smiled the sweet smile again. "I don't think I want this on my posters. It's too special. Thank you." She leaned over and kissed me on the forehead.

All I could do was shrug. “I think it turned out pretty good.”

“I’m going to find a nice frame for it and keep it in my room. I don’t care if anybody else ever sees it. I love it”

I went ahead and did her posters with just the words surrounded by stars and lightning flashes. I got real creative on the football banner, putting an Ashton High jersey on the panther and made the words look like flames. I thought it was pretty cool.

Sarah Jane won her election and pushed her way into being involved and being a leader in all sorts of things at the school. She was just as bossy as always and always got me involved when she needed something drawn or hand lettered. I complained a lot, but I secretly appreciated her reliance on me,

Sarah Jane and I rode to school together every morning. Her mother drove on Mondays and Fridays and Mama drove the rest of the week. We seldom spoke on the way to school because I usually took that time to finish homework assignments. As soon as we pulled up in front of the school, she went her way and I went mine. Her way was to the wing where all of the smart kids went for their homerooms and advanced classes. I went a different direction. The only time we might see each other during the day was at the door to the cafeteria. Of course, we didn’t sit together at lunch. She sat with a bunch of other smart girls from both sides of the river and I sat with Ricky Stillman and a couple of other guys I knew from junior high. Because Sarah Jane had band practice after school, her mother picked her up and I rode the bus home. It took forever because the West Ashton kids had to change over to another bus at a park downtown. The second bus went across the river to our side of town.

Sarah Jane wasn’t a cheerleader, but she might as well have been. Even when she was in the marching band, she was always down on the field before the games, making sure that there were people holding up the banner I had painted. I went to the games alone and sat behind the band, actually right behind Ricky Stillman's tuba. Sometimes there was a sock hop after the home games. A couple of times, I went for a little while just to hear the music and watch people dance. I didn't see any shagging. There was still a lot of twisting, jerking, monkeying and watusi-ing. I swore that if I ever heard "Sixty Minute Man" or "Dance With Me" or a new one just released in August called "It's Alright" by The Impressions at the sock hop, I would grab Sarah Jane and show people some real dancing.

The football team did pretty well and finished first in our conference. That meant playoff games would determine what team would go to Chapel Hill and play for the state championship.

We won our first playoff game in an upset and that meant we would play the second one on our home field. The game was scheduled for Friday, November 22.

Chapter 15

The day was cool and cloudy and I was sitting in Miss Carson's English class wondering if it was going to rain during the football game that night. I hadn't yet decided if I was going to the game or the dance afterwards. A bunch of seniors had put together a band and were going to play at the dance and I kind of wanted to hear them. I wasn't paying attention to the student reading her boring essay at the front of the room, and I was about to nod off because the class was right after lunch and the room was too warm. I sat up straight when the P.A. system crackled and buzzed.

"This is Principal Joyner. I have a very serious announcement." We all turned around and looked at each other wondering what was going on. When I looked out the window and saw dark grey clouds, I thought it might be getting ready to start snowing and they were going to dismiss school.

"We have just learned that President Kennedy has been shot in Dallas, Texas."

There was an audible gasp from the students and Miss Carson threw her hands to her face and screamed "Oh no! Oh no!" Like everyone else in the room, I just sat there with my mouth open, trying to comprehend what we had just heard.

The voice on the P.A. system changed from Principal Joyner's to a radio announcer's with a strange accent. "At approximately 12:30 p.m., central time, President John F. Kennedy was shot while riding in an open car through the streets of Dallas. Texas Governor John Connally was also wounded. Mrs. Kennedy was in the car, but does not seem to be wounded. The President was rushed to nearby Parkland Hospital. We will report when we have further details."

We all stared at the brown P.A. speaker box on the wall, waiting for something else, waiting for good news that it was all just a mistake and that our handsome young president and his beautiful wife were okay.

I don't remember how much time passed before the silence in the classroom was broken again by the radio announcer whose voice cracked and waivered. "We have learned through witnesses at Parkland Hospital that President Kennedy was uh, um pronounced dead at approximately 1:00 p.m. central time. That was confirmed by the priest who gave Mr. Kennedy his last rights."

There was complete silence in the room for what seemed like an hour. No one moved. No one said a word. No one knew what to do. Finally, the girl who had been reading her essay and who had not moved from the front of the room began to weep. It was as if her tears gave us all permission to react. Miss Carson laid her head on her desk and moaned. Some of the girls cried out loud and a few of the boys, trying to be cool, acted like it was no big deal. I didn't cry. All I could think of was Mrs. Kennedy. She and the president had just lost a baby in August who only lived for one day. I think his name was Patrick, and then, Mrs. Kennedy was alone with little John and Caroline. It made me think of Sarah Jane's mother having to raise her after her father was killed.

The P.A. came to life again. This time it was Principal Joyner in a low, somber voice. "We will dismiss all classes at 2:30 p.m. Bus students will wait at their normal spots. Other students will meet their rides at the drop-off and pick-up point at the west side of the school. All school activities, including the football game have been canceled. Please be respectful while leaving the building. God bless you all and God bless America."

We sat in silence until a bell rang at 2:30. Without being prompted, we all got up from our desks and filed out the door. Miss Carson never got up from her desk. The silence in the hallway was eerie. Usually, when classes changed or at the end of the day, the sound of lockers being opened and closed, people laughing and talking, and the shuffling of hundreds of feet on concrete floors was deafening. There was no such noise that day. Even outdoors, where everyone waited for their busses or rides, no one spoke above a whisper.

I waited for my regular bus that would take me downtown where I could catch the connecting bus for West Ashton. I was lost in thought and didn't notice Sarah Jane come and stand beside me. "You not going to ride with your mom?"

"I didn't try to call her to tell her to pick me up. I knew she would be listening to the radio in the car and I didn't want to hear it all again. I just wanted to ride the bus and think."

We boarded the bus and sat together without speaking. We didn't speak on the second bus to West Ashton either. Our bus stop was about three blocks from our street and we walked slowly and silently for a while until Sarah Jane stopped and started to cry. "How could they do this to us? How can they take him away from us? This changes everything in the world for me. Nothing will ever be the same!" She sobbed uncontrollably.

Without thinking about it, I put my arm around her shoulders and pulled her close to me. "I know, I know," is all I could say. I did know. I knew exactly what she meant. Up until that moment, even with the Cuban Missile scare, the civil rights marches and a strange war being fought somewhere a long way away, life for me and life for most of us was pretty simple and safe. A new pair of shoes, a new record to hear, an invitation to a party and a passing grade in math were the most important things in many of our lives. Now death, hatred, sorrow and doubt had entered our protected little worlds — our innocence had been destroyed down in Dallas along with that young man we all adored. Sarah Jane climbed her front steps and went into her house without turning around. I stared at the closed door for a few moments, wondering what might come next.

I didn't leave our house Friday night or all day Saturday. I watched TV off and on and saw Mrs. Kennedy on an airplane with the new president. A reporter said she was wearing the same clothes she was wearing when her husband was shot. I couldn't tell on our black and white TV, but the reporter said her dress had blood stains all over it.

I saw the news about the Dallas police finding the man they thought had shot the president. I saw him at the jail and when his wife and mother came to see him there. Mostly what I saw were news people jostling each other to find any kind of new information for a story or get another picture. I would watch for a while and then go up to my room to listen to music and draw in my sketch book.

On Sunday morning, Mama, Becky, Grandma and Sarah Jane's mother went to the 11:00 service at the Baptist Church near our house. Daddy and I stayed home and watched TV. Naturally, both of the channels we got were filled with anything that had to do with President Kennedy's death and the man who shot him. The man had been a Marine and belonged to the Communist Party. He was married to a Russian girl and the police had already found out that he had bought an Italian rifle for $12, probably the one he used to shoot Mr. Kennedy. Daddy could hardly sit still he was so mad. He would get up and stomp around, go to the kitchen and get another cup of coffee and swear the whole time. "Damn commies! Damn Cubans! No way the S.O.B was working alone. Russians or the mob have got to have something to do with this. Got to. I can't believe the bastard was a Marine."

I didn't know my father liked Mr. Kennedy. I think I remembered him saying that he voted for Mr. Nixon in 1960. I guessed he disliked Russians and Communists more than he liked Republicans. Anyway, he sure was upset about Mr. Kennedy.

After church, Mama, Becky and Grandma had stopped at Sarah Jane's house to have a cup of coffee and talk some more about how sad everything was. Grandma said she hated most Yankees because her grandfather was wounded by one in the Civil War, but she liked Mr. Kennedy even though he was a Yankee because he had been in the Navy and fought in World War II. She said it didn't bother her too much that he was Catholic. Mama and Becky both thought Mr. Kennedy was wonderful. They all came into our living room about 1:15 or so, just as Daddy and I were watching a bunch of policemen in cowboy hats leading Lee Harvey Oswald through a crowd of reporters and other policemen. Daddy yelled at the reporter on TV because he kept calling the man Lee Harold Oswald. Mama shook her head and sighed "Look at him. He's just a boy really. He's not much older than Becky. What in the world could make him do such a…"

Suddenly, a man in a dark hat and suit jacket stepped out of the crowd and shot Mr. Oswald in the stomach. I couldn't figure out what had happened, but Mama knew immediately. "My God, he just shot that boy! That man there, the one the other man tackled, he just shot that boy!" Daddy and I stood up and all five of us stood around the TV watching chaos unfold on our little black and white set. The man with the gun was tackled and dragged away. Mr. Oswald lay on the floor with people standing around looking at him until a white station wagon drove up and took him away. They took him to the same place they had taken Mr. Kennedy on Friday. Sarah Jane started to cry again and she and her mother left without saying anything. Grandma thought Mr. Oswald probably deserved to get shot. Daddy agreed.

Later in the day, the news reporter told us that Mr. Oswald was dead. So the man who probably shot Mr. Kennedy got shot himself while handcuffed to a policeman. Another news reporter said that a man named Jack Ruby shot Mr. Oswald. Mr. Ruby owned a night club or something in Dallas and the police knew him. As soon as Daddy heard that, he started stomping around the house again. "I knew it! I told you I bet the mob had something to do with this. I'll bet Ruby is tied up in the mob and the Russians! Damn country is going to hell in a hand basket!"

I didn't know where the country was headed, but the direction I thought my life was headed sure changed. I no longer felt as safe as I had just a few days before. I no longer felt like my future would eventually turn out okay. I would look at things a lot differently. I was only 15 and a half, but had grown up a lot in the past 36 hours.

Schools and a bunch of other things including Daddy's factory were closed on Monday. I guess it was so people could watch Mr. Kennedy's funeral on TV. It started a little before 11:00 and Mama invited Sarah Jane, her mom and her grandmother to come to our house and also eat lunch with us. Mama said it was because our TV set got better reception and our living room was bigger. I think it was because she didn't want Sarah Jane's family to be alone on such a sad day.

We watched mostly without talking, except an occasional "oh dear" or "look at that poor thing." We saw the flag-covered coffin on a wagon pulled by horses. We saw a horse with no rider and with a boot turned backwards in the stirrup. We saw Mrs. Kennedy dressed in black, surrounded by the president's brothers and other important people walk down the street. We watched straight through to the end without stopping to eat lunch. We were all exhausted. Afterwards, there were so many images to remember, all sad and all hard to believe. Two that kept coming back to me were little John John saluting his father's casket and the other was the brief image of a young Black girl crying as the funeral procession passed her spot in the crowd that stood four rows deep along the curb.

There was a lot of back and forth discussion on the local radio and TV about whether the annual Ashton Christmas Parade scheduled for the next Wednesday should be canceled. City leaders finally decided to go ahead with the parade. Becky and I rode the bus downtown and found a spot to watch the parade. We went partly because Sarah Jane was marching with the band and because we always loved watching the city's Black high school band march. They always danced and pranced to the upbeat music they played and a lot more people came to watch them instead of Santa Claus. There was no excitement from any of the floats or bands, especially the Black school band. They marched silently with only a simple drum beat pacing their steps.

Chapter 16

Thanksgiving was only six days after Mr. Kennedy was killed. Although none of us saw a reason to give thanks, Mama decided to go ahead and have everybody over for a big turkey lunch. In addition to my family, the group included Sarah Jane, her mother and grandmother. Uncle Al also came but stayed sober for the whole day.

Nobody said much during lunch and after we finished eating we all just sat around the table for a while. I don't know if Becky chose that time to make her announcement because Daddy would be embarrassed to yell and get mad in front of the crowd or if Mr. Kennedy's death gave her the courage to do something she had dreamed of doing. Mama was in the kitchen when Becky spoke. "Mama, can you hear me? I've got something to tell all of you. I've decided that I really don't want to be a dental hygienist. I want to learn about computers."

Daddy's eyes narrowed and he started to say something. "Daddy, just listen for once before you start yelling. I found out that a community college in Conway, South Carolina offers a two year program in computer programming. That's something our college doesn't offer. I have applied down there and can start second semester in January."

"Rebecca Emmerson, you listen to me!"

"No, Daddy, you listen to me for a change! Math and science are things I have always loved and am good at doing. It was you who decided that I should be a dental hygienist. There's nothing wrong with that, except it's not what I want. Can't you understand?"

Daddy's fist came down on the table and I saw surprise and fear in Sarah Jane's eyes. "Young lady, I'll not stand for you talking back to me and I'll..."

Mama cut him off. "But, Becky, what will you do? Where will you live? How can you afford to…? You're too young."

"Come on, Mama. I'll be 20 in a few months. Daddy fought in a war when he was 18 and you were married when you were 19. I really can take care of myself."

The rest of us sat in silence, watching this family drama unfold. All of our guests stayed seated, afraid to move.

Daddy started in again. "So, just how will you support yourself when I decide to cut you off? Have you thought of that?"

Mama cut Daddy off again. "Oh, Frank. Don't say that. You know you wouldn't do such a thing." That made Daddy mad and he hit the table again.

"No, Mama, let me answer. I have a friend down there and he has found me a job as an assistant manager at a record store in Myrtle Beach." Becky looked over at me and grinned. I knew the friend was Eric, the boy she met on the beach. "My friend also found me a place to stay with some other girls who go to the community college. I have enough money saved up to live on for a while. Besides, you had already paid for a whole year for school up here. I or uh you get a refund on the second semester tuition."

It took Daddy a couple of seconds to take it all in. Becky had obviously been planning this move for a while and made some real adult decisions on her own. He finally came up with another objection. "You know, I'm making the payments on your car and I pay the insurance. If you are so grown up, don't you think you should be doing that?"

Becky resorted to something I had seen her use before. She started to cry and that always made Daddy crazy. "Well, I guess if you really love me, you will keep paying those things until I get out of school. If you won't, I'll just get a second job and figure out how to pay it myself."

The "if you really love me" line did it. Daddy was still spitting mad and would make Becky's life difficult until she left, but he did love her almost more than anything else and he couldn't stand for her to doubt it.

Without another word, Daddy and Uncle Al got up from the table and went into the living room to watch the Packers and Lions on TV. The rest of us helped clear the table, also without saying a word. Finally, Sarah Jane's mother hugged Mama and thanked her for lunch. Sarah Jane smiled at me and headed out the door with an aluminum foil covered platter with leftover turkey and dressing.

Mama and Grandma put on coats and went out on the porch while Becky and I went upstairs. I turned on my radio but *Big WASH* had already started playing Christmas carols even though Christmas was still a month away. So, I put "Dance With Me" on the record player and stretched out on my bed.

Becky knocked on my door and came in before I answered. "So, Donno, what do you think of my news?"

She was smiling, but I could tell she had been crying. Becky and I were a lot alike. Neither of us could stand arguments and confrontation, especially in the family. I knew it took a lot of courage to challenge Daddy and his plans for her.

"Can you take me with you? I don't think it's going to be a lot of fun here when I don't have you around to take part of the blame."

"Ah, you can take it. Just say 'yes sir and no sir' and then do what you think is right for you. But you know something, little brother? Daddy is a good man. He grew up during the Depression and didn't have a thing."

"Yeah, I know, but I just wish he could look at things kind of like we do instead of an old guy."

Becky hesitated before going on. "Um, you're not supposed to know this and I only know because Mama slipped up and told me. Daddy didn't have much of a childhood. His daddy left him and Uncle Al when they were just babies. They both were in and out of foster homes. And also,

Daddy didn't graduate from high school. He dropped out to join the Marines when the war started."

That news shocked me, yet it explained a lot of things. Daddy was a proud man and worked hard for everything he had. I just didn't think he understood me very well.

"I know I'm making him both mad and sad by going a different way than what he has planned for me. Maybe one day he will understand that. But for you, you still have at least three more years here. Just remember that he loves you and only wants you to have more than he ever had." That was something I would struggle with for years to come.

"I guess Eric is the friend you are talking about down there."

She nodded and smiled again. "Yes. We've been writing back and forth for a while. He calls me sometimes when I know Daddy won't be home. Turns out, his father owns the record store where I'll be working. Eric runs it for his father. He only DJs at The Shack part-time because he loves to hear the live bands. His store has a section of nothing but shag music records by the bands that play at The Shack."

"You'll be the beach music queen before long. Maybe I can come down and visit sometime."

Becky punched me on the shoulder and said, "We'll have to see about that."

Becky left my room and I put a stack of shag songs on the record player. I thought about getting up and practicing my dance steps, but decided against it.

Still reeling from Mr. Kennedy's assassination and Becky's upcoming move, December was pretty gloomy around our house. To make things worse, the week before Christmas the temperature dropped down into the low20s and the wind blew all the time. That would have been okay if it had snowed, but it didn't.

Mama did her best to cheer things up by getting a big cardboard cutout Santa Claus holding an open sack of toys for the front porch and several strings of a new kind of

Christmas lights for the tree and the bushes in front of the house. The lights were smaller and brighter than the old ones and the whole string didn't go dark if one bulb burned out. We also got a real live tree instead of a cut one. It had a big heavy ball of dirt on the bottom wrapped in a burlap bag and Daddy and I had to struggle to get it into a metal wash tub. Mama said Daddy and I could plant it in the front yard after the holidays. Daddy didn't seem too excited about that idea. Daddy didn't talk to Becky very much during Christmas, yet he did take the 1958 Impala he bought her in high school and had it tuned up and had four new tires put on.

We kept the same Christmas morning tradition we had since I was little. As always, Becky and I came down the steps to see what Santa had brought us after Mama and Daddy had built a fire and turned on all the Christmas lights. I was 15 and Becky was almost 20, but we still talked about Santa Claus and were almost as excited as we had been as little kids. Becky *ooh'ed* and *ah'ed* over a suitcase and some new clothes.

I really was surprised by my gift. It was a small metal easel that could sit on a table. It was just big enough to hold the 11 by 14 inch canvases that came along with it. In addition to the easel and canvasses, I got three nice artist paint brushes with long handles. I looked up at Daddy, wondering if he had anything to do with the gift. He must have known what I was thinking because he shook his head and nodded at Mama. It didn't matter. At least he didn't forbid her from getting me something art related. Of course, I got socks, underwear and a sweater with a reindeer on it. Becky gave me a book on oil painting that showed how to mix colors.

Sarah Jane, her mother and her grandmother came over for lunch and our gift exchange tradition with them. I gave Sarah Jane a nice wooden frame with a mat for the picture I did of her and a 45 of "Monkey Time" by Major Lance. It wasn't exactly a shag song, but I heard it on the juke box at the pool pavilion right before school started and liked the beat. I was pretty sure Sarah Jane didn't have it.

Sarah Jane must have known that I was going to get the easel, canvasses and brushes because she gave me a small set of oil paints. There were tubes of red, yellow, blue, white and black and a bottle of turpentine. I had learned in art class that I could mix those colors together and come up with almost all other colors. After I opened that gift, Sarah Jane gave me another gift. By the shape, I could tell it was a record and figured it was another beach tune to add to my collection. Instead, it was "Please Please Me" by a band called The Beatles. I had never heard of them and quizzically looked at Sarah Jane.

"You just wait," she said. Then she took a pencil and a piece of the wrapping paper and drew four simple faces that had long hair down over their foreheads. "You just wait and see."

After she left, I played the record. I kind of liked it, but wasn't sure. It wouldn't be long before I would hear a lot more songs by The Beatles. It also wouldn't be long before my new art supplies would cause a big problem.

Chapter 17

The first few months of 1964 were wild and weird for me. First of all, Becky left for South Carolina just after New Year's Day. She cried, Mama cried, I cried, and even Daddy sniffed a little. Right before she got in her car, she hugged me and said, "Listen, little brother, you keep on drawing and keep on dancing. I'll write you and maybe we can figure out a way for you to visit me at the beach. I love you, Donno."

Although Becky had seldom been home for the past year – being busy at school, work, going out with her friends, her leaving for good left a big empty feeling at our house. Things were not as joyful with her gone. There wasn't as much laughter. I couldn't help thinking about visiting her sometime.

Before school started back after the holidays, I used my new oil paints and did a small painting, really just trying to learn how to use the brushes. First, I mixed black and white paint to make a pale gray and coated the whole canvas, giving it a gloomy, eerie feel. Without really having a plan, I started sketching a figure on the canvas using only the black paint. Because of the shape and size, it started looking like a young boy in a coat. I guess I couldn't get the Kennedy funeral out of my head. So, I painted the boy's right arm into a salute and as I added paint, the little boy changed into John John Kennedy saluting his father's casket. It was not a likeness of his face, but anyone who had watched the funeral would have recognized him.

The figure of John John was on the right side of the canvas leaving an open space on the left. As I looked at the painting, I knew what should fill that space. It was an image that stuck with me just like John John's. I painted how I remembered the little Black girl I saw crying as the TV camera passed her in the crowd on the street during the funeral procession. The only difference was that I painted her with one hand covering her mouth and the other holding little John John's hand. Both figures were loosely painted in black and their edges blended into the still wet gray background.

It was the first stylized, abstract painting I had tried. The figures were almost like smoke rising from a dying fire. It took me a while to decide if I liked it or if I should paint it out and start over on something else. I decided I liked it, but something was missing. I thought about it for a while and came up with an idea that seemed to fit the rest of the picture. In very small letters that were just as smoky and indistinct as the two children, I added the words "I have a dream" above the children's heads. I remembered that Black preacher, Mr. King, saying that on TV during a big event in Washington. I put the painting on a shelf to dry and didn't think about it too much until I decided to take it to school and show it to Miss Walincourt, my art teacher. I didn't even show the painting to my parents first.

Miss Walincourt got all excited about the painting and actually hugged me. "Oh, Mr. Emmerson, this is the best thing I have seen from any of my students in a long, long time."

I thought it was pretty good and I liked the misty smoky style of it, but I didn't think she would get so excited about it.

"Mr. Emmerson, Donald, you know that the city wide student art contest is coming up soon. May I enter this piece for you? I think you have an excellent chance of winning again this year."

"Sure," I said. Why not? It was certainly different than the picture of the red bird I had entered the year before, so I didn't think the painting would win. That was around the middle of January. In a few weeks, I wished I had told Miss Walincourt no.

On February 9th, something else happened that changed my little world some more. The Beatles appeared on

The Ed Sullivan Show. Sarah Jane had warned me about them and I had heard one or two of their songs on *Big WASH* radio, but nothing prepared me for what I saw and heard on our old black and white TV that Sunday night. When Mr. Sullivan introduced them, the screaming started and lasted all through "All My Loving," "Till There Was You" and "She Loves You".

You could barely hear the music for the screaming coming from the TV and from Sarah Jane who had come to our house to watch it with us. Mama even clapped along with the music and danced a bit. Daddy said he wished they would hurry up and finish so a magician named Fred Kaps could come on. Grandma turned off her hearing aid and fell asleep.

In the 30 minutes between their first and second set, I decided that if that many girls could go that crazy over guys with funny accents and long hair, I wanted to be part of it. By the time The Beatles came back to *The Ed Sullivan Show* on February 16, I had already quit using wax to make my flat top stand up and started hoping my mousy brown hair would grow faster so I could comb it down over my forehead and ears. I also tried to imitate that funny English accent Paul McCartney had. I didn't think my thick southern accent would be much of a problem.

I spent all the money I had on Beatles records at McMurray's. I had to buy 45s because that's all my little record player could play. At school, boys wearing short boots with pointed toes and higher heels started showing up, as did dark pants with tight legs and fewer haircuts.

On *Big WASH*, the DJs started sounding British and every other song was from The Beatles first album. At least three or four times every night, you would hear "Please Please Me, "I Saw Her Standing There," " Do You Want To Know A Secret" and "Twist and Shout." I liked the original "Twist and Shout" by The Isley Brothers when I heard it on the juke box at the pool and felt a little guilty singing along on The Beatles version. It didn't take long before I could sing along with all of The Beatles songs. I was hooked. Marvin Gaye, The Drifters, The Dominoes, The Marvelettes and The Temptations were replaced by Ringo, George, John and Paul. Eventually, records by The Rolling Stones, The Dave Clark Five, The Kinks and The Byrds joined The Beatles collection. All of my beach music records got pushed to the back of my little wire record holder or to a box under my bed.

If Becky leaving, The Beatles coming to America, and the ongoing trauma of the Kennedy assassination were not enough, a storm created by my entry into the student art contest nearly got my art teacher fired and Daddy arrested for assault. It also got me labeled as a trouble maker by a few people in West Ashton.

One day after art class, Miss Walincourt stopped me at the door. "Mr. Emmerson, I was not able to enter your painting into the school district art contest."

"Oh, okay. Thanks for trying." I figured there was some rule about previous winners entering or something like that. With everything else going on in my head, it wasn't that big of a deal.

"No Donald, it's not okay! The administration would not let me enter it for you because they say the painting is too controversial. They say it might incite racial strife, maybe riots." Miss Walincourt threw up her hands when she said that.

"Uh, they think my painting is bad? I mean, do they think I am trying to cause trouble with Black people or something?"

"Donald, you probably never heard the word Beatnik. Well, I'm an old Beatnik who thinks anyone in power should be challenged. Beatniks are rebels. The bigots in charge of this school district are afraid of anything that might suggest that white and Black children can get along in school. They want to keep Black children out of white schools just as long as they can." Miss Walincourt was almost shouting.

I didn't really understand it all, but I heard that before he was killed, President Kennedy had been working on something called the Civil Rights Act. He wanted Black people to be treated fairly and not kept from doing things just because they were Black. Part of what the president wanted to do was to start allowing Black kids to go to schools that had always been for white kids only. After Mr. Kennedy died, Mr. Johnson, the new president, kept working on the same thing.

On February 9, 1964, the very day that The Beatles were on *The Ed Sullivan Show,* the U.S. House of Representatives voted in favor the Civil Rights Act. According to Miss Walincourt, when that happened politicians and others in the South realized that the 100 years of keeping Black people from being treated equally might be over, so they tried to fight it any way they could.

"Gosh, Miss Walincourt, I didn't mean to cause any trouble. I just started painting and that's what it turned out to be. I thought it was pretty neat, but I understand if it can't be in the contest."

Miss Walincourt got all red in the face and started waving her arms. "This goes way beyond the art contest, Mr. Emmerson. It has to do with the first amendment freedom of speech! It has to do with the Constitution! It has to do with the Bible! It has to do with, with, I don't know! It has to do with everything that is fair and good and I won't let it happen."

I knew that Miss Walincourt was a little on the crazy side so I wasn't sure what I should say. "Well, uh, if it would do any good, I can do another painting of a bird or horse or something and you can put it in the contest."

"No sir, Mr. Emmerson! I'm going to make a stink about your wonderful little painting and we'll see what comes of it." She got all red in the face and kicked one of the wooden easels.

I sure wish I had been brave enough to stop her right there. If I had, it might have avoided a lot of problems. But, she was a teacher and I was a confused tenth grader. As it turned out, Miss Walincourt went before the school board and asked for the painting to be accepted in the contest. When they refused, she went to the local Ashton daily newspaper and they printed a story about the painting including a picture of it. The headline read "Local Student Artist Denied Access to Art Contest Because of Interracial Painting." I wished that hadn't happened and really wished she hadn't given them my name. The local TV station got a hold of the story and interviewed Miss Walincourt on the air. They showed my painting too. I guess it was due to all of the news about the Civil Rights Act and what it would do for Black people because the story about my painting even got on the Greenville, SC and Charlotte TV stations. A TV station from Raleigh called and wanted to interview me on the air. Mama wouldn't let me do that. Luckily, none of the TV stations used my name. That didn't matter too much at home because a lot of people read the newspaper article and found out that it was me. At school, a few kids came up and patted me on the back and told me how much they appreciated my stand for equality. I wasn't sure what they meant. A few more kids came up to me, especially in the boys' bathroom and pushed me around some and called me names. I knew exactly what they meant and I avoided going to the bathroom unless it was absolutely critical. Most of the other kids just ignored me as usual. Sarah Jane was the only one who said that she understood what I was trying to say with the painting. I wasn't really sure I knew what I was trying to get across.

Miss Walincourt was given the choice of resigning or getting fired. She got a lawyer and worked it out for her to keep teaching until the end of the year. She told me that she had planned to quit then anyway.

A big bully at Daddy's job stopped him in the break room one day and in front of a bunch of other men, asked Daddy how he had punished his "Nigger-loving, fagot artist son.".After he got out of the hospital with eight stitches in his face, the bully tried to have Daddy arrested. The other men in the break room told the police that the bully started the fight. The bully was transferred to another department and moved to the night shift.

Daddy didn't stand for the insult from the bully, but he wasn't happy with me either. The whole thing just added to his belief that art was a waste of time and that I should forget about it. However, with all of the news coverage about the painting, two different people called our house and offered to buy the painting. One even offered me $200. Daddy left selling it up to me. I thought about taking the money — I could afford to buy a new record player that would play 33 rpm records. I could get all of The Beatles albums and have enough left over to get a Nehru jacket with no collar like The Beatles wore. Finally, I decided not to sell it. It didn't seem right to make money off of a painting of two kids who were so upset over the president's death. I ended up giving it to Miss Walincourt.

Chapter 18

Daddy wasn't pleased with all the fuss about my painting and told me that my art wasn't worth the trouble it caused. However, by the time school was out in June, he had stopped the lectures about art and started in on my appearance, especially my hair. It finally grew long enough to touch the top of my ears and cover my forehead. I actually had need of a comb for the first time in my life. Along with the new hair length, I started taking on a new attitude about things, sort of an artsy, rebellious, smart-alecky attitude. The way Miss Walincourt described being a beatnik and the way the Beatles acted during their press interviews was the pattern I was after. I didn't want to be a hoodlum or juvenile delinquent, but rather a cool, smart, rebel artistic genius who was above all the trivial stuff most teenagers thought to be important, like popularity and acceptance. Everybody knew that artists were so connected to their creative nature that they didn't bother with anything else. I considered The Beatles to be genius artists and poets, so adoring them was okay.

I started working on the new attitude before school was out. I began pretending that being a loner and subject of some abuse by the popular crowd was my choice — as if I couldn't care less what others thought of me. To my surprise, I started finding myself among other kids who were trying the same change in their attitudes. Suddenly nerds and losers were a group with some recognition. You could tell who we were by the long hair, slouchy posture and disinterested facial expressions. We were still the targets for abuse from jocks, cheerleaders, and square dance team members, but that slowly became a badge of honor rather than one of shame and failure. We actually believed that the "in crowd" popular kids were upset that we no longer seemed to care about achieving their social status. Of course, we were kidding ourselves. The popular kids cared nothing about what we thought of them.

I was too smart to try my new "don't care, cocky" attitude around my parents, especially my father. I was having a hard enough time avoiding his ultimatum of keeping my hair trimmed or getting a military style buzz cut. Wearing a baseball cap pulled down over my eyes helped. I don't know if it was the hair or if he sensed my change of attitude, but Daddy decided that grass cutting and other chores at home were not enough "character builders." According to him, I needed the responsibility of a real job where I had to show up on time, take orders from a boss and learn respect for the hard work it takes to earn a paycheck. I promised him I would do my best. Of course, having a job didn't relieve me from the home chores.

Castle Drugs and Sundries was one of the five drug stores scattered along the three miles of Main Street of West Ashton. Like all of the other drug stores, Castle Drugs was locally owned and operated by the druggist himself. It was where my family bought everything from aspirin to Pepto-Bismol and toothache medicine as long as I could remember. It also had a soda fountain that featured real hand-dipped ice cream and huge banana splits. It was fun to sit at the fountain on stools that spun around like a top.

Doc Farmer, as he was known, was the crusty old druggist and owner of Castle Drugs and was known to swat teenagers on the butt with a yard stick when they hung out at the fountain longer than he thought necessary. Doc Farmer and my father had been friends ever since they sold brooms together for the West Ashton Lions Club to help blind kids. Working for Castle Drugs was my first real job.

Daddy went with me on my first day to assure Doc Farmer that he could treat me anyway he pleased. "Well, young Emmerson, are you ready to enter the world of retail pharmaceuticals, home remedies and in-demand sundries?"

"Uh, yeah, I guess."

Daddy punched me in shoulder. "You say yes sir to your employer, boy."

"Uh, oh yeah, uh, yes sir, I guess I'm ready."

"That's outstanding, young Mr. Emmerson. You are going to be my alternating rapid distribution coordinator and transportation expeditor."

I didn't know what all that meant, but it didn't sound much like the job I was expecting to get. I had figured I would be working behind the soda fountain making milk shakes and ice cream cones. "Uh, sir?"

"Young Mr. Emmerson, you will be my part time, daytime delivery person."

I assumed that Doc Farmer knew I wasn't old enough to drive a car, so when he saw the quizzical look on my face, he explained. "Look right outside the side door there, young man, and see your work implement."

Leaning against the wall beside the door was the oldest, most beat-up bike with the fattest tires I had ever seen. The thing was huge. In addition to the fat tires, it had a basket on the front that was big enough to hold two or three bowling balls. The rear fender was gone and the seat was falling apart. It must have weighed 200 pounds. Painted on the center tank were the words "Castle Drugs and Sundries — FAST FREE DELIVER WITH A SMILE." I wasn't smiling.

"Yes, young man, this bicycle has been part of Castle Drugs since 1951. Thousands of West Ashton families have been served by it and by strong riders like you. You join a long line of West Ashtonians who have pedaled this beauty through our fair community. Your compensation will be $2.50 per four hour shift and a generous ten percent discount on all soda fountain products except Cheerwine. It is too hard to get to be wasted on employees. Oh, and Castle Drugs delivery personnel do not accept gratuities. Remember, fast, free delivery with a smile. Welcome to the team."

I still wasn't smiling, but when I looked up at my father, he was. "Gonna be good for you Donno. Gonna get you out of the house and away from that art stuff and that long-haired Limey stuff you've been listening to." I had to look it up to find that "Limey" was a slang word for British people. Daddy had learned it during the war and I guessed he was talking about Beatles music.

Doc Farmer would have me deliver anything from prescriptions to a tin of aspirin to almost anywhere in West Ashton, all the way down to where Main Street turned toward the river and out the other direction toward the swimming pool. That included all the side streets and little neighborhoods along the way. Being in the mountains, no street in West Ashton was flat. There were steep hills everywhere I had to ride and the summer of 1964 was one of the hottest anybody could remember. Doc Farmer wouldn't allow me to wear shorts or jeans and I had to wear a little white jacket over my shirt. Doc Farmer said it assured customers that I was really working for him. Every time I came in from making a delivery, I would be exhausted with sweat dripping off my longish hair. To cool off, I would have the kid working behind the fountain make me a big lemonade with cherry syrup and lots of crushed ice. With my employee discount, the lemonade cost 20 cents each and I drank three or four during a four hour shift. All of those 20 cents were written down on a ledger and added up at the end of the week. When I eagerly opened up my first pay check, I thought there must have been a mistake. Between tax and something called FICA and 20 cherry lemonades, I only made $4.25 for the whole week. I drank ice water after that.

My first real job only lasted about a month. The Fourth of July was on a Saturday, but that didn't stop Doc Farmer from opening the drug store for half of the day. There wasn't much business and I mostly sat around chatting with the kid behind the fountain or sweeping the front steps. Around 11, an hour before we were supposed to close, a customer called in an order for something they absolutely had to have before that afternoon. Doc Farmer gave me an envelope with four one dollar bills, three quarters, two dimes and a nickel so I could make change in case the customer gave me a five dollar bill. Off I went. I immediately recognized the address of an older lady who lived on a street one block from the swimming pool. I was supposed to collect $1.35 for some kind of ointment or something. I made the delivery just fine and the customer had the exact change which I put in with the $5 in the envelope in the pocket of my little white jacket. Of course there was no tip.

Instead of going straight back to the drug store, I swung by the pool to see if anybody was there. The pool and the pavilion were packed. I thought out loud, "What the heck. I'll just run up to the pavilion and see what's happening." I parked the bike, took off my jacket and laid it across the handle bars. I certainly didn't want anybody to see me in it and give me a hard time about being a "delivery boy."

As soon as I get to the top of the steps, I saw Sarah Jane trying to show some kid I didn't recognize how to shag. I didn't pay attention to the kid, because Sarah Jane was wearing a bathing suit I had never seen before. It was a bright red two piece thing that left a lot of skin uncovered. She caught me staring and hollered at me. "Hey, Donno, I'm playing some new shag songs by The Tams. Please come and dance with me and show these guys how it's done."

I suppose it was either the lure of the red two-piece or the fact that I knew I could shag better than any kid there, but when "What kind of fool do you think I am" blasted out of the juke box, I went against my life long pledge to not let Sarah Jane show me up. I danced.

Sarah Jane looked at me and I could see her starting to count under her breath, "One and two, three and four, five six." It wasn't hard for me to pick up the rhythm and we started. First, I pulled her to me and we spun around. Feeling the warm skin of her bare back was disconcerting, yet I managed to push her away and we went through another series of "One and two, three and four, five six." After that, I tugged her right hand with my left and she responded by going past me, twirling twice as she went by. That was pretty much the extent of our routine and for the rest of the song — only doing the basic steps with no spins.

When the song ended, I looked up and there was a group circled around us and they were clapping. Of course, we were not anywhere near as good as them, but hearing the applause reminded me of how I felt about the adulation the god and goddess couple had gotten on that faithful day I first witnessed the shag.

Absent mindedly holding hands, Sarah Jane and I stood in the center of the admiring circle for a moment or two until the next song came on. It was "I Should Have Known Better" by The Beatles with John Lennon singing lead that shocked me back to the present. It reminded me that, even though I was a pretty good dancer, I had made the psychological leap from old time rock and roll, beach music and shag and had moved on to something I thought was much more modern and artsy. I would not want John Lennon or Paul McCartney to see me dancing to The Tams and I wouldn't want any of the other nerdy kids who formed my new group of friends to consider me a "sell-out." Life was so confusing.

When I got back to my bike, reality gave me another smack in the face. My little white jacket was gone. I looked all around, under bushes, behind trees, and on the other side of the building. The jacket was gone. *Why would anyone want to steal a jacket with 'Castle Drugs and Sundries' stitched across the pocket? Why not steal the bike?* I looked at the bike and said out loud, "Naw, nobody would steal that thing, not even somebody dumb enough to steal my little white jacket." Then I remembered the $6.35 in the pocket. This was not going to end well. Pedaling back to the drug store, I tried to come up with a good excuse, but there was none. I had really screwed up.

As I rode down Main Street toward the drug store, I could see a solitary figure standing outside the front door. It was Doc Farmer. He was looking at his watch. I looked down at my watch, It was 12:45. *Oh crap, the store was supposed to close at noon.*

"Well, young man, explain yourself." Doc Farmer stood there in his suit and tie, glaring down at me as sweat dripped down my forehead.

"I'm sorry, Doctor Farmer, I uh, uh made a mistake." There was no denying any of it. I told him everything, stopping at the pool, leaving my jacket on the bike and losing $6.35. "I promise, I will pay for the jacket and the lost money, I promise."

"You certainly will. It will be deducted from you final paycheck. You are terminated, Mr. Emmerson. Are you going to tell your father or shall I?"

Oh damn! Daddy's going to kill me. I got down on my knees and begged. "Doctor Farmer, please. I'll work for free and uh, I'll clean the bathrooms. I'll pay full price for sodas. Please don't fire me. Please!"

"No, young man, you betrayed a trust and you must face the consequences. Perhaps in the future you will look back on this incident and make better decisions."

Why was my life getting so messed up?

Chapter 19

"You'd better get your head out of your duffle bag, boy! You foul things up now, you're gonna keep doin' it! When I was your age, I worked two jobs just to make enough to put food on the table for me and Al. You got to learn some responsibility." Daddy got so mad, he had a coughing fit. He did that a lot when he got excited about something.

Daddy yelled and coughed, Mama wrung her hands and Grandma just shook her head. She kept going on about the 'good for nuthin' younger generation. Long ago, I had accepted that Daddy wasn't always pleased with me and the things I did, but this was the first time I felt that I truly dis-appointed him. I had broken a promise and I had embar-rassed him in front of his friend. It was going to take a long time to make up for my mistakes, if I ever could.

I was grounded for two weeks. That was not such a big deal because I wouldn't be going any place other than the swimming pool anyway. I did go to the barber shop and get a haircut, not short, but shorter. I thought that might appease Daddy a little. It didn't.

Mostly, I stayed in my room, listened to the radio or my records and drew in my sketch book. About the only time I went outside was to cut the grass or do some other chore like sweeping down the spider webs from under the porch roof or watering Mama's flowers that always looked like they were dying.

One day, when I was sitting on the front steps taking a break from grass cutting, Sarah Jane came over. She was on her way to the pool. I couldn't help wondering if she had on the red two piece suit under her cover-up.

"Hey, Donno."

"Hey."

"Are you still grounded? I guess your father is still upset, huh?"

"Yeah." I guessed that Sarah Jane knew all the details of me getting fired. Mama probably talked to her mother.

"Sorry you can't go to the pool."

"No big deal. Wasn't thinkin' about goin' anyway."

"I think the dance we had that day was pretty good. Don't you?"

I was in no mood to hear Sarah Jane's always cheery, always positive, always in charge and upbeat attitude. Instead of just nodding agreement and sending her on her way, I assumed my 'don't give a damn' attitude. I leaned back on the steps and looked up at the sky like I had other stuff to think about and said, "You know, Sarah Jane, I was about to quit that silly job anyway. And, uh, gettin' pretty bored with goin' to the pool and the shag thing, you know. I mean, it's okay for you and your little group of friends, but I'm about done with it."

Sarah Jane exploded. "Donno Emmerson, you're such an idiot! You talk about my little group of friends, do you? Well, your group of real friends is pretty small, too. It's only me. If you keep up with this silly way you have been acting, you're going to lose that friend too." Sarah Jane turned on her heel and marched down the sidewalk, flaming red ponytail bouncing side to side.

I knew she was right, but I was so confused about my life, the best I could do that day was finish cutting the grass then go inside and listen to The Beatles and draw.

Chapter 20

The two weeks of being grounded ended about three days before my 16th birthday. Daddy hardly spoke to me during that time other than criticizing the way I trimmed around the sidewalk and driveway. He didn't even look up when Mama announced that she had gotten a call from Becky inviting me to come down to Myrtle Beach for a few days as sort of a birthday present. I guess Daddy was just glad to get me out of the house and out of his sight. To my astonishment, he agreed to let me go. That was good, because Mama had already bought my ticket.

I was to ride the bus down to the beach and then Becky would bring me back when she came home to get some more of her clothes and to see the family. I was glad to get away from the tension at home. On the day before I was to leave, Mama packed me a suitcase with some new underwear, a couple of pairs of new shorts, two pairs of khakis and all of my knit Polo shirts. She also bought me a brightly colored short sleeve Madras shirt that she said was from India. I wasn't sure I would ever wear it since I wasn't much into the preppie look any more. I took another little bag and put in my tennis shoes and my sketch pad and pencils. The Weejuns that I had almost quit wearing were the only other shoes I took.

I left on my birthday. It would be the first time I had not spent it with all of my family. It was also the first time I had not seen Sarah Jane on our birthdays or gotten a present from her. Daddy was mad at me and so was Sarah Jane. I didn't know if I could ever change that. There was a lot of stuff running around in my brain about all of it. My trip to Myrtle Beach, beginning with the ride to the bus station and the bus ride itself added to my confusion.

Even though my bus didn't leave until 9:30, Daddy drove me to the Greyhound station in downtown Ashton before he had to be to work at 7:30. He must have smoked three Chesterfields during the 20 minute drive to the station. Daddy didn't say a word to me until I was about to get out of his truck. "Boy, don't get into any trouble that I have to get you out of. Here take this. Pay for your sister's supper once or twice." He handed me a 20 dollar bill. I decided against telling him that Mama had already given me 20 dollars. There was no "happy birthday" or "have a good time." I saw him light another cigarette as he pulled away.

There were some interesting people in the bus station at 7:00 in the morning. There was a young Black couple who kept hugging and kissing. I overheard them say something about getting married once they got to Charleston. There was also a man who couldn't have weighed more than 100 pounds. He had long greasy hair and a scraggly beard and no luggage that I could see. His eyes darted around like he was afraid someone or something was going to sneak up on him. Then there was a boy I recognized who just graduated from my school. I wondered if he was going on to the beach too. I started to take out my sketch book and do some quick drawings of the people. I was really trying to get better at drawing people, but then I figured they might get curious about me looking at them and back down to my pad, so I didn't draw any.

I was scheduled to change busses in Columbia, SC. It took us about five hours to get there because we made a stop in Gaffney, SC so the driver could eat breakfast and the rest of us could go to the bathroom. I got off the bus and walked around a little. There was a fruit stand selling peaches right next to the bus station. I got a big juicy peach and sat on a bench outside the station to eat it. The boy I recognized sat down near me and pulled a sandwich out of a brown paper bag. He looked up at me and nodded and I nodded back. We didn't speak so I don't know if he recognized me or not. I doubted if he did. I had to go to the bathroom to wash the peach juice off my hands and face.

We had a two hour layover in Columbia. The station was much busier than Ashton or Gaffney. It was crowded with soldiers with short hair and either dressed in green uniforms with coats and ties or khaki uniforms with short sleeve shirts and no ties. There was another group of young men not in uniforms who were lined up in front of an older, big Black soldier with a funny hat that looked like what Smokey Bear wore. He was holding a sign that read, "Fort Jackson Bus." The boy I recognized from Ashton was in that line.

Right before that group was ready to leave, the older soldier holding the sign yelled at me, "Hey you, kid. You with the long hair, you going to Fort Jackson for basic training?"

At first, I didn't know what he was talking about. Then it hit me, he thought I was supposed to be going into the Army. "Uh, no, uh sir. Just 16. Going to the beach." He smiled and answered back, "That's okay. We'll get you eventually." I realized that the guys getting on the bus to Fort Jackson and the ones in uniform didn't look any older than me. Later, as I was waiting for my next bus, I overheard one of the boys in uniform say, "I'll be glad when I finish infantry training. I hope the war in Nam ain't over by then. Lookin' forward to wasting a few gooks."

I got an RC Cola and a pack of Nabs and sketched a little to spend the time until my next bus came. I drew a few young soldiers, but I didn't draw them with faces.

The bus station in Myrtle Beach was a lot smaller than the one in Columbia and just as crowded. Unlike Columbia, there were only a few guys in uniforms — most of the people there were tanned or sun-burned college aged kids wearing shorts and t-shirts. I collected my suitcase and sat on a bench outside, waiting for Becky to pick me up.

I was enjoying the sun and admiring the girls in shorts when a bright red Mustang convertible drove up and honked the horn. The first time I had seen a Mustang was back in April when there was a story about the New York World's Fair on TV. Ford was using the World's Fair to introduce this new sporty car and had a big display of three different models, a convertible being one of them. Even though it was a quick grainy photo that was not so great on our little black and white TV, I immediately fell in love with the car and decided that I would own one someday. Although I was changing into the non-materialistic artistic rebel who was supposed to have given up the desire for flashy things in favor of truth and beauty, I still wanted a Mustang convertible. I rationalized that the car was actually a work of art, so I decided it would be okay to have one someday. Every teenage boy starting at age 12 has a dream car. I started out loving '32 Fords, then changed to '57 Thunderbirds and became pretty good at drawing them, but when I saw that black and white photo from the World's Fair and then a color picture of a Mustang in Mama's *Saturday Evening Post*, I was hooked. All of my car doodling switched from hot rods to Mustang convertibles with a happy couple in the front seat. Strangely, the girl in the doodles looked a lot like Sarah Jane.

I looked back at the Mustang idling at the curb and realized the driver was waving at me. That didn't make sense. Then I heard, "Donno! Wake up and get in the car!"

It was Becky! She was driving my dream car! "Wow Sis, is this your car. How did you…?"

"Oh, don't be silly. This is Eric's car. He thought you would enjoy riding in it being your birthday and all. So, he stayed at the record store and sent me in his new Mustang. Pretty cool, huh?"

I hadn't much cared for Eric when I first met him during our beach trip the year before, but the Mustang changed my attitude. "Cool for sure, Becky. I love Mustangs! Can't believe your boyfriend has one. And listen, thanks for inviting me to come down here. Things are pretty testy at home."

Becky pulled out on the main highway headed north toward Ocean Drive and the wind washed the smell of the ocean over us. "Well, Donno. It wasn't exactly my idea to invite you. Mama called me at the store and asked me to. She was afraid you or Daddy would do or say something that you couldn't take back. She thought you coming here might cool things down some."

On the radio, I heard the beginning of "A Hard Day's Night". Becky said it was a local station that played mostly beach music, but that started adding in some of the British Invasion and people like Bob Dylan. She turned the volume down so we could talk. I would have rather listened to The Beatles than talk about how I screwed up and how it upset Daddy. "I know, I know. I made a dumb mistake and I don't blame Daddy for being mad, but it's like he was never a kid and everything is so serious with him. If maybe he would just once say he liked my art or be proud of something I do."

"Oh, I think he is proud of you and I'm sure he loves you. He just doesn't know how to show it. Besides, I think he's scared. You know, I have basically left home for good and look at you. You're already taller than him. In a couple of years, you'll be out of high school and headed to art school or something. Daddy won't have any kids to protect."

"Yeah, or to boss around."

"It's All Right" by The Impressions came on and Becky turned up the radio. She said, "I love this song. It has a good slow shag beat and it's sort of happy. It says just have a good time because everything is going to be alright. We sell it a lot to the beach music crowd at the store."

We listened to the whole song without speaking. I wasn't so sure I believed the lyrics. Was everything going to be alright for me?

When the song ended, Becky turned down the radio and asked, "Speaking of shagging, you and Sarah Jane dancing any these days?"

I wondered how Becky could possibly know about the one time Sarah Jane and I danced when I should have been on my way back to the drug store. Did she know about me pushing Sarah Jane away with my "little friends" remark? "Uh, no. She's kind of getting on my nerves again. You know, bossing me around and stuff." Not wanting to get into all the reasons why Sarah Jane was mad at me, I changed the subject. "So, how's it going with you? You learning all about those computer things?"

"Trying to, but it's kind of complicated stuff. I am actually taking part-time classes here in Myrtle Beach at a business school rather than driving all the way to Conway every day. That works out better with my job at the record store."

When Mama told me I was going to spend a few days with Becky, I wondered where I was going to stay because of Becky's roommates. "Are you still living at the same place? Weren't you living with some other students?"

Becky looked at me for a second or two like she was trying to decide how to answer my question. "Well, that's something I need to tell you about. I have a new roommate. It's, uh ,Eric."

That news took a little time to sink in with all that it implied. "Oh, I guess he must have a pretty big place then."

"Nope. Just a one bedroom apartment." She cleared her voice. "But, uh, we, uh, he has a pullout couch where you can sleep."

I wasn't thinking where I was going to sleep. I was trying to wrap my brain around Becky and Eric's sleeping arrangements. " Uh, that's uh, well uh, cool, uh I guess."

"I know, Donno, I know what you're thinking. But I love him and we're talking about getting married and he's really good to me."

I couldn't come up with an adult response like, *Well, if it makes you happy"* or *You're an adult and can make your own decisions.* The best I could do was "He must be okay if he lets you drive his cool car."

Becky laughed out loud, "Oh, you big goof!" Then she got serious. "Listen now, the only way Mama can get in touch with me is at the store, so I can keep this a secret for now. Donno, I don't want Mama or Daddy to know about this yet. Okay?"

It was another one of those moments that proved I was quickly slipping away from my childhood, where parents provide protection and control, and was moving into a place where I had to live with the consequences of my own decisions. "I won't say anything. You can count on me."

"Thanks little brother. It's you and me. Like always."

On the Mustang's radio, the disc jockey announced, "Listen to this one, beach music fans. It's a new one from The Tams who are headlining at The Shack tonight. Here you go. It's called, "You Lied To Your Daddy." I looked over at Becky and she looked back at me. Then, we both broke up laughing.

"Did you hear what he said about The Tams being at The Shack tonight?"

"Yeah!" Again I was reminded of dancing to a Tams song with Sarah Jane.

"Well, that's part of your birthday present. We're going to The Shack tonight to see them in person."

"Cool!"

"And guess what else. Britney McMurray and her husband are going to be there."

There I was, riding in my dream car that would probably be unattainable for me until I was at least 30 and too old to enjoy it. And then, I hear that my dream girl, who was absolutely unattainable for me, would be helping me celebrate my still sub-adult childish birthday.

"Turns out, Eric and Britney's husband Jeff have been buddies since high school. Isn't that cool?"

"Yeah, cool."

"We hang out with them a little and when I told Britney you were coming down, she said she and Jeff would love to say hello. They come to The Shack to dance a lot anyway."

"Oh, good."

Becky took me to Eric's apartment so I could change clothes. It was in the middle of a golf course and just a block away from the beach. I decided that shorts, my new Madras shirt and my Weejuns with no socks would be the best outfit. I saw the couch where I would sleep for the next few days, but I couldn't bring myself to look in at the bedroom where Becky and Eric slept, together.

"Let's go, little brother. We need to pick up Eric at the store and then get to the club. He is working the door tonight. Plus, there's another band called The Catalinas. They play The Pavilion a lot. They will come on before The Tams and are pretty good, even though they're white."

Eric met us in the record store parking lot and he was just as I remembered him. He was good looking, tall, tan, had neatly trimmed blond hair and had really white teeth.

After giving Becky a quick kiss, Eric grabbed my hand and pumped it up and down. "Hello, little brother Donno. Welcome to the beach and happy birthday. Let's go PARTY!"

If Eric kept calling me "little brother" and "Donno," he would soon use up all the good will the Mustang had created. "Hey, uh hi, Eric. I uh really like your Mustang. Cool car."

"Yeah, very first Mustang convertible sold in the state of South Carolina. What do you think of that?"

What could I think? The guy had it all — looks, car, and my sister. "First one? That is cool."

When we got to The Shack, there was already a crowd waiting to get in, but we didn't have to wait. The man at the door shook Eric's hand and waved us in. Like before, there was no problem with a 16-year old getting in. The crowd outside and the crowd inside looked alike and looked a lot like Becky and Eric — well groomed, good looking, tanned and wearing what looked like a beach music club uniform, Madras or Polo shirts, shorts and loafers with no socks. I smiled at the conformity before I remembered that besides my long hair, I was dressed exactly like everyone else at the place.

Eric gave Becky a big hug and said, "Okay, guys. I have to go do my thing at the door for a while. And Donno, I told the bartender to give you one PBR in honor of your birthday, but it has to be in a cup. Wouldn't want the alcohol and tobacco guys to come in and see a juvenile drinking."

Eric did it again, he called me a juvenile, worse than little brother or Donno. "Hey, Becky, what is a PBR?"

"Never heard of PBR? That stands for Pabst Blue…oh, look, there's Jeff and Britney."

Becky waved at a couple making their way through the crowd on the dance floor. I first saw a guy who was the spitting image of Eric. Jeff was tall, tan, mouth full of shiny white teeth and dressed like every other male in the place. Then I saw Britney and my heart stopped. Her face was just as beautiful as I remembered, but something was wrong. *Oh no, she was fat. No wait, she was…my dream girl was pregnant!* Of course I knew all about how babies were made, but to think of my angel Britney, the girl that came to me in my dreams, doing something like that with a guy like Jeff instead of with a not so tall, not so good looking guy like me, well, it was almost too much.

"Hi, Becky, good to see you again. And who is this? Is this your little brother? Could he be the one I teased and called playboy?"

I cringed, waiting for Britney to pat me on the head and pinch my cheek.

"Why, he has grown up. I'll bet you really are a playboy now, aren't you?"

Before I could say anything, Jeff slapped me on the back." Right on, little bro. Glad to meet a real playboy."

I was pretty sure Jeff didn't drive a Mustang, so I could dislike him all I wanted. I started to say something to Britney, but a guy on the stage took the microphone and announced, "Alright shaggers, let's give these boys from Charlotte, NC a big welcome and then get out there and dance as they bring you their version of Billy Stewart's beach classic 'Fat Boy.'"

Jeff dragged Britney away and as the horns and guitars opened up, they danced. Even in her condition, my dream girl could dance.

Becky put her arm around me, "Come on, Donno, let's dance."

"I think I'll sit this one out, Sis."

The Catalinas were on stage for about 45 minutes and I didn't dance once. I inched my way back away from the dance floor and toward an empty stool at the end of the bar. After The Catalinas had stopped playing and The Tams were setting up their equipment, Eric and Becky walked over to me. "Here you go, little brother. I promised you one in a cup. Don't drink it too fast." Then they walked away, leaving me with a cup full of beer and a decision to make. *Would I drink it or not?* I was pretty sure Mama would be very upset if she knew and I was certain that Daddy would be mad because he had told me not to do anything that would get me in trouble. But, Mama and Daddy weren't there. "What the hell?" I said out loud. After all, I was 16 now. Surely a lot of 16 year olds had drunk beer before. Besides, Daddy was only 17 when he went in the Marines and started killing people. The Shack was packed with people and it was hot. I'm not sure it was air conditioned, which probably wouldn't have done much good anyway with all of those warm bodies dancing around. I turned up the cup and took a sip. The cold liquid hit the back of my throat and it felt good. The next sip was more like a gulp and it felt even better, especially after a big belch. Becky said to not drink it fast. I figured four gulps wasn't too fast. The opening notes of The Tams' first song covered up a really loud belch. The song was "You Lied To Your Daddy." It seemed appropriate at the time.

I watched Becky and Eric dancing. He would kiss her every time he pulled her close. Even though my eyes were blurry and my head was spinning a little, I could see how happy that made her and wondered if there would ever be a girl that would care for me like Becky cared for Eric.

The song ended and one of the singers said their next song was going to be "What Kind of Fool Do You Think I Am." *"Oh yeah",* I thought. That was the song Sarah Jane got me to dance to at the pool the day I got fired. "Yep, I was a fool that day for sure."

"Hey, kid" A guy behind the bar was holding a cup and trying to get my attention over the loud music.

"Uh, me?

"Yeah, you. The tall dude at the end of the bar said to give you this." With that, he stuck a full cup of beer in front of me and walked away.

"Excuse me, but uh, I'm only supposed to get one." The bartender didn't turn around so I looked toward the end of the bar to see who had made the mistake. With Britney leaning on his shoulder, Jeff was giving me a big grin and a thumbs up.. I sort of waved back. He must not have gotten the word from Becky about me only getting one birthday celebration beer. My hesitation on drinking the first beer disappeared and I gulped the second even faster.

Then an old guy, maybe 25 or 30 sat down beside me. He was probably more than a little drunk, sort of like me. "What's up buddy, where you from?"

I guess the two beers made me a lot friendlier than usual. "Hey, yeah. I'm from West Ashton, North Carolina and it's my birthday." I didn't mention which birthday.

The old guy saw my empty cup and waved to the bartender, "Hey, give this guy another of whatever he's been drinking on me. Can't have any empty cups on his birthday." He raised his right hand and we exchanged high fives.

The next thing I remember was sitting up in the back seat of the Mustang with cool night air hitting me in the face.

Becky turned around from the passenger seat and shook her head. "You've had quite a birthday celebration, haven't you, little brother?"

I groaned, "What happened?"

"You don't remember dancing with Britney when the band played "Silly Little Girl Come Back to Me?" "

"Uh, I what? Oh no."

"So you also don't remember giving her a big kiss on the cheek after the dance?"

My stomach did a flip as I tried to remember what I had done. Images of the night mixed with images from my fantasies about Britney. "Oh crap! What did she do? What did she say?"

Becky laughed out loud. "She thought it was cute. Jeff, I'm not so sure about." Becky laughed again. "And by the way, you and Britney put on quite a show. It was the best shagging I have ever seen you do."

A few things started coming back to me. "Did I do something in front of the bandstand?"

"Oh you mean when you kept yelling for The Tams to play "Hard Day's Night" by the Beatles?"

"I don't remember that."

"What about throwing up all over your Weejuns out in the parking lot?"

I groaned again and slid back down on the back seat, waking up long enough to fall fully clothed on Eric's couch.

When I woke up about 9:30 the next morning, the apartment was quiet and dark. I lay still for a few seconds slowly trying to get my eyes to focus. My biggest mistake was sitting up quickly. "Oh wow." A base drum was pounding in my head and the cymbals were crashing in my stomach. I would have lain back down but my mouth was dry as cotton and the taste was nasty.

I staggered to the kitchen to get a glass of water. There was a note from Becky on the counter. "Good morning party boy. Eric and I had to go to work so you will be on your own until 6:00. There are bagels in the cabinet and OJ in the refrigerator. Aspirin in the medicine cabinet. Hope your head is okay. Stay out of trouble and NO MORE BEER! Love ya! Becky"

The orange juice helped my cotton mouth and nasty taste. One bite of bagel was enough to prove my stomach wasn't ready for anything solid. Two aspirin may have helped, but the hot shower did the most good. I stood there so long, I used up all of the hot water. When the water turned icy cold, my head started to clear and slowly, I remembered bits of things from the night before. The tune of " Hard Day's Night" keep popping into my slowly recovering brain.

"Well, I guess I can't hang around here all day thinking about how stupid I am. Let's get moving, Donno, my man." I put on my shorts, a Great Smoky Mountains t-shirt and my sneakers, grabbed a pencil and my sketch book and headed out the door. As soon as I got outside, I knew I was going to have to do something about the unbelievably bright sunshine. My eyes just couldn't take it. I walked down to the beach road where there were dozens of gaudy shops selling beach towels, t-shirts and air mattresses in the shape of dolphins. I used $6.99 of my $40 and got a pair of really dark sunglasses with plastic lenses and a baseball cap that had "Ocean Drive, Home of The Shag" stitched across the front. The sun glasses made me feel a whole lot better.

I could hear the sound of the ocean and went that direction. I had no plan in mind, but figured a walk on the beach would do me good and it did. The warm sand and the ocean breeze in my face seemed to be good medicine, so I walked and walked, not caring how far. Zoned out, I didn't pay much attention to anything around me until I looked up and saw that I was almost to a long wooden pier sticking way out into the ocean. "Humph. Never been on a pier. Let's see what it's all about."

Because I wasn't carrying a fishing rod, the man at the pier gate didn't charge me the two dollars the fishermen had to pay. The fishermen must have been having good luck because there was a strong fishy smell mixed with the salty sea breeze. The smell didn't do my stomach any good and neither did seeing a man cut open a still flapping fish and pull out its guts with his hands. After that, I walked down the middle of the pier and didn't look from side to side until I got to the very end. On one side was a young couple listening to a transistor radio playing "Glad All Over" by The Dave Clark Five. On the other side, a Black teenager was singing along with his radio to The Drifters' "Under the Board Walk." It was like the British Invasion and American rhythm and blues were dueling.

As I looked out over the breaking waves and toward the empty horizon, I imagined jumping off the end of the pier and swimming eastward. Would I end up in England or Africa? Would either be a better place to grow up than West Ashton, North Carolina? I did a few rough sketches of the fishermen standing in rows along the pier and one pretty good one of a little boy who was holding a tiny fishing rod right beside his father.

I didn't go back to The Shack with Eric and Becky. The thought of it made my stomach boil and I was afraid Britney would be there. I couldn't face her again. So, I either stayed in the apartment watching TV or I walked on the beach. In a couple of days, it was time to head back home. I was hoping that Eric would let Becky drive his Mustang, but we took her old car instead. We didn't talk much on the way, mostly listening to the radio. The further we got away from the ocean, we heard less and less beach music and more country and gospel. Not being a fan of either, I kept changing stations trying to find some rock and roll which meant a lot of static because the radio only got AM stations. Finally, Becky yelled at me, "Donno, quit that! You're driving me crazy. Find a station or turn the radio off!"

Just as we were going through Florence, South Carolina, the last few notes of "Love Me Tender" by Elvis Presley came through loud and clear. Then a disc jockey with a twangy voice announced "That's right, Elvis fans, it's our Sunday afternoon Elvis marathon brought to you by Low Country Funeral Home and Ambulance Service. Now here is "Don't Be Cruel" also from 1956."

Becky squealed, "Leave it there. I still love Elvis." I remembered Elvis on the "Ed Sullivan Show" when I was nine or ten. I think he sang two or three songs, but the only one I could remember was "Hound Dog". Mostly I remembered Becky, Mama, and even Grandma clapping and squealing just like the audience and just like the audience did when The Beatles were on The Sullivan show. Later, Grandma said she thought Elvis was a fine Christian boy and that his mother must be proud. I remember Daddy saying Elvis needed a haircut.

For the next 30 or 40 minutes, Becky and I listened to Elvis sing "All Shook Up," "It's Now or Never", "Your Teddy Bear" and several more. Becky sang along and knew every word. After each song, the disc jockey would announce a recent or soon to be held funeral, all customers of Low Country Funeral Home and Ambulance Service. We didn't pick up another radio station until we were about 20 miles from home and could get *WASH*.

When we pulled into the driveway, Becky stopped me from getting out of the car. "Remember, Donno, say nothing about me and Eric. Okay?"

"Okay, as long as you won't say anything about me getting, uh, getting drunk."

"It's a deal. Now let's go inside and tell them what a great time you had at the beach."

With that, I took another step toward independence and detachment from the authority of my parents, especially my father. I was a little ashamed that the step involved lies.

Chapter 21

The Monday after I got back from the beach, I started a week of behind the wheel drivers training. It was taught by Mr. Gordon, the JV basketball coach. He always smelled like onions and favored athletes and girls. Guess which girl was my driving partner for the week? I didn't think Sarah Jane would have requested me as a partner, so it must have been fate that put us together in that old Plymouth sedan with hot sticky plastic seat covers and a manual transmission.

Because I had taken art for two semesters my sophomore year, I didn't take the classroom drivers training course. That meant I couldn't get a learner's permit. Of course, Sarah Jane had taken the classroom course, had her learner's permit and her mother had been letting her practice driving all summer. With Sarah Jane being 16 soon as she finished the-behind-the-wheel course, meant she could get her drivers' license. Mr. Gordon treated her like she was already a seasoned driver while he treated me like the idiot I sometimes was.

On our first day, we went to an old airport runway near town and practiced starting and stopping. Sarah Jane went first. Because her mother's car was a straight drive, she already knew how to release the clutch smoothly, how to change gears at the right time and how to push in the clutch and brake pedals when stopping. Mr. Gordon was ecstatic. "Young lady, you make my job much easier. You're ready to drive on the street now. Let's see what Mr. Emmerson here can do."

Having a male ego, I believed that I was naturally better at all things mechanical. I figured if she could do it, certainly I could do it better. I should have known not to think I could do anything better than Sarah Jane other than draw.

It was a good thing that the old Plymouth had seat-belts. If we hadn't been wearing them, we all would have gone through the windshield when I let out the clutch and hit the brakes at the same time. Luckily, that killed the engine and we stopped. Once he recovered from fright, Mr. Gordon asked, "Um, Mr. Emmerson, do you have some sort of affliction that causes your feet to act independently of your brain? Or maybe that's the problem. Your feet are getting directions from your brain." Sarah Jane snickered in the back seat.

The second try wasn't much better. I let out the clutch too quickly without giving the engine any gas. The car jumped and lurched forward like a bucking bronco. It kept doing it until Mr. Gordon yelled, "Push in the clutch! Push in the clutch and apply the brakes smoothly!" Sarah Jane snickered again.

On the third try, I managed to synchronize the clutch and the gas pedal, but with way too much gas. The rear tires squealed and billowed smoke as we left a 20 foot long black stripe down the runway. Sarah Jane laughed out loud when Mr. Gordon asked if my family had a car with an automatic transmission because he doubted I would ever pass the driving test with a stick shift.

The fourth and fifth tries were better and by the sixth I could finally get moving in low gear without lurching and could change gears with only a minor bit of grinding. I was starting to get pretty confident until Mr. Gordon called it a day and suggested that Sarah Jane drive up back to the high school.

On the last day of the week, I had finally mastered starting and stopping, changing gears and even a fair amount of success with parallel parking I was not as good as Sarah Jane, but I only knocked over the orange warning cone once. I figured I was as good as I was going to get until I could get a learner's permit. Sarah Jane and I had both taken turns driving through town to get some experience in city traffic when Mr. Gordon made an announcement, "Alright Miss Allison and Mr. Emmerson, we have one more test to perform before I will consider you ready to get behind the wheel alone and terrorize the pedestrians of our fair city. It's what I like to call the 'Hill Climb'." He gave an evil little laugh that even made teacher's pet Sarah Jane shutter. I had heard stories of this torture, but didn't believe it could be true.

Sarah Jane was first. Mr. Gordon directed her to drive back through town and to turn left onto the steepest street in the city that had a stoplight at the top of the hill. The whole idea behind Mr. Gordon's test was to see if we could stop on the hill, push in the clutch with our left foot and hold the car from rolling back by keeping our right foot on the brake until the light changed. It would have been easier if we could have ridden the clutch, but Mr. Gordon forbade that. He also forbade allowing the car to roll back even an inch. The way I saw it, to do what he was saying, you had to have three feet, one to release the clutch, one to release the brake and one to hit the accelerator all at the same time to get the car moving forward. Without the third foot, the only solution I saw was to move to a town with no hills.

Sure enough, the light turned red and Sarah Jane had to stop. From the back seat, I could see her narrow her eyes, grit her teeth and take a vice-like grip on the steering wheel. The light turned green and in an instant, we were smoothly moving forward with no roll-back at all. Somehow, she had done it. She figured out how to do all three things at one time with only two feet. Mr. Gordon gushed. "Excellent, Miss Allison! Excellent! You make me proud."

Sarah Jane gave me a wicked smile when we changed places and I got behind the wheel. We circled around and I turned onto the test hill. The light at the top was green and I thought I had gotten a temporary reprieve. But no such luck. The light turned yellow and I started to run through it anyway until Mr. Gordon stopped me. "Oh no, Mr. Emmerson. A caution light is as good as a red light. Never run through it."

So there I was, sitting at the top of the hill with my left foot holding down the clutch and my right on the brake. I was calculating how fast I would need to move my right foot to the accelerator, when to my horror, not one, but three more cars pulled up behind me. The one directly behind me was only a foot or so from my back bumper. If I screwed up and let the Plymouth roll back, I was going to cause a four car collision and worst of all, Sarah Jane would never let me forget it. Sweat was pooling in my arm pits and trickling down my nose when I remembered a recurring dream. I had dreamt I was in my hot new Mustang, sitting at a drag strip starting line. In the lane next to me was a red Corvette driven by a little girl with an equally red ponytail. In my dream, when the starter dropped his flag, I popped the clutch and launched the Mustang forward, smoking the tires and leaving the Corvette still sitting at the starting line.

It took a second or two to slow the Plymouth down after exploding through the intersection. When I looked in the rear view mirror, all I could see was Sarah Jane's wide-eyed expression and a cloud of blue tire smoke obscuring the cars still sitting on the hill. Mr. Gordon was trying to say something, but couldn't quit stuttering. "How about that, Mr. Gordon? I didn't roll back any at all. Did I?" He could only nod his head. Mr. Gordon gave me a passing grade for the week. I figured he was afraid that if he didn't pass me, he would have me in the class with him again. I passed the test, but I still had to take the classroom part. That meant I wouldn't get my license until after Christmas.

Chapter 22

After the week of drivers training, I started to work at the A&P. Getting fired from the drug store had done nothing to stop my father's insistence that I needed a job. Because I had turned 16, I could get a real workers permit and work for a big company like the A&P. I didn't apply for the job myself. Daddy knew the assistant manager through his bowling league team and arranged for me to get hired. Until school started back, I was scheduled to work three days a week from 8:00 a.m. until 1:00 p.m. That was okay with me because I still had afternoons off to go to the pool or other stuff. The store was only a few blocks from my neighborhood, so it was no big deal to walk or ride my bike there. Besides, the job paid $1.25 an hour and I figured, how hard could it be to put groceries into a paper bag? What a stupid thought that was.

My training lasted about ten minutes and consisted mostly of how to tie the white apron we were required to wear around my waist. In addition to the apron, we were required to wear black pants, a white short-sleeve shirt and a black clip on tie. There were no special requirements on shoes so I wore my beat up Converse Chuck Taylor All Stars.

I probably should have figured it out on my own, but nobody told me not to put a loaf of bread at the bottom of the bag underneath two family size cans of pork and beans. I also didn't know that I was supposed to put ice cream in a special bag that would keep it from melting. The worst thing that happened the first day was a runaway buggy. The A&P parking lot wasn't flat and the buggies didn't have breaks. As I was trying to put two huge bags of dog food into the back floorboard of a 1956 Dodge that was also holding an unfriendly German Shepard, the buggy with the rest of the lady's groceries rolled away. In what seemed like slow motion, the buggy hit the curb in front of the store and tilted over just enough for the bag with two dozen eggs to fall out.

The assistant manager that hired me must have been Daddy's really good friend because he didn't fire me. Over the next couple of days, with the help of another bag boy, I finally got the hang of it all and discovered that if I was nice to the little old ladies, they would give me a quarter tip when I carried their groceries to their cars. Several ladies gave me 50 cents and suggested that I get a haircut with the money.

On the first Saturday I worked, I got off at 1:00. Although I still had on my dorky work clothes, I decided to stop by the pool and pavilion for a hot dog and Pepsi. Plus, I had a pocket full of quarter tips so I could feed the juke box.

For the middle of August, it was an unusually cool and cloudy day. That meant nobody was around the pool and even the little kids were up in the pavilion. It was very crowded and I didn't see Sarah Jane until Martha and The Vandellas' song called "Come and Get These Memories" started to play. Although I had sort of dropped out of Motown and beach music in favor of The Beatles, The Animals and The Rolling Stones, I still liked some rhythm and blues groups like the Vandellas, Temptations, and Four Tops. I looked over toward the juke box to see who might have chosen that song. Sarah Jane and some guy I had never seen before were dancing right in front of the juke box. She was wearing white shorts and a bright yellow blouse that really set off her tan. She looked pretty good. The stranger was wearing khaki shorts, a t-shirt with HARVARD across the front, and wouldn't you know it, Weejuns with no socks. Sarah Jane had become a very good shagger and the stranger was keeping up with her. He was actually pretty good too. I watched for a few seconds and then turned toward the food counter when I heard, " Donno, Donno, wait. I want you to meet someone."

I turned back to see Sarah Jane leading a tall, dark haired guy with big shoulders and a toothy grin toward me. "Donno, I mean Don Emmerson, this is Robert Langdale. He just moved into that neat house over on Maple Crescent. He'll be a senior and he's transferring into our school. Isn't that great?"

Before I could respond one way or the other, toothy Robert grabbed my hand and nearly crushed it as he pumped it up and down. "Glad to meet you, uh, Donno, is it? My friends call me Rob."

Before I could correct "Rob" and let him know that my real name was Don and not Donno, Sarah Jane jumped in. "His dad is the new pharmacist at the Castle Drug Store. He bought part of it from Doc Farmer. Isn't that neat?"

Hm, I thought. *This was starting to sound like a disaster in the making. There was a new good looking guy in town who could dance almost as good as me or maybe better and his father was going to be working side with the by side man who fired me from my first job. Could this get any worse?* Yes it could.

Sarah Jane jumped up and down with even more excitement. "Oh! Oh! I almost forgot. Guess what? Mama bought me a car! I just got it today." Sarah Jane drug me to the street side of the pavilion and pointed to a line of cars parked on the street. "See it! It's the baby blue Volkswagen bug. It's used, but it sure is fun to drive. Aren't you excited for me?"

"Uh, uh, excited? Uh."

"And guess what, Donno. Rob has his own car and we've decided to take turns driving to school, and you can ride with us. Isn't that just groovy great?"

If Rob had a Mustang, I planned to shoot myself.

Sarah Jane had her license and a car before me. Another tall, good looking guy with straight teeth had entered my life and I either had to ride to school with these two or ride a bus there that smelled like my daddy's Lucky Strikes and football players after a game. "Yeah, uh, groovy."

I used up all of my quarters playing "House of the Rising Sun" by The Animals and "You Really Got Me" by The Kinks over and over. Nobody could dance to those songs. I didn't want to see new boy Rob and Volkswagen girl Sarah Jane shagging in front of me again.

School started right after Labor Day and being a junior, I was sort of in no man's land. I wasn't a lowly sophomore anymore, but nor was I a senior and a member of the elite. The seniors didn't pick on me like they had the year before, yet the sophomores weren't scared of me either. Even though I hated to admit it, riding with Sarah Jane and Rob wasn't too bad. We got to school on time and we could listen to the radio on the way there. Ricky Stillman rode with us too. He had his license but no car. When we were in Sarah Jane's bug, Rob was always in the front and Ricky and I had to cram into the back seat. Luckily, he didn't have to bring his tuba along. It was better when we were in Rob's car. (Thank goodness he didn't have a Mustang.) His '58 Impala was pretty cool and the back seat was huge. It even had radio speakers back there. I tried to ignore how close Sarah Jane sat to Rob.

Ricky and Sarah Jane both got into the symphony band and didn't have to practice with the marching band after school anymore. Rob was big enough to play football, but said he was going to try out for the tennis team in the spring. I didn't know we had a tennis team. That meant they could leave in the afternoon like everybody else. That was pretty cool, because both Sarah Jane and Rob dropped me off at the A&P on days I worked. I kept my white shirt and clip on tie in my back pack. Who would want to wear that stuff to school?

Because of drivers training class, I couldn't take art first semester and I missed it a lot. On the second or third day of school, I stuck my head in the art room while on my way to another class. The new art teacher, Mr. Wertz, was setting up an easel at the back of the room. "How may I help you, young man?"

Mr. Wertz was 50ish, had closely cropped grey hair and a neatly trimmed goatee. He wore a starched white shirt and a dark red and blue striped tie. He was the complete opposite from the casually dressed Mr. Fontain from junior high and the wild beatnik Miss Walincourt. “Uh, I really like art and uh, I’ll be in your class second semester, I hope.”

“And what is your name, I might ask?”

I swear he sounded like one of the German officers I had seen in war movies. “Uh, Don, Donald Emmerson, uh sir.”

“Ah, your reputation precedes you, Mr. Emmerson. You are the young phenom who cost the previous instructor her job, I believe.”

I didn’t know what “phenom” meant, but I figured it was bad because he knew the trouble my painting caused Miss. Walincourt. “Well, uh I uh…”

“Not to worry, Mr. Emmerson. I look forward to exploring and sharpening your raw talent when you join my class after Christmas. In the meantime, try not to pick up any more bad habits.”

I wondered what bad habits he thought I had. Grandma did fuss at me for slouching at the dinner table and Daddy said I mumbled a lot. I didn’t think that was what Mr. Wertz was talking about. I guessed that I would find out second semester.

Chapter 23

Most of the drivers-ed class was on laws and stuff like how many spaces you were supposed to stay behind the car in front of you. The one thing I remember the most was the gory film the teacher showed about halfway through the semester. It showed the aftermath of a bad wreck and was in color. It was supposed to show us how serious wrecks could be in order to scare us into driving safely. It did that to me and more. The car in the wreck was a '58 Chevy, a lot like Rob's car. The driver, a teenager, tried to get across a railroad track just ahead of a speeding train. The driver and a girl in the car were killed instantly. The film showed their bodies being pulled from the car and put into ambulances. I immediately thought of Rob and Sarah Jane and hated Rob for the chance that he might put Sarah Jane in danger like that. I knew it was foolish and I knew that Rob seemed like a pretty good driver. *Was I really concerned about Sarah Jane's safety or was I just jealous? Did I care that much about her or did I just not like Rob's interference in my already complicated life?*

The homecoming game and homecoming dance were set for the third Friday of October and of course, Sarah Jane was in charge of planning for the dance. And of course, that meant that I was drafted to do art work for the some of the decorations. Mama let us work on stuff with poster paints and scissors on the dining room table once she put a leaf in the middle and covered the table with a big piece of canvas she usually used for covering her tulip bulbs in the basement during the winter.

The week before the dance was also the first week of the Summer Olympics in Tokyo, Japan. One night, when Sarah Jane and I were cutting out big red, yellow and orange oak leaves I had drawn on poster board (her theme for the banner at the game and the dance was “Autumn Leaves Must Fall, But Not the Mighty Black Panthers”), we heard Daddy yelling in the living room. “Damn Japs! Damn um all! We should’ve nuked every last one of um!”

Wide eyed, Sarah Jane looked at me and asked, “What’s that all about? Why is he mad at the Japanese?”

“He’s thinking about the war, I guess.” The Winter Olympics had been in Austria back and February and Daddy got a little upset about people he called “Jerrys” being on TV. I didn’t tell Sarah Jane, but he wasn’t crazy about her driving a Volkswagen either. He said that just 20 years before, a lot of American boys had been shot down in B17s trying to bomb the factory that made VWs and now they were selling their damn cars to us. Daddy was annoyed about the Germans being on TV. Seeing the Japanese was different. He hated them.

“He doesn’t talk about it, but according to Mama, Daddy saw a lot of hand to hand combat and lost a lot of good buddies on some little island out in the Pacific Ocean. She said some of Daddy’s closest friends were captured and tortured before they were killed.”

“If it upsets him that much, why is he watching the Olympics?”

“He says he wants to see the American athletes crush Jap athletes.”

Daddy started yelling again. “Look at ‘em! Smilin’ like they are regular human beings! They’re nothin’ but animals. I’ll bet there are bastards in that crowd that tried to kill me back on …”

Daddy didn’t finish what he was trying to say because he started coughing violently. His cough had gotten worse in the last couple of months, bad enough that even I noticed it. The front door opened and I heard Daddy go out on the porch.

“Where’s your dad going? Is he that upset?” Sarah Jane put down her scissors and looked in the living room.

"No, he's out on the porch smoking. That's what he does sometimes when he is mad or needs to think."

We heard another deep hacking cough episode out on the porch and Sarah Jane asked, "Don't you think your dad should quit smoking?"

"Do you want to tell him that? Do you think he would listen to me?"

We worked on the decorations for the dance for another hour or so. As Sara Jane gathered up all of her stuff to leave, she hesitated for a second and then asked me, "Would you be mad if I go to the homecoming dance with Rob?"

I was shocked. *Had she thought I might ask her to go with me? Did she think I cared enough about her that I would be mad for her to go with Rob?* Even worse, *was I upset with the idea that she would be dancing with Rob and probably kissing him when he brought her home? Did I really care? Have I been avoiding thinking about her and Rob?*

I tried to be cool. "Why should I care? Uh, besides, I'm going to work late that day so a couple of the other bag boys can go to the game. I might not even go to the dance." I lied.

The look on Sarah Jane's face was hard to interpret. I couldn't tell if she was relieved or sad. Had she wanted me to answer her question differently? *Damn*, I thought. *Why does stuff have to be so screwy, especially when it comes to Sarah Jane?*

Even though I got off from work early enough, I didn't go to the game. I had decided not to go to the dance either until Mama asked why I was still home. "You and Sarah Jane worked so hard on those decorations, aren't you going to see how they look in the cafeteria?"

"Aw, you know. I had to work and I don't have a ride. Everybody else has already gone, I guess." I didn't mention that I also didn't have a date or plans to meet anyone there.

"Well, I hate for you to miss it. Go change your clothes and I'll take you to the school. I am sure you can get a ride home with somebody. Maybe Sarah Jane and Rob will let you ride back with them."

I had visions of sitting in the back seat watching Rob and Sarah Jane laugh and carry on in the front seat or watching him give her a good night kiss at her front door. "Aw, Mama, I don't know. I'm kind of tired and uh…"

"Nonsense. Go upstairs, put on some nice clothes and go have a good time."

Reluctantly, I did what my mother said, but in a weird rebellious way I wore my Sunday lace up black shoes instead of my Weejuns. I didn't even want to think about dancing.

Mama dropped me off near the side entrance to the school cafeteria. When I got out of the car, I could hear people laughing and talking. I could also hear The Beatles blasting away with "A Hard Day's Night." I figured that every other song the DJ played would be something from The Beatles with a few "Twist" songs mixed in. The "Twist" was still the most popular dance.

After stopping to check in with the chaperon at the door, I slipped in the cafeteria and worked my way around the wall until I could see the DJ and the dance floor. The decorations looked pretty good, especially with the rotating spot light that changed colors. The cafeteria looked like a real night club, although the only real night club I had seen was The Shack at the beach.

After a bunch of sophomores tried to twist to "Surf City" by Jan and Dean, the DJ announced that there was going to be a dance contest. There was a little applause and a lot of groans. The DJ went on, "Oh come on you guys, it will be fun. Principal Joyner and Miss Carson will be the judges and the winning couple from each class will get Ashton High Fighting Black Panther sweatshirts and free tickets to see *My Fair Lady* at The Roxie downtown. The overall winners will also get a Chinese dinner for two at The Paradise Restaurant on Broadway."

The dance contest sounded a lot like a Sarah Jane idea. The DJ went on. "Let's see what all of you dancers can do to "The Way You Do The Things You Do" by those temptin' Temptations." When I heard that song start, there was no doubt the dance contest was a Sarah Jane Allison idea. The song had an unmistakable shag beat.

One sophomore couple tried to twist to the song and were terrible. I think they realized that they were the only couple from their class in the contest and if they finished the dance, they would win prizes. Three senior couples entered the competition and two of them actually shagged. One of the senior couples wasn't too bad and would probably win for their class. Sarah Jane and Rob was the only junior class couple to enter. I believe Sarah Jane threatened all of the other juniors so they wouldn't compete.

It was all very dramatic. The lights were dimmed and a spot light moved back and forth between the couples. Principal Joyner and Miss Carson made it even more dramatic by asking the crowd to applaud when they were near a dancing couple. I don't know if it was by design or just chance, but Rob and Sarah Jane were right in the middle of the dance floor and the spotlight stayed on them much longer than any other couple. They were also the best dancers by far, doing shag moves that even impressed me.

I had seen enough. I wasn't about to watch smiling Rob and perky Sarah Jane be announced as the overall winners of the contest. I said good night to the teacher at the door and headed outside. I figured it would only take me three hours to walk home as long as I didn't get run over while crossing the bridge over to the West Ashton side of the river.

"Hey, Emmerson. Where you headed?"

It was Ricky Stillman, leaning up against the wall smoking a cigarette. I immediately wondered how that affected his tuba playing. "Ah, this gig is getting pretty lame. I think I will head out."

"You drive here?"

Ricky knew good and well I still didn't have driver's license."Nope, uh, hoofin' it, I guess."

"Uh well, that's cool, but I have my old man's Falcon and don't have to have it back until 10:00. Let's go check out the strip."

I looked at my watch. It was 8:00. Mama said she was sure I could get a ride home with someone. She didn't say that ride had to come straight home. "Sure, let's do it.".

The strip was about a half a mile long and was anchored on one end with a drive-in theatre and on the other end was Buster's Burgers, the home of the *Big WASH 'Rockin Tower of Rhythm'.* In between the two anchors were other restaurants, a bowling alley and a new place that sold hamburgers for 15 cents. It was called McDonald's.

The usual procedure for cruising the strip was to start at one end and drive up and down the road as slowly as possible with the radio turned up just below the eardrum bursting level. No matter how cold or rainy, you always drove with the windows down with your arms draped over the window frame. Slouching down so your head was barely visible was part of the ritual. If you had a really cool car, at stoplights revving your motor and squealing the tires was also cool. Ricky's dad's Falcon didn't qualify for that kind of cool.

"Uh, Emmerson, old pal. Let's go request some tuneage at the Tower. What do ya say?" Ricky was obviously just as alone as me and looking for some reason not to be at home on a Friday night.

I nodded in agreement. It was Friday night and I was an American teenager. Why the hell not? The dance must have let out because the traffic on the strip really picked up. There was a line of four cars ahead of us waiting to drop their song requests in the bucket.

"What are you gonna request, Emmerson? I'm gonna request "Teenager In Love" by Dion and The Belmonts."

"Oh, man, Ricky. That thing is ancient. It must be at least five years old." Of course, the song was an anthem for almost every teenage boy who never had a girlfriend or who had lost his true love to someone else. Even though that applied to both Ricky and me, I decided on something a little more contemporary. I requested the Bob Dylan version of “Blowin’ In the Wind” and “You Lost That Lovin’ Feeling” by The Righteous Brothers. Both songs sort of fit the mood of the night for Ricky and me.

Ricky pulled into a parking spot and we shared an order of fries. After that we cruised the strip a couple of times until we heard our songs and then headed across the river to West Ashton and home.

Chapter 24

Christmas of 1964 was surreal — I guess that's the best word for it. A week after Thanksgiving, Grandma caught the flu which led to pneumonia. She was in and out of the hospital a couple of times until finally, her 80-year-old body just gave up. She died on December 19th. Mama's daddy had died of the flu back in 1919 and Grandma was buried right beside him in a church cemetery out in the country. Mama's daddy died when she was only a baby, so Grandma was the only family Mama ever knew until she married Daddy. Mama was so upset, we didn't even put up a Christmas tree. Becky got home just in time for the funeral on the 23rd and on Christmas Eve, she announced that she and Eric had gotten married back in October and would be living in Myrtle Beach. Becky was 20 and there wasn't much Mama and Daddy could say.

We silently exchanged gifts on Christmas morning and just as silently ate a lunch of ham salad and tuna casseroles left over from the food the neighbors and church friends brought to the house after Grandma died. None of us could help looking at Grandma's empty chair. Becky stayed until the day after Christmas and then went back to South Carolina. Mama didn't stop crying for nearly a week.

Sarah Jane and her mother were at our house a couple of times. On Christmas day, Sarah Jane gave me a new kind of felt-tipped pen called a Sharpie that would write on almost anything and a sketch pad with very slick paper. I gave her a snow globe with a hula dancer in it that I got at the dime store on Main Street. I also gave her a box of candy I had originally planned to give to Grandma. We didn't have much to say to each other. She was wearing a new charm bracelet and I figured it came from Rob, but I didn't ask. I wondered what she gave him in return. Sarah Jane and her mother left town to go visit a cousin in Charlotte on Christmas day, so I didn't have to think about her until after New Year.

Daddy's gift to me added to the weirdness. On Christmas night, he told me that he planned on getting Mama a new car right after the first of the year and that I could have her station wagon as long as I paid him $15 a month until I graduated from high school. He said the money would help cover the higher insurance premiums it would cost him because I was a teenage driver and teenage drivers had a lot of wrecks. He also said nothing worth anything was ever free. You had to work for it. I guess he also thought that after I graduated, I would find a full time job somewhere and make enough to support myself. I figured I made about $95 to $100 a month at the A&P after taxes and all. Because I was also going to be responsible for gas, oil and tires for the car, I would have about $30 a month left over for records, art supplies and other essential stuff. I didn't worry too much about paying for dates. I wasn't going out with girls then.

In my wildest dreams as a 15-year-old, my first car was going to be a white Mustang 2+2 with blue racing stripes and a black leather interior. But as a 16-year-old aspiring artist and non-conformist, a four-door compact station wagon better fit my image. With a bike rack on top and a painting easel permanently in the back, my car would stand out in the school parking lot for sure, especially if I painted something cool on the tailgate. Miss Walincourt, my beatnik art teacher, wore a thing around her neck that she called a peace symbol. She said it started back in the fifties as a symbol for people trying to do away with nuclear weapons. She said that it just became a symbol for people who were against all wars. It was pretty simple and looked like an upside down Y with a line through it. I thought that might look pretty good on the back of the wagon and I doubted anyone but me would ever know what it stood for.

In addition to the $15 a month, Daddy attached one more string to the car gift. He personally had to make sure I was a competent driver before I could get my license. With finishing the classroom drivers-education course, I could take my driving test and get my license anytime. I had hoped to do it the week after Christmas, but Daddy wouldn't allow it until he passed on all of his knowledge of driving to me. Because his plant was closed down between Christmas and New Year, he chose that time to teach me. He also chose to teach me in his four in the floor, straight drive truck with a sticking clutch and squeaking brakes. I tried to convince him that I learned everything I needed to know in drivers-ed — he wasn't convinced. I also tried to tell him that it would be better if he taught me on the car I would actually be driving. He said if I could drive his eight-year-old truck, I could drive anything. He was right.

On the first day, he smoked a half of a pack of Lucky Strikes as I ground through the gears or stalled the engine because of the balky clutch. At the end of the day, he was coughing so badly that he could barely yell at me for almost running over the mail box as I pulled into the driveway.

On the second day, we did nothing but drive in reverse. Daddy said I needed to know that in order to back into a loading dock or something. The coughing was just about as bad as the day before.

On the third day, he had enough and said he thought I was ready to take the test except for one other stipulation. I had to take the driving test in his truck. I couldn't decide if he really wanted me to fail or if he thought I would impress the grouchy highway patrol lady that gave all the area teenagers their driving tests.

I passed the written part okay and did pretty well on the first part of the driving test, only grinding the gears a little. The one last thing I had to do was parallel park. Daddy's truck was huge compared to Mama's station wagon and I wasn't sure I could get it in the only spot designated in the highway patrol station parking lot for parallel parking. Just as I stopped and tried to figure out how to get the truck in that tiny spot, a fancy Cadillac convertible zipped into the spot and the driver rushed into the building without even looking at us. The test lady said something about "rich SOB's" and then looked at her watch. "Oh what the hell?" she said. "Forget about it. You'll probably never have to parallel-park in your lifetime anyway. Besides, it's time for lunch."

I pulled the truck into a regular parking spot, went in the building, got my picture taken and eventually got my license with a goofy looking picture of me. Then Daddy and I drove home. Without much fanfare, I had reached one of the milestones in any boy's life. I was a licensed driver in the state of North Carolina.

Chapter 25

School started back Monday, January 4 and I was looking forward to it. It was good to get away from the gloom at home and good getting back to art class. Daddy hadn't decided on what kind of car to get Mama, so I still didn't have her old station wagon to drive. That meant I was still dependent on riding with Rob or Sarah Jane. Ricky and I were still relegated to the back seat of Sarah Jane's bug or Rob's Chevy and it was like we were in two different worlds. The two in the front seat laughed, giggled, gave each other flirty little looks and sang along with the radio. The two of us in the back seat sat silently, trying to ignore all of the sugar sweet stuff in the front seat. When I got my car, at least I was going to be in the front when it was my time to drive. That didn't work out either.

On the same day we started back to school, President Johnson made a big speech about a "Great Society." It was on the 6:00 news and Daddy was standing right in front of the TV watching it when I walked in from work. The news reporter said that Mr. Johnson wanted the government to do more for poor people, especially poor Black people. He said the president wanted more Black children to go to school with white kids and poor people to have the same chance at good jobs as white people. When the reporter said that Mr. Johnson wanted Black people to be able to buy houses wherever they wanted, Daddy shook his head. "I don't know about this. Givin' stuff to people who haven't worked for it just doesn't sound right. What about us hard workin' slobs? What do we get out of this so called "Great Society" Mr. President? What's in it for us?"

Daddy lit another Lucky Strike and looked at me. "Donno, you're gonna have to bust your tail to get ahead.

Ain't nobody gonna give you anything. You're too white." As Daddy walked into the kitchen, I stared at his back and realized that my father was probably a racist.

I turned back toward the TV thinking about what Daddy had said and almost missed the reporter say that at the end of 1964, the US had over 23,000 soldiers in Vietnam and 216 of them were killed there during the past year. The last thing the reporter said before switching to the weather report was, "The Pentagon announced today that United States Marines will be deployed to Vietnam in the coming months to bolster the South Vietnamese Army's struggle against Communist insurgents." I thought about the boy from Ashton I saw in the bus station in Columbia who was headed to basic training in the Army.

Walking up the stairs, I heard Daddy try to tell Mama about what the president had said, but he could hardly talk through his coughing.

My art class met on Wednesdays and Fridays and I could hardly wait to go. When I walked in, Mr. Wertz was standing at the front of the room checking people off his list. "Ah, Mr. Emmerson, so glad you will be with me this semester. Perhaps you will actually take art seriously now."

I couldn't quite figure out what he meant by that. Then he went on. "I am partnering you with Miss Goldstein. She is new at Ashton High and a gifted artist. So please be a gentleman. Now take your seat." Except when we worked at an easel, the art students sat in pairs at long tables.

I looked around the room and all of the tables had two people behind them except one. I'm sure my mouth dropped open when I saw the girl seated beside the spot I was to take. Looking at me with deep set dark, almost black eyes was a beautiful oval face with olive, nearly golden skin surrounded by straight coal black hair down to her shoulders. I immediately thought that this girl looked exactly like my fantasy images of Cleopatra.

Mr. Wertz stood beside me and whispered, "Mr. Emmerson, it is impolite to stare even if it is at lovely young woman. Now go take your seat."

I made a loud scraping noise pulling out my chair and dropped one of my books when I sat down. I was too embarrassed to look at the goddess beside me until she spoke. "Hello. My name is Liana Goldstein, but almost everyone calls me Lilly."

Her voice was even goddess like with an accent that sounded exotic to my southern down-home ears. "Uh, hi, uh. I'm Donno, I mean Donald, uh Don Emmerson. Glad to meet you." She smiled and I think I gulped.

I heard very little of what Mr. Wertz said the rest of the class. I did catch something about the class being all juniors and seniors and that meant that we were advanced students. He was expecting us to take art class as seriously as we would English or math. I think he said there would be homework and difficult assignments. I spent most of the hour sneaking peeks at Lilly and trying to figure out how I could learn more about her. She gave me the opportunity.

"My next class is chemistry. This school is so large, I've only been here three days and I keep getting lost. Can you tell me how to find the chemistry laboratory area?"

"Oh, uh, sure. Why don't I just take you there? I'm going that way too." That was a lie, I had never been anywhere near the chemistry labs. I had satisfied my science requirement the year before with geology. Everyone called geology "rocks for jocks" because it was a sure passing grade for football players and others like me who weren't into chemistry or biology. I passed with a C minus.

"Thank you. That would be wonderful. My old school at the kibbutz only had 80 students and the building was very small."

I had no idea what or where a kibbutz was, but I was determined to learn more about the beautiful Lilly. We walked slowly through the crowded halls to the science wing. Kids in the hall stared at us. I don't know if they were staring because of Lilly's striking beauty or surprised that a long haired, sweatshirt and jeans wearing slob with old high-top tennis shoes was walking and talking with such a pretty girl.

My next class was Latin and on the opposite side of the building — I knew I would be late getting there. I didn't care. Walking and talking with a goddess was worth a late slip for a class I could barely understand anyway.

In our five minute walk, I learned that Lilly was born in America but grew up in Israel because her father took her and her mother there to help establish Israel as a country after World War II. Lilly was sent to Ashton to live with her grandparents because there was a lot of fighting with Arab people near where she lived. It took me a while to figure out that Lilly was Jewish. I don't think there were any Jewish people in West Ashton and the only ones I had heard of in Ashton proper were the rich owners of clothing stores and a few doctors and lawyers. Lilly's grandfather was a lawyer.

Lilly didn't want to be late for her chemistry class and rushed in right as the bell rang. I stood there for a minute or two staring at the closed door where she had disappeared. Was she real? Was there really a girl like that who actually talked to me and would sit beside me for a whole semester in art class?

I loafed along toward my Latin class, thinking of Lilly's beautiful face and not paying attention to what I was doing until Principal Joyner stopped me. "Emmerson, why aren't you in class? Where are you supposed to be?"

I was so stunned that I couldn't come up with an excuse so I decided to tell the truth. "Uh, Mr. Joyner, uh there is this new student from Israel in my art class and she didn't know how to get to her chemistry class. Uh, she's uh, she's real new and I walked her to her class so she wouldn't get in trouble for being late."

"Do you mean Miss Goldstein?"

"Uh, yes sir. That's her."

Mr. Joyner looked at me as if he was wondering why someone as beautiful and sweet as Lilly would even speak to me much less accept my help. “Well, um Mr. Emmerson, that’s very nice of you. You be sure to treat her like a lady.” He pulled out a pad of paper, wrote something down and handed it to me. “Here’s a hall pass. Give it to your teacher so you won’t be in trouble for being late.”

“Thank you Mr. Joyner.” Perhaps telling the truth did have its advantages.

When Daddy bought Mamma her 1964 metallic blue Pontiac Catalina Safari station wagon, I got her old Chevy II wagon. I had assumed that I would be part of the car pool rotation with Rob and Sarah Jane. They decided differently. They both had extracurricular stuff like student council meetings and French Club Valentine dance planning in the afternoons. Ricky Stillman and I didn’t have stuff like that and could leave right after the last bell (Ricky had dropped out of the band and no longer had after school practice), so it made more sense for Ricky and me to ride together and Rob and Sarah Jane to ride together. Ricky didn’t have a car, so that meant I drove to school every day. That also meant that by default, Ricky and I became best buddies and best buddies always sat together at lunch in the cafeteria — that is until the day I met beautiful Lilly.

All through Latin and my business math class, I daydreamed about Lilly and looked forward to sitting beside her in art class. I was still daydreaming as I made my way through the cafeteria line with my carton of milk, bowl of tomato soup, dry grilled cheese sandwich and an even dryer piece of cake. I turned in the direction of my usual table with Ricky when I spotted Lilly sitting all alone at a table on the other side of the room. I forgot about sitting with Ricky.

It was one thing to be assigned to sit beside her in class and another thing to help her find her next class when she asked, but to walk right up and ask if I can sit with her at lunch took some guts. “Hi, Lilly. Do you mind if I join you? My regular crowd doesn’t seem to be eating today.” Of course, my regular crowd consisted of Ricky, who I feared was already searching for me at our normal spot.

"Oh, hello Donald. Please join me. I really hate eating alone."

The only reasons I could figure she didn't have a table full other kids around her was that other girls were jealous of her beauty and the boys were afraid to approach a girl who looked like her. I looked around and several people at nearby tables were staring at us.

"Uh I see you bring your lunch." I couldn't tell what she was eating. It certainly wasn't a peanut butter and jelly sandwich. It looked more like a pancake rolled up with cheese or something inside. "What exactly is that you're eating?"

"Ah, this is a blintz. We eat them a lot of different ways in Israel. This one has fried potatoes and melted cheese in it. My grandparents' maid fixed it for me because she thought I might be missing home."

After I sat down, the first thing I noticed was her cool Beatles lunch box and thermos. Then I heard her say her grandparents had a maid. I figured her grandparents must live on the other side of the river. "Are you? I mean, are you missing home?"

"Well, I miss my parents and worry about them. I missed being with them at Hanukkah back in November. I was already here by then. I guess it will get better once I know my way around and get to know more people. So far, you are the nicest person I have met."

I'm sure I beamed with pride. "Lilly, you are a good person to be nice to." I surprised myself for being brave enough to say that. I really wanted the conversation to continue. "What is Hanukkah? Is it some kind of holiday or something?"

"Yes, it's a celebration. We call it the Festival of Lights and it has something to do with the old temple in Jerusalem. I'm not completely sure of all of the history. I guess it is sort of like how you put lights on an evergreen tree at

Christmas. We light candles in a thing called a Menorah. We light one candle each night for eight nights. We also give gifts, play games and eat a lot food."

I was so enthralled with the way she talked, I had to concentrate to understand what she was saying. She went on and told how her grandparents came to America from Germany at the beginning of World War 1. Lilly's father was born in the United States so he was an American citizen automatically. When World War II broke out, Lilly's father enlisted in the U.S. Army and fought all through France and into Germany. He helped liberate some of the concentration camps where Jewish people were being killed. After the war, he came home and married his high school sweetheart, Lilly's mother. Lilly was born in 1948, the same year that Jews from all over the world came to their old home land to start the country of Israel. Lilly's father was so angry about what he had seen in the concentration camps, he wanted to help Israel become a safe place for the surviving Jews to live. He took Lilly and her mother to Israel and he joined the Army there. Lilly said her whole family had what she called "dual citizenship."

I was so taken by her voice and her story, I only took a bite of my sandwich and drank a little milk. After she had opened up about her family and life, I wanted to hear more, I just wanted to hear her speak. "That's a neat lunch box you have. Do people in Israel know about The Beatles?"

"Of course, silly. We love The Beatles. My favorite songs are "I'll Follow The Sun" and "Eight Days a Week" on the "Beatles For Sale" album."

I was impressed. "Oh, wow! You are up to date. That album only came out last month."

"And, guess what, we also eat with knives and forks and most people wear shoes." We laughed out loud together.

We continued to talk and laugh until Ricky showed up. The look of astonishment on his face was priceless. I could tell he couldn't believe I was sitting with such a beautiful girl. Truthfully, I couldn't believe it either. As I expected, Ricky grilled me for all of the details during the ride across the river back to West Ashton after school.

Chapter 26

On the second day the art class met, I was still so mesmerized by Lilly's beauty and sweet personality that I had a hard time listening to Mr. Wertz. I think I heard him say something about how it was going to difficult to earn an A in the class and that being a true artist took hard work and sacrifice. He also said that most of us would only treat art as a hobby and that was okay. But, if any of us wanted to be serious artists, we must first learn the basics before we could be truly creative. He paused for a moment and I looked up to see him staring right at me.

When the class ended, Mr. Wertz stopped me. "Mr. Emmerson, please stay for a moment. I am sure Miss Goldstein will be fine." That made me mad. I was really looking forward to walking with Lilly. She smiled and said she would see me at lunch.

"Mr. Emmerson, I noticed that you were more attentive to Miss Goldstein than you were to my declaration of my expectations in this class and the work required to succeed here and beyond. I want you to know that they were directed at you and Miss Goldstein specifically."

"Uh, I uh, I'm sorry I guess."

"Mr. Emmerson, you have some raw talent and have been praised for it. The painting you did of a cardinal that won the scholastic contest was fine for a junior high student. However, when I look at it with a critical eye, it is very amateurish. The lighting is fractured and the colors are muddy in much of the background."

"I thought it was pretty good, I guess."

"For a ninth grade student, yes. Better than many — yet could have been much better. The monochrome painting that caused so much trouble for your previous teacher is another example. It showed a bit of creativity unusual for a young artist, however, technically it is not well done. The perspective is wrong and the proportion of the children's hands to the rest of their bodies is atrocious."

He was starting to make me mad. I wasn't all that great at a lot of things, but I thought I was pretty good at art. It was my one distinguishing attribute other than being able to dance a little. "Miss Walincourt thought it was good. She liked it a lot."

"Miss Walincourt was a children's art instructor who was pleased when a student could draw a straight line or one of those infantile smiley face things. Anything advanced of that excited her beyond reason. She was not a serious art instructor. Most art instructors, including myself, have limited artistic talent ourselves. We know basics but lack a truly creative spark. Our greatest talent is recognizing and nurturing it in others. "

When he said that, I realized that I had never seen anything painted or drawn by any of my three art teachers.

"Now, Mr. Emmerson, you can stop your art education at this level and still be able to impress a few people when you doodle and sketch. However, if you truly want to expand your creativity beyond the high school level, you must master the basics." He opened a folder and handed me three sheets. In bold type were the words Form, Perspective, Anatomy, Composition, Rule of Thirds, Value, Lighting, and Color. Under each of the bold headings was a paragraph or two briefly explaining the meaning of the words. Some of the explanations also had sketches in addition to the words.

" If you choose, learning to use what is described on these pages, you will then be able explore your creative talents fully. You will have the basic knowledge that will equip you to discover if you are a fine portrait artist, a landscape painter, an illustrator, an architect — ha!, even cartoonists use these same principles in their work. Esteemed artists such as Picasso, Dali', van Gogh, all of the popular abstract and impressionist masters knew and used all of the principals on those sheets I gave you. You should research those names and see some of their early work. This a great deal for you to consume right now, Mr. Emmerson. Please be prepared to give me a decision at our next meeting."

I was overwhelmed. It was like he was asking me to make a plan for the rest of life right then and there. Did I really want to work that hard? Did I really think I could learn these things? I didn't know.

"As you know, this class only meets three times a week for less than an hour per meeting. There is no possible way I can cover any of these topics in depth or give each of you one on one attention. You must take some of the initiative on your own. You must work at home."

Homework was bad enough for my academic classes. What he was describing was scary. With my job and other stuff, I wasn't so sure about any of it.

"Now, I didn't pair you with Miss Goldstein by accident. I think you will see why." He pulled a large black portfolio from under his desk and opened it on one of the tables. "These are drawings and pastel paintings that Miss Goldstein showed me when she asked to be in this class without having taken the prerequisites normally required by the school board."

I gasped. The first was a pencil drawing of a young girl with her arms around a goat's neck. The expression the girl's face was so real, so full of life, I first thought it was a black and white photo. The second drawing was of a woman using a hoe in a garden. I actually felt the movement of her arms and the strain on her back even though it was a simple sketch with white chalk on brown paper. The third was best. It was color pastel of two girls and a boy dancing hand in hand. It was not a realistic portrait, but stylized and free, yet the look of pure joy on the children's faces jumped off the page. All I could say was "Wow!"

"Wow indeed, Mr. Emmerson. As I have learned, at the small school where Miss Goldstein attended, art is more than encouraged. It is cherished. The children begin serious art education when they are five or six-years-old. Miss Goldstein mastered the basic concepts I gave you before she was 12. I don't know if you have the talent she displays, but I am certain you will never know unless you try. I would suggest you find some way to communicate about art with Miss Goldstein outside of art class. She has highly developed technical skill while you have some unrefined power and depth. Find some way to learn from each other."

At lunch, I told Lilly of my conversation with Mr. Wertz and that I had seen some of her art work. "Lilly, those drawings are great. I don't know how you did some of those things with the pastels. I thought I could draw a little, but you are way better than me."

"I really enjoy drawing the people living at the kibbutz, especially the children. I'm glad you like them. I look forward to seeing your work."

"Mr. Wertz gave me all of these things to work on and suggested that we get together and help each other. Is that okay with you? "

"I would like that very much. Here, let me give you my phone number and you can call me tonight. We will make a plan." Lilly wrote down her grandparents' phone number and address. She added a tiny heart at the end.

Ricky had been silently eating his beanie-weenies while trying to follow our conversation. With a mouthful, he asked, "All that's cool, but what's a kibbutz?"

That night, right after supper, I decided to call Lilly. There was no privacy when you were on the phone at my house. We only had one phone and it was on a little table at the foot of the stairs near the front door. We also only had one bathroom and it was upstairs. It was a busy spot because there was always somebody walking by or going up the stairs to the bathroom when you were on the phone. Becky complained about it all the time when she talked to her boyfriends. Sometimes, she would stretch the cord far enough to go out on the porch. I never worried too much about people overhearing my phone conversations because they never were very important. I was just talking to Sarah Jane or Ricky Tillman most of the time.

"Hello?"

"Uh, can I? Uh, May I speak to Lilly, uh please?"

"And who might be calling my granddaughter?"

"Mr. Goldstein, this is Don, I mean Donald Emmerson. I'm a friend of uh, Lilly and I are in the same art class. And, and, the teacher told us to work together."

"I see. I will ask her if she wishes to speak with you."

"Thank you, Mr. Goldstein."

Daddy walked down the stairs and gave me a strange look.

Lilly's sweet voice calmed my nerves. "Hi, Donald. I hoped you would call tonight."

"Hey. Is it alright to talk? Your grandfather didn't sound like he much cared for me speaking to you."

"Oh, don't let Gramps bother you. He likes to think he's mean and scares people. He's really just a big matzo ball."

"Well, he did sort of scare me." I didn't know what a matzo ball was, but I figured it had something to do with being a Jewish lawyer or a Jewish grandfather.

Lilly and I talked about all of the stuff Mr. Wertz gave me and she explained what she thought they meant. We talked about painting with oils and drawing with charcoal. We talked about her life in Israel and what it was like for me growing up in West Ashton. We talked about The Beatles and we talked about being a little scared of growing up.

After I hung up, I was sitting there looking at the phone and thinking of Lilly when Daddy walked up. "Who've you been yacking at for so long?"

"Uh, Lilly Goldstein. She's in my, she's in one of my classes at school. We were working on uh, an assignment." I didn't want to mention art class and get that argument started again.

"Goldstein, huh. Sounds Jewish to me. Is she a Jew?"

The tone in Daddy's voice sounded the same as when he talked about the Japanese. "She's from Israel but lives here with her grandparents. Oh, and her father was in the Army during the war." I thought that might change Daddy's tone.

"Must be one of those rich Jew families across the river. Well, isn't that something? I'm going to bed. See if your mother needs any help with anything."

It was only 7:30 when Daddy wheezed and coughed going up the stairs.

Chapter 27

Lilly and I talked on the phone almost every night. Her grandfather must have figured it was okay because Lilly always answered the phone when I called at our regular time. We did talk about our art assignments some. Mr. Wertz made us draw hands and feet a hundred different ways. Other times we drew faces with different expressions. Every assignment included drawing cubes, cones, balls and tubes with shading on different sides to indicate volume and light source. In class, we used little figures that had moveable arms, legs and heads that had the perfect proportions of a human body. Mr. Wertz let Lilly and me take ours home to use as models for assignments. There was nothing very creative about the assignments and I started getting bored with it until Lilly reminded me that she did the same kind of drawing when she was eight or nine. She also reminded me that even Leonardo da Vinci practiced drawing like that. "Donald, if you want to be another Leonardo, you have to wear down a lot of pencils."

We usually ended our phone calls talking about something funny that happened at school or some new song that we heard on the radio. Lilly liked "Downtown" by Petula Clark and "How Sweet It Is" by Marvin Gaye. She really liked Motown. I told her that my favorite new song on the radio was "The Sound of Silence" by Simon and Garfunkel, but she didn't want to hear it anymore because it was so sad. She said silence scared her sometimes because Arabs had attacked her kibbutz more than once during the early mornings when there was no sound except a little wind blowing through the olive trees. Lilly laughed when I told her that I also liked "Love Potion Number 9" by The Searchers.

One night, Lilly asked me why there weren't any Black students at the high school. I didn't have much of an answer. I knew that a lot of people were trying to change things and President Johnson had passed laws that made it possible for Black people to do things they never could do before. That still didn't explain why our school was still all white. "Maybe the Black kids like their school a lot more than ours. They've sure got a good marching band. Did you see them at the Christmas Parade?" Lilly said her grandfather thought Negro people weren't ready to compete in the white world other than in sports and popular music. Mr. Goldstein sounded a little like my father. I thought it was kind of strange that a Jewish man was biased against someone else.

During a lunch in early February, I told Lilly I wouldn't be able to call that night because Sarah Jane wanted me to help with some signs and decorations for the French Club Valentines dance.

"Your neighbor certainly is active in a lot of things."

"Tell me about it. And somehow she usually gets me involved. I've been drawing stuff for her projects since elementary school."

"When is the dance? I mean, is it just for members of the French Club?"

Deep in my gut, I felt something monumental was about to happen. "No, anybody can go. I've never been, but I think it's pretty fancy and people dress up for it. They have it at one of the big hotels downtown."

I could hear the coy teasing in Lilly's voice. "Oh, I would love to go. It sounds like so much fun. And I speak French."

What could I do? There was nothing else I could do. I was about to ask a real girl, a girl I really liked, out on a real date, but she could actually say no and I would be destroyed. "Uh, would you uh, would you like to go with me?"

"Oh Donald, that would be wonderful. Of course I'll have to ask my grandparents for permission. Knowing Grandfather, he will probably want to talk to you first."

"Uh, okay. Sure." The thought of being interrogated by a rich Jewish lawyer from the other side of the river was almost as scary as asking his granddaughter for a date. I decided that Lilly was worth it.

"Thank you, Donald. Call tomorrow evening at our regular time and I will put him on."

It was a little difficult to finish my meat loaf and green peas thinking about what Lilly's grandfather might ask me. I looked at Ricky who had heard our entire conversation and he rolled his eyes. I nodded in silent agreement.

That night, Sarah Jane was all bouncy and excited about the dance. She didn't stop talking while we cut big hearts out of pink poster paper and she wrote sayings in French that I didn't understand. My main job was to draw a giant picture of the Eiffel Tower with a couple holding hands on the top.

"Oh Donno, isn't this going to be wonderful? A real disc jockey from the radio station and a real dance floor. I can't wait. You are coming, aren't you? You and Ricky can come together."

I wasn't going to mention that I was bringing Lilly to the dance, but I couldn't let Sarah Jane automatically assume that Ricky and I would come and stand along the wall to watch others dance. "I have a date."

"Really?"

I could tell Sarah Jane was searching for a face or a name of some girl that I might ask to a dance. I guess she finally remembered I had been sitting with a girl at lunch every day since school started back.

"Oh, are you going with that pretty girl I see you with sometimes?"

"Her name is Lilly. She just came here from Israel."

Sarah Jane frowned slightly and I couldn't come up with a reason for it.

"Well, I'm sure you'll have a good time. She sure is a pretty girl. Now, let's get all this finished. I still have calculus homework to do."

The next day at school, I worried all morning about talking to Lilly's grandfather that night. At lunch, I almost backed out, and considered telling her that I had to work the night of the dance so I really didn't need to talk to her grandfather. However, when she sat down at the table, she was excited about getting a new dress if her grandparents said it was okay if she went to the dance.

"Oh, Donald, I'm sure Grandpapa will let me go after you talk to him. He will hear what a great guy you are and how sweet you have been to me."

Ricky rolled his eyes again.

"Sure, well uh, I will call tonight, and uh everything will be good, I'm sure."

I piddled with my supper and only ate a bite or two of the last of the casserole brought to us when Grandma died. I went to the bathroom and then made the call.

"Hello, Donald, Grandpapa is right here. I will put him on."

"Yes sir, Mr. Goldstein, Lilly is a very nice girl."

"Yes sir, I understand that she hasn't had time to learn about American boys."

"Yes sir, I respect her a lot."

"Yes sir, there will chaperones at the dance."

"Yes sir. I know she is only 16. So am I." That probably wasn't a good thing to say.

"No sir, I don't drink alcohol." I didn't mention drinking beer at the beach.

"Yes sir, I am a safe driver." I hadn't even thought about actually driving to the dance. I would have to give the wagon a really good wash job.

"Yes sir, I will have Lilly home by 10." I didn't know when the dance would actually end.

"Yes sir, I understand that you will still need to approve of me when you meet me in person the night of the dance." I saw a haircut in my immediate future and my only suit would have to go to the dry cleaners the next week.

"Thank you, Mr. Goldstein."

Lilly got back on the phone. "See, Donald, I told you he would like you. I am so excited about the dance. I need to finish my art assignment, so I will talk to you tomorrow."

Did Lilly's grandfather like me? I felt like he was about to sentence me to jail time or something. I needed to go to the bathroom again.

Ricky was either too scared to ask a girl at our school for a date or he asked a few and they turned him down. As a last resort, he asked his second cousin Martha to come to the dance with him. Martha was a sophomore at one of the high schools out in the county. It was okay with me — I knew I would run out of stuff to say before too long. Lilly said it would be fun to have Ricky and his date to join us. Ricky made me promise not to mention that Martha was his cousin.

On the night of the dance, Mama was helping tie my new striped tie. There would be no clip-ons that night. When she looked down at my shoes, she frowned and said, "Maybe you ought to wear your lace up Sunday shoes. Your loafers are a little run down in the heels."

She was right and the Weejuns had also gotten a little tight after two years. But, I wasn't going to wear wing tips to a dance and the Weejuns were my dancing shoes anyway.

Daddy walked in as I put on my jacket. "So, you're takin' out that Jewish girl tonight, huh?"

"Yes sir. Her name is Lilly."

"Goldstein, right?"

"Yes sir."

"Well, you're sure movin' in high society aren't you? Just don't get too used to it. Those rich Jews, uh those rich people over there, they're different than us. They care about nothing but money."

Mama stepped in and rescued me. "Frankie, stop that. Just let Donno go and have a good time. He's not planning on marrying the girl. They're just friends. It doesn't matter who's rich and who isn't."

"I'm just sayin' you get to runnin' around with that crowd, you'll be sorry."

Mama gently pushed Daddy away. "Oh pooh, Frankie. Quit being so negative all the time." Mama reached into the Frigidaire and got the corsage she had bought for me to give to Lilly. I never would have thought about that.

Daddy was right about one thing. The Goldsteins were rich, really rich. In the neighborhood where they lived, I drove past a golf course with a big swimming pool and tennis courts. There were mansions with white columns and houses surrounded by big walls with closed gates on the driveway. West Ashton seemed a long long way away.

Ricky and Martha both whistled from the back seat when we drove up in front of Lilly's house. It was as big and grand as any others in the neighborhood and I was scared to death walking up to the door. If a maid or butler had answered the door, I would have turned around and run away. Thank goodness, Lilly came to the door but I could hardly say hello. She was beautiful. The first time I saw her, I thought she was one of the prettiest girls I had ever seen, but standing there in that doorway, she was, well, I didn't have the words. Her long hair was tied up high on her head, showing her slender neck. I didn't know much about makeup on girls, but I could tell she had done something to her eyes and her lips. She looked like a movie star, like pictures I had seen of Natalie Wood when she was a teenager. Her dress was pure white with a little black band across her shoulders. I stood there and stared until she broke my trance.

"Hi, Donald. Don't you look nice. I like your haircut."

"You look really, uh really great. I like your hair too. Uh, here. This is for you."

Lilly took the corsage from me and grabbed my hand. "Well aren't you sweet. Come in and meet my grandparents and then you can pin this on me."

Mr. and Mrs. Goldstein weren't anything like I had imagined. I thought he would be about six foot four and 200 pounds. Instead, he was a little scrawny guy. Mrs. Goldstein was much taller than her husband and outweighed him by 50 pounds at least.

Lilly's grandfather may have been small, but he had a strong grip when he shook my hand and his voice was deep and menacing. "Mr. Emmerson, do you remember our phone conversation?"

He wouldn't turn loose of my hand. "Yes, uh, yes sir."

"In by 10 and no alcohol, isn't that our agreement?"

My hand was beginning to ache. "Yes sir, that's our agreement."

Like Mama had done, Mrs. Goldstein rescued me. "Jacob Goldstein, you old so and so. You're about to crush the boy's hand. Turn him loose so he can pin this lovely corsage on your only granddaughter who you are embarrassing."

Lilly's grandmother rescued me again. I had no idea how or where a corsage should be pinned. I was also pretty certain there were places where my hands shouldn't go while searching for a spot. Mrs. Goldstein did it for me. Mrs. Goldstein also made Lilly and me pose for a picture in front of a huge fireplace in the biggest living room I had ever seen. I had also never seen a Polaroid camera before. We didn't stay to see the picture develop.

I did know enough to help Lilly with her coat with a furry collar. Mrs. Goldstein said to have a good time and Mr. Goldstein just said "Remember, Emmerson, 10:00." as we walked out the door.

I had to admit that Sarah Jane and her committee did a pretty good job of decorating the hotel ballroom for the dance. All of the tables had tiny Eifel Towers as center pieces and the big Eifel Tower I drew was behind the disc jockey and had different colored lights shining on it. The pink hearts were everywhere.

As we stood in the doorway looking at the decorations and looking for a place to sit, The Beatles version of "Twist and Shout" was blasting away. Out of the entanglement of couples twisting away on the dance floor, I saw Sarah Jane waving madly at us. I waved back. After the song ended, Sarah Jane and Rob rushed up to us. Sarah Jane had on a short pink dress with ruffles around the top and around her knees. Her hair wasn't in her normal ponytail but was on top of her head like Lilly's. She looked pretty good. Rob wore a tux and had a rosebud in his lapel. Rob really could be irritating.

"Isn't this great, Donno? Look at your drawing. It's just the best."

"Yeah, turned out okay, I guess."

Sarah Jane turned to Lilly. "Hi, I'm sorry I haven't had a chance to meet you, but we have saved a place for you at our table."

Always sweet and agreeable, Lilly said, "Oh, that's wonderful. Thank you."

I mumbled, "Yeah, wonderful." Then I remembered Ricky and his cousin standing silently behind us. "Is there room for Ricky and Martha? We're together."

"Of course. We'll pull up a couple of chairs and make room."

Just as we sat down, the disc jockey announced the next song. "Here's one that will get this party rockin'. From 1963, by The Kingsmen, get out on the dance floor and do your thing to "Louie Louie."

Lilly clapped with joy. "I love this song. I can't understand a word they say, but I just love it."

I started to tell her that I had heard some rumors about the lyrics being dirty and tried to figure them out every time it came on the radio. We turned to watch the dance floor where every possible variation of the twist, swim, monkey and Watusi were being attempted.

I couldn't tell how Ricky and Martha felt about sitting with Rob and Sarah Jane. Martha hadn't and didn't say a word the whole night and when Ricky wasn't at the refreshment table, he was tapping out the rhythm to the songs on our table. The music and Ricky's tapping were so loud, we couldn't hear each other across the table, so Rob and Sarah Jane talked to each other and Lilly and I talked to each other. Ricky and Martha just sort of stared at each other.

In a little while, Sarah Jane got up and walked to the stage. I could see her talking to the disc jockey. I figured she made a request. After another Beatles song ended, the disc jockey said "This one is for you beach music and shag fans. Pretend you are down at Myrtle Beach and hit the floor to "No Place to Hide" from Martha and the Vandellas."

The words "shag" and beach music cleared the floor except for Rob and Sarah Jane and a few other couples who didn't know what they were doing. Lilly watched Sarah Jane and Rob intently as they twirled and slid across the dance floor, smiling and flirting with each other. "I like that dance. It reminds me of a swing dance we do back home. It's so smooth. Do you know how to do it?"

"I'm okay, I guess but I don't much like that song. I'll go request a better one." I didn't want to be out on the floor at the same time as Sarah Jane and Rob. I requested "How Sweet it Is" by Marvin Gaye.

After the twangy surfing song, "Walk Don't Run" by The Ventures finished, the disc jockey got back on the microphone. "Looks like there is another beach music fan out there. Listen to the sweet tones of Mr. Marvin Gaye with his "How Sweet It is"."

Lilly grabbed my hand. "You knew I liked that song. Come on and show me how to shag."

We walked out on an empty dance floor and I whispered "Just follow me. On one, and two, three and four, five six. Just make steps in place without moving either forward or back. On five, move your left foot back a little and on six move your right foot forward a little. Here we go. Hold my left hand. One and two, three and four, five six." It only took Lilly a second to catch on. She even kept up the steps as I twirled her. She was a natural, like she was with everything else she did.

When the song ended, Lilly hugged me and said she loved to dance. She also said the word shag meant something completely different in Israel. I didn't know what she was talking about.

Sarah Jane clapped loudly when we came back to the table and complimented Lilly on her dancing. Amongst songs by The Four Tops, Bobby Freeman, The Dave Clark Five, Dionne Warwick, Ricky Nelson, The Kinks, The Rolling Stones, The Shangri-Las, The Four Seasons and at least six by The Beatles, the DJ did manage to play "My Girl" by The Temptations and "Lonely Drifter" by The O'Jays. When those songs played, it was Lilly and me and Sarah Jane and Rob shagging alone. After a while, I forgot about them and just had a good time.

Toward the end of the dance, the disc jockey played several slow songs. With her head on my shoulder and the smell of her hair filling my senses, Lilly and I danced our last dance to "People" by Barbra Streisand. Lilly reminded me that Barbra was Jewish.

We collected Ricky and Martha and drove toward Lilly's house. I had thought we might drive through the *Big WASH* Tower of Rhythm to request a song, but I knew that would make us late getting Lilly home on time. I didn't dare do that. However, we did do a Chinese fire drill at a stop light. I had to explain the process to Lilly and we didn't make it back in our seats before the light changed back to green. Lilly and Martha both wondered if Chinese people really did something like that. Ricky and I laughed and laughed, drowning out the beginning of "Let It Be Me" by Jerry Butler and Betty Everett.

I pulled into the Goldstein driveway at exactly 10:00. It was freezing cold outside, so we rushed to the door. "Donald, I had such a good time. The best time I have ever had. Thank you." Lilly pulled my face down to hers and kissed me, kissed me on the lips.

I didn't notice the cold as I floated back to the car. I was only 16, but I thought I knew exactly what love was all about.

Chapter 28

Just after Valentines, a series of storms came through and it snowed every Wednesday for three weeks in a row. The snow never melted and piled up to almost three feet deep. We didn't go back to school for what seemed like a month. I was stuck at home most of the time. The roads were so bad, the A&P didn't have any customers, so I didn't go to work in the afternoons. I would have had to walk there anyway. Ricky and I did go sledding some, but that got kind of boring after a while. Daddy was home most of the time too. He had the flu or something and the company doctor said he should stay in bed for a while. Mama fixed him a place on the couch in front of the TV. He really had a hard time breathing and coughed a lot. About the only time he talked to me was to tell me to shovel the sidewalk and to go start the cars so the batteries wouldn't die. I mostly stayed upstairs in my room, drew in my sketch book and listened to records or the radio. About every hour, *Big WASH* would run a recorded news story. I usually ignored them, but after a while I paid attention. I learned that George Harrison had his tonsils removed, so I wondered if he would still be able to sing. I learned that a famous Black man named Malcom X was shot and killed and I wondered why he was famous and why he was shot. I learned that we were sending Marines to Vietnam and we would soon start bombing things over there. I learned that we were testing atomic bombs on little islands in the Pacific Ocean and I learned that "My Girl" had reached number one on the Top 100 list.

I talked to Lilly every day for hours at a time until her grandfather or my father told us to get off the phone in case a really important call came in. Lilly said she liked the snow at first and enjoyed sledding down a hill at the country club. After a while, she got tired of it. She said it was just like the desert where she lived except it was white and cold rather than sandy and hot. We talked about all kinds of stuff. I found out that she had a big brother in the Israeli Army and if she went back, she would have military training next year. She said everybody in Israel over the age of 17 had to know how to use a gun. I told her about how my daddy didn't like for me to be so interested in art. I even told her about thinking I was in love with Britney McMurray when I was 14. Mostly we talked about how tough it was to be different. She said she felt different in North Carolina because of her accent and her religion. She also said if it weren't for me, she would have been terribly home-sick. I told her I had always felt a little different from the rest of the kids my age and my family, especially my father — maybe because I was always looking at things through an artist's eyes. She agreed that she felt that way too sometimes. I had never opened up to a girl, or anybody else like that before.

One night, when we were talking on the phone, I could hear her radio playing "I'll Follow the Sun" by The Beatles in the background. It had been released in December and like all their songs, became a hit. "Lilly, turn up your radio so I can hear it." Together, we started singing along, laughing because we hadn't seen the sun for a long time. I stopped when the lyrics talked about the lovers breaking apart when one of them left to follow the sun. It reminded me how Lilly described how the sun shown so brightly in Israel and how the cold weather made her miss it.

In the first week in March, the sun did come out and the temperature climbed into the 60s. Just like magic, the piles of dirty snow melted away, birds showed up, dead looking things turned green and I was glad to go back to school — especially because I could see Lilly. She had cut her hair during the snow break and mine had grown back down to my collar. We laughed that our hair was almost the same length. We laughed about a lot of things. Just seeing her in person almost made up for the dark mood at home.

Daddy went back to work even though he was still pretty sick. When he came home he ate dinner, watched the news and went to bed.

The first day back in art class, Mr. Wertz asked to see what all of the students had done in their sketch pads while out during the snow. He made a few comments to the other students before he got to Lilly and me. "Mr. Emmerson, I see you spent a good deal of time doodling. However there are some presentable preliminary sketches. The drawing of the figures beside the automobile has some merit." It was from a picture Becky took of Mama and Daddy beside Mama's car when we were at the beach. It was a happy time before Daddy started getting sick.

"And Miss Goldstein, I don't suspect you have doodled at all. What great work have you created?" As he flipped through the pages of Lilly's sketchbook, he smiled and nodded. When he got to the last page, he looked up at Lilly and said, "As I expected, Miss Goldstein, outstanding work, especially the last one." Lilly quickly took the book and closed it. I only caught a quick glance of the last drawing, but could not see what it was.

Mr. Wertz announced to the whole class that we were to take one of the sketches done during the snow break and fully develop it first in charcoal and eventually in oils or watercolors. Those finished pieces would be done outside of class and would be our final exam for the year. In the meantime, art class was still mostly working on basics and practice. If I hadn't been sitting beside Lilly, I would have gotten bored with it all.

At lunch, I asked Lilly if I could look at her sketch book. Just like Mr. Wertz had said, there were some wonderful drawings. I didn't ask Lilly why there was a page torn out.

Chapter 29

By the end of March or beginning of April, I had spent so much time on the phone with Lilly, I guess her grandparents sort of figured I would be around for a while, so why fight it? They let me take her to the movies on Saturday nights, but we had to be in by 9:00. They didn't know we went to the drive-in one time. They also let me take Lilly to the library to study. While there, she got me to look stuff up for a history term paper and I made a B+. Lilly's grandparents even invited me to dinner once at their house. It was for a special holiday meal. They called it Passover. Lilly tried to explain it all to me and said that her grandparents kept kosher and that the meal might be a little different than what I was used to. I didn't know what kosher meant. I decided it was some sort of Jewish food they kept in the freezer and ate it only on holidays. I still don't know what part of the dinner was a piece of kosher, but the chicken and vegetables were good. I couldn't say much for the bread. It was flat and tough.

I wanted to ask Lilly to come to our house for Easter lunch, but Mama didn't think Daddy was up for guests and she said she didn't think Jewish people liked ham very much. Becky didn't even come home for Easter. It was pretty sad. Grandma was gone, Becky was in South Carolina and Daddy wasn't in any kind of holiday spirit. The three of us ate our ham and potato salad in silence. Sarah Jane and her mother brought over some peach pie and homemade ice cream later. Sarah Jane was all excited. Rob had asked her to go to the prom with him in May.

At our school, only seniors and their dates could go to the prom. I had figured Rob would probably ask Sarah Jane. They were always together anyway. What I didn't figure on was some other senior inviting Lilly to the prom. There were a few other Jewish kids at the school and one of them was the son of Mr. Goldstein's law partner. Isaac Cohn was a shy, pimply faced kid who would probably never even speak to a girl, much less invite her to a dance. It turned out that Isaac's father and mother didn't want him to miss his senior prom, so they asked Lilly's grandfather for a favor. They ask Mr. and Mrs. Goldstein to have Lilly to go the prom with Isaac just so he wouldn't be alone and left out. Lilly didn't have much choice and besides, her grandmother said she could get a new dress if she agreed to go with Isaac.

When Lilly told me about Isaac's invitation, I put on like I was hurt and a little mad. I really wasn't either. I mean, we weren't officially "going steady." I hadn't given her a ring or charm bracelet — and because I wasn't a football player, I couldn't give a cleat off of a shoe either. Only football jocks did that.

"Oh, Donald, I hope you understand. I have to do it for my grandfather and Isaac is so shy, he won't even look me in the eye at the synagogue. I doubt he will speak to me the entire night. I expect we will leave early anyway."

"Well, I guess it's okay. Like you said, it's a favor for your granddad. Anyway, next year we will both be seniors and I can take you to the prom myself." Lilly didn't respond to that and there were a couple of seconds of silence before she spoke again.

"Besides, Donald, you know you are my favorite dance partner."

How could I be angry after hearing that? "And don't you forget it. I promise we will find a special place to dance together, better than any old prom."

The prom was on a Saturday night and I knew that Lilly would be going to services on Sunday morning, so I didn't talk to her until Sunday night. I asked her in jest, "Well, did you and Isaac dance every dance?"

She answered in jest, "Oh sure, we never sat down the whole night. Actually, I did dance a few times. The band was called Ricky and the Shades and they played a lot of "Twist" music. They must have played "Peppermint Twist" five times. You know, with the twist, you don't really have to have a partner. They did play a song called the "The Stroll" by a band called The Diamonds. I had never seen that before, but the other kids said they used to watch it on *American Bandstand.* It was fun."

"What did Isaac do during all of this?"

"He talked to Mr. Bowers, the math teacher who was chaperoning the dance."

"Well, I'm sorry you didn't have a good time."

"It was okay. I'm glad I went for Isaac's sake. I would have rather gone with you, but at least I can say I've been to an American high school prom. Oh, and by the way, Sarah Jane and Rob must have been having a big argument. Sarah Jane looked upset and they left early."

"Huh, I wonder what that was all about. I'm sure she will tell me sometime soon. She always does on stuff like that."

About a week after the prom, Sarah Jane called and asked if she could ride with me and Ricky for a couple of days a week until school was out. Because of all the days we missed due to the snow, the school year wouldn't end until the middle of June. After what Lilly had told me about Sarah Jane and Rob getting in an argument at the prom, I guessed she didn't want to ride with him anymore. "Uh, sure, I guess. What's going on with you and Rob? Something wrong with his car? And uh, I thought you had a bunch of stuff in the afternoons at school."

"All of my afternoon stuff is over except being an usher and marshal at graduation. And no, there's nothing wrong with Rob's car. I'm just mad at him right now."

I really didn't want to get into her love life with Rob so I didn't respond, but Sarah Jane went on anyway. "We had it all worked out. He was going to Hillside College next year and that's only 30 miles away. We could see each other every weekend and maybe even during the week. But now, he has been accepted at the university and that's five hours away. I'll never get to see him."

"Well, you know, maybe he'll change his mind or something. I mean you can always talk to him long distance."

That didn't help Sarah Jane's mood. "You don't really understand, do you? Anyway, thank you for letting me ride with you. Pick me up in the morning and don't be late."

I thought about how hard it would be to be separated from seeing Lilly like that.

We had final exams the week before graduation and I passed them all with Cs and a couple of Bs. My final grade in art was the only one I truly cared about. Lilly and I had turned in our art projects separately, but were together when we went by the art room after school to get our grades and pick up our projects. There were several other art students there and Mr. Wertz asked Lilly and me to wait until he finished with them. I was first. "Mr. Emmerson, your pen and ink with water color over wash was the only use of that medium in the whole class and well done. Technically, you were precise. I was especially impressed with your use of white space to create the effect of bright sunlight on the windshield of the automobile and the eye glasses of one of the figures."

I had added glasses to Mama's face even though she seldom wore them. They just added a little extra contrast to her face.

"Mr. Wertz went on. "I have given you a grade of A minus, the second highest grade in the class and one of the few I have ever awarded to a junior student."

At first, I was excited about the A and was starting to feel pretty good about myself until I thought *Why the minus*?

Mr. Wertz must have sensed my confusion. " Mr. Emmerson, do you like music?"

"Uh, I guess, yes, sure." I had no idea what he was talking about.

"Do you sing along with the lyrics on songs that you like, or tap your foot to the rhythm? Do you dance?"

Lilly joined in. "He's a wonderful dancer, Mr. Wertz."

"Yes sir, I like all kinds of music and I like to dance, but what does this have to do with my drawing?"

" When you feel the rhythm of a piece of music or identify with the lyrics enough to join in, you have allowed the piece to join your artistic soul. The same is true of creating a piece of art. You must feel what your subjects are feeling or transfer your feelings to them. If it is a landscape, you must feel the sun on your face or the movement of the trees. As I said, your work is technically superb, very advanced for a high school student. However, art should interpret reality, not just reproduce it. Your painting did not tell a story. There is no emotion in the faces of the two subjects. It might as well have been a photograph. You should work on that this summer and next year we will see how you have progressed. Now, let's look at Miss Goldstein's work." He flipped over the cover sheet of Lilly's pastel and colored pencil mixed media drawing and it was spectacular. "Miss Goldstein, you, and at times, even Mr. Emmerson, are the reason why I choose to teach art. With a minimum of strokes and a unique use of light and shadow, you have captured pure joy and sadness all at once. I and any viewer of this piece can feel the emotion with just a glance." Lilly's drawing was of two little girls. One was holding a yellow balloon and her smile and blue eyes are reflected in the balloon. The other little girl had lost her grip on the string of a red balloon and it was flying away from her outstretched hands. She looked heart broken. The girl with the yellow balloon was black and the other was white. I was equally impressed and jealous — could I ever be that good?

"Mr. Emmerson, do you see what I mean by emotion? And Miss Goldstein, the other drawing you showed me was equally as good as this, but I believe this one displays all of your skill in a different way, an extremely pleasing way. I hope you and Mr. Emmerson will allow me to keep these works as examples of my top students' accomplishments."

Lilly and I left the art room together and walked down the hall. "Lilly, that pastel was, I don't know, it was probably the best thing of yours I have ever seen. It was the best thing by anybody I have ever seen."

"You're so sweet. But yours was just as good. I loved it."

We walked a little further until I remembered something else Mr. Wertz had said. "What was the other piece of yours Mr. Wertz mentioned? Have I seen that?"

"Oh, it was another mixed pastel and colored pencil drawing I tried. Maybe I'll let you see it later. Can you take me home? I have probably missed my bus."

Chapter 30

I had no interest in going to graduation, but Lilly wanted to go. She said she had never been to an American high school graduation and wondered how different they were from Israeli graduations. All of the graduations in our county were held in a big old auditorium downtown. It either had no air conditioning or it wasn't working that night. It was the middle of June and was really warm. Mama made me wear a suit and the only one I had was made of wool. She said graduations were important and special occasions. The suit and the heat made staying awake hard. The principal, the chairman of the school board, the student body president, the senior class president, the valedictorian and the salutatorian all announced that graduating from Ashton High School was a great achievement and that there was a "glorious future" awaiting the seniors if they used all of the "great skills" they learned in the last 12 years. After the third or fourth speech, I saw a lot of the seniors who were wearing heavy robes over their new dresses and sport coats nodding off. I probably would have fallen asleep if Lilly hadn't been so enthralled with it all. She clapped loudly after every speech. She also said if I studied hard, maybe I could be one of the speakers my senior year. I laughed at her and she punched me on the shoulder.

After the speeches, it was time to hand out the diplomas. There were more than 500 graduates that year. A lot of babies born nine months after their fathers got home from the war had made it to the 12th grade. The schools would be filled with baby boomers for years to come. As the names were called and the graduates walked across the stage, there was applause and yells of "Atta boy" and "That's my girl." Some students got very little applause while kids in the popular groups or star athletes got such loud acknowledgements, it drowned out the next name called. Lilly made sure every graduate got at least some recognition. She clapped for everyone.

Most of the kids walked across the stage, shook hands with the principal, accepted their diplomas from the school board president and walked straight off the stage. A few raised their diplomas in the air to show their families. There was a couple who spun around in a pirouette to the delight of the crowd. Rob did a big fist pump after he got his diploma. Lilly couldn't figure out why it was such a big deal when the principal told the graduates they could move the tassels on their hats to the other side. I told her it was just an Ashton thing and nobody else in the world did it. Lilly surprised me by knowing all of the words to the school's Alma Mater. I didn't have a clue what they were.

Rob and Sarah Jane must have made up because I saw her standing with Rob and his parents after the ceremony and they all looked happy. He was holding her hand. There was a lot of hugging and picture taking and little brothers and sisters wearing their siblings' black graduation hat. I heard a lot of the graduates talking about how a whole group was going out to the Maple Lodge to celebrate. I knew that Becky went out there after her graduation and didn't get in until 2:00 in the morning. Daddy wasn't happy. I told Lilly about it and she wanted to go too.

"No, not now. You're supposed to be 18 to get in and it's a long way out there. We would never make it back by your 10:00 p.m. curfew." Lilly faked a pout. I didn't tell her I only had three dollars with me and not enough gas to get to the Maple Lodge and back. "Maybe another time. But, I'll tell you what, let's go cruise the strip and put in a request at the *Big WASH* Tower."

"Ooh, let's do that. And then you can show me the Mistletoe Overlook I keep hearing people talk about."

I wasn't sure I believed what I had just heard. The Mistletoe Overlook was a pull-off spot on the mountain that overlooked the strip on one side and downtown on the other. It was called Mistletoe because girlfriends were supposed to pretend it was Christmas and give their boyfriends a special gift when parked there. I had never been up there at night, but I understood that on most Friday nights you had to wait your turn to get a parking spot. It was always crowded. I hoped that because it was graduation night, all the other kids in town were at a party somewhere or eating out with their families. "Uh, okay. But do you know about what goes on up there?"

Lilly gave me her coyest grin and nodded. "I'm pretty sure I know what to do. Do you?"

We pulled into Buster's Burgers and with $1.20 of my $3.00 got one strawberry milkshake and two straws. After we finished the shake, we got in line to drop our song requests in the bucket. Lilly said she was in a Motown mood and requested "Back In My Arms Again" by The Supremes. I wanted something different that wasn't by The Beatles. I requested "Mr. Tambourine Man" by The Byrds. Then we headed up the mountain to find a parking spot.

Every parking spot was filled as I came around the last curve on the narrow two lane road. I was afraid we would have to go back down on the strip. I was also afraid that if I did find a spot, what was I going to do? What was Lilly expecting? We had kissed briefly a couple of times and held hands other times. But if we parked at the Mistletoe Overlook, how far would we go? What would Lilly think of me if I went too far or not far enough?

"Oh crap! No place to park. I guess we'll have to go. "

"No, Wait! Look Donald, someone is pulling out. Quick! Pull into that spot."

A black T-Bird spun the tires as the driver pulled away from the gravel parking spot and onto the asphalt. I figured he was either mad that something didn't happen or glad that it did. I whipped into the spot and Lilly immediately leaned across me to be able to see the lights down below on the strip. I turned off the engine and the lights, rolled down the window and turned up the radio. Her request was playing. As The Supremes sang “Back In My Arms Again” Lilly got up on her knees and kissed me. And I let her. I leaned against the door with the steering wheel against my ribs so she could get closer to me and we kissed again. The smell of her hair, the sweet taste of strawberry ice cream on her lips and the touch of her hand on my face caused feelings I had never felt before and I returned her kiss.

I was still wearing my suit coat and tie and even with the window down, Lilly’s closeness and all of the heat our bodies were creating, I started sweating. “Lilly, I’m going to take off this jacket and throw it in the backseat.” Looking at the big open space in the back, big enough to lie down and after having my arm crushed against the steering wheel in the front, I wondered— would she?—does she want me to?—would we?. “You know, we would have a lot more room in the back seat. Do you want to move back there?”

Lilly looked at me for a moment and nodded, saying nothing. I opened the driver’s side door and helped her out. While still holding her hand, I reached for the back door. Suddenly, Lilly pulled away. “Donald, you know I care for you, don’t you? You know I love being with you, don’t you?”

I could only nod.

“As much as I would love for you to be my, uh my first, I can’t do it, not yet.”

I had to think about what she was saying. First at what? Oh, that first. “Lilly, it would be my first too.”

“Then can we wait a little longer? I promise, when I am ready, you will be my only choice.”

Different emotions swirled around in my brain: anticipation, disappointment and finally relief. I wasn’t ready either. “I understand, Lilly. Let’s wait until we are both ready.”

Just then, the radio DJ announced a new song. ”Here’s a new one for you beach music fans from Mr. Gene

Chandler. Get out there and shag to "Nothing Can Stop Me"."

Lilly laughed out loud at the title of the song. Lilly took my hand and we danced right there on the side of the road at the Mistletoe Overlook. As we drove back down the mountain, my requested "Mr. Tambourine Man" came on and we sang along.

We got to her house a little before 10:00 and we lingered on her front porch. "Thank you Donald. I had a great time. And thank you for understanding. I will keep my promise." I leaned into kiss Lilly again, but the porch light came on and her grandfather opened the door.

Chapter 31

For the most part, the summer of 1965 was okay. Daddy's cough wasn't any better, but he kept on going to work every day. Mama spent a lot of time doing banking and other stuff Daddy usually did. He had lost some weight and didn't have much energy. He also didn't have much interest in what I was doing as long as I kept the grass cut and the bushes trimmed. Daddy stopped fussing about me seeing "that rich Jewish girl from across the river."

Seeing that Jewish girl sure made the summer bearable. If it weren't for her, I probably would have spent all of my time working at the A&P, cruising the strip with Ricky, and drawing up in my room. I doubt if I would have gone to the pool or the teen-center below the fire station either. Thankfully, Lilly's grandparents had gotten used to me and figured I wasn't going to do their granddaughter any real harm. I guess they trusted me. That turned out to be a mistake.

On days I didn't see her, Lilly and I talked on the phone for hours. We also went to the movies a lot. We saw *Shenandoah,* a Civil War film with Jimmy Stewart, Katharine Ross and Doug McClure. Lilly didn't like it. She said it was too sad and reminded her of the fighting in Israel. After that, we only went to see comedies. Lilly's favorite was *What's New Pussycat* with Woody Allen, Peter Sellers, Peter O'Toole, Richard Burton and Ursula Andress. It was okay, but my favorite was *The Great Race* with Peter Falk, Keenan Wynn, Arthur O'Connell, Jack Lemmon, Tony Curtis and Natalie Wood. Lilly laughed out loud when I told her I thought she looked just like Natalie Wood. She laughed, but I think she liked it.

On July 4th I didn't have to work so I picked Lilly up and we went to the pool. Seeing her in a bathing suit made me proud she was with me and made me want to punch all the other guys that stared at her. Lilly couldn't believe how cold the water was. She said the place where she lived was close to the Jordan River and she swam there a few times, but the water was always warm from the sun. I asked Lilly if the water in the pool at the country club near her grandparent's house was heated. She said she didn't know because Jewish people weren't allowed to join the club. Lilly and I would only swim across the pool a couple of times and then head upstairs to the pavilion to get something to eat, listen to the jukebox and maybe dance.

Mrs. Bronson was still in charge of the snack shop and the pavilion. When I introduced her to Lilly, Mrs. Bronson said she didn't recognize Lilly's accent and wondered where she was from. I told her that Lilly was from Argentina and was here as a summer exchange student. Lilly snickered when I said she was from Argentina. I explained to her about how Mrs. Bronson felt about Black kids coming to the pool and I didn't want to get into the whole Jewish thing. Lilly said that if that was the case, she probably shouldn't ask if the snack shop had kosher hot dogs.

There weren't many kids our age at the pool that day. Ricky was on vacation up in the mountains with his family and Sarah Jane was doing a summer leadership training thing at the teachers' college two counties away. She was planning for running for class president once school started back. She also had a goal of being valedictorian. I had no idea where Rob was. For all I knew, he was with Sarah Jane.

Most of the kids were watching a doubles ping-pong game and there was no music playing. I hadn't been to the pavilion since the middle of June and I figured there were some new songs on the jukebox. Lilly looked over my shoulder, sipping her Cheerwine, as I flipped through the titles. "Hey, look. There's Dylan's "Like a Rolling Stone"." I had started to really like Bob Dylan's cross between folk music, rhythm and blues and rock and roll. I also liked his sort of goofy voice and rebellious attitude. Lilly reminded me that Dylan was Jewish and she wondered what Mrs. Bronson thought about Jewish music being played on her jukebox.

"Donald, find something we can dance to. You've told me about seeing some really good dancers here. How about dancing with me at your special place?"

"Do you want to "Twist" or "Shag"?"

"Didn't you say this was the first place you ever saw anyone shag?"

"Okay. Let me find a good shag tune." I knew we would probably be the only ones dancing, but that was okay. I would be dancing with Lilly and the other kids would stare at her because she was so beautiful. "Let's see. Here's one from Maurice Williams and the Zodiacs. Have you ever heard of them? They had a big hit three or four years ago called "Stay"."

"I have heard of them. I remember the song was really short. What is this one called?"

"It's called "May I". I bet it is a good shag tune." I put in a nickel and pushed the button. I was right. It was a good dance tune. I took Lilly in my arms and spun her around. "One and two, three and four, five six." We weren't anywhere near as good as the god and goddess couple who made me want to learn to dance, but it didn't matter. I was dancing with Lilly, and she was my goddess. Lilly loved that song.

On the way home, we sang along with "Ticket to Ride" by The Beatles and "Help Me Rhonda" by The Beach Boys. Neither of us paid much attention to the news reporter talking about a big push by American soldiers in Vietnam and B-52s dropping bombs on villages where they thought the enemy might be hiding. They called it Rolling Thunder.

Mr. and Mrs. Goldstein asked me to stay for supper and to watch the Fourth of July fireworks the country club shot over the golf course near their house. I called Mama and she said it would be alright. She said Daddy wouldn't be eating supper anyway.

My 17th birthday was on Thursday the 15th of July and Lilly's was Tuesday the 20th. We knew that our families and Sarah Jane's family would want us around on our actual birthdays, so Lilly and I decided to celebrate together on the Saturday in between. Lilly got permission to stay out later than 10 because I wanted to take her to dinner at the Crystal Cafeteria downtown and then to see *Cat Ballou* with Jane Fonda, Lee Marvin and Nat King Cole at the theatre right down the street from the cafeteria. I didn't get off work until 6:00, so there was no way we could eat and make it to a 7:00 movie. That meant going to a 9:00 show, putting us home way after 11:00. Mr. Goldstein said it would be alright that one time.

For my birthday, Mama bought a nice blue Polo shirt and a new pair of khakis. Mama had also gotten my Weejuns fixed with new soles and heels. She said they were too expensive to buy new ones. Daddy gave me a 10 dollar bill, Uncle Al surprised me with a 20 and Becky sent me a card along with five dollars. With my weekly pay of $18, I had more than enough to take Lilly out and to buy her a nice birthday gift. The little jewelry store up on Main Street was the closest and easiest place for me to find something. Rings and watches didn't make much sense and neither did earrings. I didn't even remember if Lilly wore earrings. I couldn't decide. Finally the man at the store suggested a nice heart-shaped gold locket on a chain. I wasn't sure until he said he could engrave something on the front and inside the locket and there would still be enough room for a little picture. That gave me an idea. Lilly really seemed to like the song "May I." The second verse of the song said *May I bring you joy?"* I had "May I" engraved on the front of the locket and" bring you joy?" on the inside. I thought that was downright poetic. The jewelry store man said I could pick it up Saturday on my way home from the A&P. That gave me time to draw a tiny picture of two people dancing together that fit in the locket. Mama wrapped the little box for me as I changed clothes.

Mr. Goldstein met me at the front door and reminded me about my promises to him and that even though he was allowing Lilly to stay out later, I still had to keep my promise. I said I would and I meant it, I thought.

Lilly came down the steps with a bright smile and an even brighter orange and yellow dress that left her shoulders bare and set off her summer tanned olive skin. She took my breath away as usual. How did a goofy kid like me get a girlfriend like Lilly?

Lilly and I had agreed that we would exchange our birthday gifts for each other at dinner, but the silver and gold wrapped 11 inch by 14 inch package she carried was too exciting for me to wait. We opened our gifts in the car. Lilly opened hers first. After opening the locket and seeing the drawing and engraving, she cried. "Dear, dear Donald, it's beautiful! And I am surprised that you remember how much I loved dancing to "May I" with you. You already bring me joy." Lilly leaned over and kissed me and handed me her package. "Now it's your turn."

I didn't try to save the fancy wrapping and tore into the package. It was a framed drawing of Lilly and me standing in front of the fireplace in her grandparent's home. It was us the night of the Valentine's Dance back in February. "Oh, wow, Lilly. This is, uh, it's wonderful." I remembered Mr. Wertz saying my drawing didn't show much emotion and needed to tell a story. Our faces in Lilly's pastel and charcoal drawing showed what he meant. We looked, well we looked in love. "This is the best thing I have seen you do, Lilly. I, I just can't believe it." I pulled her close and kissed her like I had never kissed her before.

"Do you really like it? I did it from the photo that grandmother took on the night of the dance. I started to use it for our final assignment for art class but decided it should just be ours. Mr. Wertz liked it and wanted to keep it. I couldn't do that."

"It's the best gift I have ever gotten. Thank you!" I started to say that it would always remind me of her, but that would almost sound like we wouldn't be together forever. I didn't want to think about that.

"Well, this beautiful locket is the sweetest and most thoughtful gift I have ever gotten. Now, let's get going so we can have a nice dinner and see a good movie."

I kissed her again and started the car. The radio was already on and tuned to *Big WASH* and "I Can't Get No Satisfaction" by The Rolling Stones was just finishing up when the DJ came on with a couple of commercials for a dry cleaners and a sale at an appliance store or something. We didn't pay the commercial any attention. Then he started to announce the next song, "Here comes "Can't Help Myself" by The Four Tops, but before I spin that one, don't forget that Maurice Williams and the Zodiacs are out at the Maple Lodge tonight. Here's your chance to hear and see one of the top bands around up close."

I stopped the car in the middle of the street. "Lilly, did you hear that? Did you hear him say that Maurice Williams and the Zodiacs are in town? The Maple Lodge was always bringing in top beach music and rhythm and blues bands.

Her eyes got big. "I did. Is it true?"

We looked at each other and knew what the other was thinking. "You know, we probably can't get in. You're supposed to be 18."

"You look 18."

"You want to give it a try? All they can say is no and we would still have time to get back to the 9:00 movie. You don't have to be in until 11:30."

"I've never seen a really famous band. That would be a wonderful birthday present, not as wonderful as my locket, but wonderful."

How could I turn her down? "Let's do it." After a quick drive through stop for burgers and cokes at McDonald's out on the strip, I headed south, looking for the Maple Lodge.

Chapter 32

The parking lot at the Maple Lodge was packed. The Lodge had a public pool and playground with swings it operated during the day. At night, the pool and playground was closed and the lodge building switched to a dance club with live bands. The parking lot was so crowded, I had to park on the grassy playground. Getting in The Shack down at the beach was easy when I was barely 16 because Becky's Eric let me in. I figured the Maple Lodge had much stricter rules and checked IDs. Lilly and I walked up to the door and merged with a big group trying to get in. There was an older man taking up money and a younger man stamping the back of people's hands to prove they had paid the three dollar per person cover charge. The older man was having a hard time making change for all of the people handing him five and 10 dollar bills. He yelled, "Has anybody got correct change, I'm out of ones." Luckily, I had six ones. I stuck my cash in his face and he took it. Never looking up, he motioned for us to go on in. The younger guy looked at us, didn't say a word and just hit the back of our hands with a purple maple leaf stamp. I guess he figured if the old guy let us in, we must be okay.

Lilly grabbed my hand and we walked into the darkness with the only visible light shining on the bandstand where musicians were setting up drums, tuning guitars and testing microphones. Somewhere, I guess it was a juke box, I could hear Willie Tee singing "Thank You John" and there were a few couples shagging on the dark dance floor.

"Isn't this exciting, Donald? I can't believe we got in so easily. Now, what should we do?"

"I guess we ought to find a place to sit." My eyes had adjusted to the darkness and the thick blue haze of cigarette smoke and I looked around. Scattered around the walls and back in smoky dark corners were round tables with red and white checked tablecloths. The tables were big enough for six or eight people, but most of them were already filled. Finally, way back behind the bandstand, I spotted a table that had several empty chairs. I figured it wasn't all filled because you could only see the back of the band from there. "Come on, let's go back there. We can probably stand in front and see the band if we aren't dancing." Once we sat down, we realized another reason the table wasn't already filled. It was right across from the entrance to the bathrooms. Every time someone went in or came out, a bright light and a foul odor would hit the table. "Lilly, do you want to try and find another seat?"

"No, this is fine. We will be dancing most of the time anyway."

In a couple of minutes, two more late arriving couples found their way to our table. They looked to be college age or a little older. They didn't ask if they could join us and just sat down. Both girls and one of the guys were holding Pabst Blue Ribbon cans. Seeing the Pabst cans reminded me of how sick I got at the beach. The other guy, wearing an untucked madras shirt, khaki shorts and loafers, was drinking from a bright red cup and had a cigarette hanging from his lips. Before he sat down, he took a bottle out of his back pocket and sat it on the table. The bottle was half empty. "Yo, table mates. What's up? Ready to party hardy with Mooorice?"

The guy was already drunk and I had a premonition. Daddy once told me about Murphy's Law —"If something can go wrong, It will." I was about to turn to Lilly and tell her that we needed to move, when the band started playing and someone with a microphone announced, "Alright, beach music lovers, here is who you came to see. From Lancaster, South Carolina, welcome back number one recording artists, Maurice Williams and the Zodiacs to the Maple Lodge stage." Six Black men wearing bright green shirts and white pants ran past our table and jumped up on the stage. The crowd went wild, and many got up from their tables and started jostling for spots in front of the stage.

We were caught by surprise and didn't move until Maurice himself announced that the group would open with their latest release "May I." Lilly squealed, grabbed my hand and started dragging me toward the crowd already gathered in front of the stage. "Come on Donald, that's our song. I want to see them sing it."

"If it can go wrong, it will." I should have known — things had gone too smoothly. I found her a gift I could afford and that she liked. He grandparents agreed to let her stay out later. Just by pure chance, the band that recorded the song she loved was playing nearby — I should have known. Drunk madras shirt guy, with his red cup in hand, got up from the table with his date just after us. She pushed her chair back and the idiot tripped over it. I watched as a cup full of dark brown liquor flew through the air. Why couldn't it have just landed on the floor, in his stupid lap or on his own bleach blonde date? But no, it landed in Lilly's hair, down her shoulder and down the front of her new dress. I have to admit that my first thought was to turn and slug the son of a bitch in the face. But then, I heard Lilly scream. When I looked at her, she had liquor dripping down her arm and on to her shoes and she had a pitiful "What just happened to me?" look on her face.

I didn't know what to do. No one else seemed to notice except for the drunk and his date. Everyone else was singing along with the band. The drunk's date did at least point toward the bathroom and said that there might be some paper towels in there. I pulled Lilly, who looked to be in shock, toward the women's bathroom and pushed her in the door. I went in the men's bathroom and got some wet paper towels from there and handed them to her through the door.

When Lilly came out, her hair and arms were wet, there was a dark brown stain down the front of her pretty dress and she smelled like she had taken a bath in bourbon. "Oh, Lilly, I'm sorry. Are you okay? What can I do?"

Lilly started crying. "I just want to go. Please, let's go."

I put my arm around Lilly's sticky shoulder and led her through the crowd in front of the stage. The band was finishing up with a version of The Tam's "What Kind of Fool Do You Think I Am?" I hoped to see the drunk on our way out so I say or do something to him, but he had disappeared.

By the time we got to the car, Lilly had stopped crying and I had realized the predicament we faced. "Lilly, I can take you to a service station or something so you wash more of that stuff off, but what can you do about your dress?"

"Oh, I'm sure most of it will come out. I was really more embarrassed than anything. Plus, we didn't get to dance or hear "May I"."

"But what about your grandparents? I mean, it's pretty easy to tell that smell is some sort of liquor. What can we tell them?"

"I hadn't thought about that. You're right. Grandfather will be furious."

My first thought was that I really didn't want to face Mr. Goldstein and his dark eyes boring a hole through me as he squeezed my hand. My next thought was and I said it out loud, "What if he stops letting me see you, Lilly?"

"I won't let that happen! Maybe I can take the dress off and hide it in the bushes before I go in the house. Then I could get it the next morning and wash it."

"How would you explain not wearing a dress if they were awake? That might be worse than the liquor smell."

"Hm, true. Well, I don't have to be in until 11:30. They're usually in bed no later than 10:30. Maybe they will be asleep when I go in. I can take care of the dress in the morning and they won't know."

I started feeling guilty. Lilly was searching for ways to deceive her grandparents because of a foolish mistake I made. Taking her to the Maple Lodge seemed like such a good idea at the time. Yet, if there was a possibility of not getting caught and not facing the consequences…well, I might just have to deal with the guilt as long as I could keep on seeing Lilly.

It was only 9:30, so we had two hours to kill before taking Lilly home and hoping her grandparents were asleep. We headed back to the strip and went into McDonald's. Lilly went to the bathroom while I got us a large order of fries and two Cokes. We sat in a booth to eat our fries when an older couple came and sat near us. Lilly and I both noticed the man and women staring at us and occasionally twitching their noses. The sweet smell of bourbon was even overpowering the smell of frying burgers and French fries coming from the kitchen. We took our Cokes out to the car and sat there listening to the radio for two hours. It would have been ironic if someone had requested "May I" on the *Big WASH* request line, but thank goodness they didn't. It was two hours of Herman's Hermits, The Dave Clark Five, Sam the Sham and the Pharaohs, Jay and the Americans and of course The Beatles. Not one shag tune was requested.

Finally, at 11:15 it was time to take Lilly home. When we drove up, the lights were all out, even the porch light — we took that to be a good sign. I guess the safest thing I could have done was just drop Lilly off and quickly drive away. Instead, I walked her to the door and whispered "I'm so sorry about tonight. I really wanted it to be special and something you would remember."

Lilly laughed under breath and whispered back "Oh, don't worry, I will remember it forever. And, I really love my locket."

"And I love my painting. I will call you tomorrow." I kissed Lilly and turned to walk away as she opened the door and crept in. It looked like we had made it, but no such luck. I was halfway down the sidewalk when I heard "Mr. Emmerson, return here now!"

"Oh crap!" I turned and walked back to where Mr. Goldstein was standing in his pajamas with his arms crossed. Lilly was standing inside just behind him.

"Oh Crap!"

"Mr. Emmerson, please explain why my 16 year old granddaughter smells like a distillery."

I started to remind Mr. Goldstein that Lilly would be 17 in just a few days, but thought that would be a bad idea. "Uh, It was an accident, sir. Someone spilled it on her. And uh, we weren't drinking anything, uh sir."

"You mean to tell me that liquor is served and consumed at an Ashton movie theatre?"

I looked at Lilly, who had her head bowed and was sobbing. "No sir, we uh, we decided to go hear a band we like instead of the movie."

"And where was this band performing, Mr. Emmerson?"

" You probably haven't heard of it, sir. It's called the Maple Lodge. They have a lot of good bands there."

"Oh, I've heard of the Maple Lodge. My law firm has defended the owner for selling alcohol to minors. You are not 18, are you Mr. Emmerson?"

"No sir."

"So you took my 16 year old granddaughter and illegally entered an adult establishment. Is that true Mr. Emmerson?"

Lilly looked up at blurted out, "But, I wanted to go too, Grandfather. I encouraged Donald to go."

"Quiet, Liana. We will discuss this later."

"Mr. Goldstein, Lilly had nothing to do with it. It was all my fault. I just wanted to impress her. Don't blame her for any of this, please."

"That's very noble of you, Mr. Emmerson, but she certainly knew better than to go and you obviously do not take promises that you make very seriously. You broke the ones you made to me about your conduct with my granddaughter."

I couldn't deny that. "Yes sir and I am sorry."

"Sorry is not enough, young man. There will be consequences for your actions and I also plan to have a conversation with your parents about this. I will call tomorrow evening. Now, please leave my home."

I made eye contact with Lilly before I left and she shook her head and sobbed.

Chapter 33

I spent most of the day on Sunday up in my room waiting for the phone to ring and looking at the picture Lilly had done for me. A couple of times, I thought about telling Daddy what had happened. Maybe if I had, things would have been better, but I didn't.

Right after supper I was back in my room when I heard the phone ring. Mama answered and called out to Daddy, "Frank, it's for you. It's Mr. Goldstein, Lilly's grandfather."

"What the hell does he want?"

I could only hear one side of the conversation but could figure out what was being said on the other side.

"I know who you are, Goldstein."

"Yes, I am his father."

"Are you damn sure about that? How do I know your girl there didn't talk him into it?"

"Well, I'll tell you what. You discipline your trouble making granddaughter and I'll take care of my son."

"You heard what I said! I'll take care of my end. You take care of yours. You got that?"

The next thing I heard was, "Donno, get your butt down here! Now!"

Daddy and Mama met me at the bottom of the steps and Daddy lit in. "Are you stupid or what? What the hell are you doing takin' that rich Jew girl to a juke joint like that?"

"We just wanted to hear a special band out there. We weren't drinking or anything."

"So you decided it was okay to take a 16 year old girl to that kind of place when you knew it was illegal for you to be there. Didn't I tell you that you were going to get in trouble messin' around with those people?"

I wasn't going to let Daddy blame Lilly for any of this. "Lilly's not like that, Daddy. She's sweet and nice. I talked her into going."

"It doesn't matter. You mess with them, you're going to lose. I'm telling you. You stay with your own kind."

With that, I kind of lost it. "I won't stay away from her! I uh, I love her! You can't stop me from seeing her."

"What the hell do you know about love? You're only 17 and an air head."

I yelled at my father for the first time in my life. "What did you know about killing people when you were 17? Did you know enough about hating people to do that? I know enough about love to love Lilly!"

"Well, maybe it would do you some good to join the God damn Marines. Maybe it would get your head out of the clouds and away from that art shit. Maybe that would make you grow up a little."

I wanted to ask, at least I am good at art, what are you good at Daddy? Instead, I yelled, "You can't keep me from seeing her, Daddy."

"The hell I can't, boy. You are grounded for a month and you will not drive that car until school starts. If you go anywhere, you'll walk or ride the damn bus. And don't you think about trying to see or call that girl. Old man Goldstein will see to that never happening."

"But that's not fair. We didn't do anything wrong. All we wanted was to listen to a band and dance."

"When are you going to learn, boy? Ain't nothin' fair in this world, especially when you are dealing with rich people."

Daddy started coughing and Mama started crying. I went upstairs to my room before I started crying.

For the next two weeks, I didn't speak to my father. I ate supper with him and Mama but that was about it. I walked to the A&P for work, came home and went straight to my room. I sat listening to music, looking at the picture of Lilly and me and drawing random things in my sketch book.

No matter what I did, I thought of Lilly and how I might get to see her or at least talk to her.

Sarah Jane finally got back from her leadership training and a side trip she and her mother took to look at some colleges. I guess my mother told her mother about what happened and Sarah Jane came over one day while Daddy was at work and I was home. Just like when we were little kids, she walked right up to my room. At least she knocked this time.

"Okay if I come in?"

"Yeah, I guess."

"Mama told me most of what happened. You know, Donno, that was a pretty dumb move on your part."

"Listen, Sarah Jane, I don't need you telling me how I messed up. Just stay out of my business, alright?"

Sarah Jane laughed out loud. "Ha, you know that will never happen. You couldn't survive without my help, could you?"

I started to tell her just to leave me alone and get out of my room, but she interrupted me.

"Oh wow! That's a beautiful picture of you and Lilly. Did you draw that or did she?"

"She did. She's a lot better than me." I looked at the picture and shook my head. I was missing Lilly even more.

"Have you talked to her since all that happened? I mean, I know you really did, uh do care a lot for her."

"I haven't talked to her since that night. Daddy said I can't call or go see her and her grandfather said she can't even answer the phone. I tried once but their maid answers it."

"Would you feel better if you could talk to her, at least on the phone?"

"Yeah, I just want to tell her that I'm sorry for getting her in trouble and that I can't wait to see her again even if it's not until school starts."

"I have an idea."

Sarah Jane was always having ideas. Lots of times they were crazy and other times her ideas meant me being part of her plan. This time, I was willing to try almost anything. "What is it? What's your idea?"

"What if I call Lilly's house and ask to speak to her about some kind of school thing? I'll bet they would let her talk to me. I will also bet your Daddy would let you come over to my house to help me with something or another. When Lilly comes to the phone, I give it to you. My mother is going to a bridge club party tomorrow, so she won't be there to interfere."

Sometimes, Sarah Jane's scheming and conniving made sense. "I'll do it. I'll come up with a reason for coming to your house."

"Okay, tomorrow night at 7:30."

Daddy got home from work at 6:00 and as he came in the door, I made sure he overheard me talking to Mama. "Sarah Jane wants me to help her with some sort of project she's doing for church. Is it okay if I go over there for an hour or so after supper?"

"It's alright with me, but you have to ask your daddy. You're grounded, you know?"

I turned and looked at Daddy. I was pretty sure Mama would say it was okay for me to go to Sarah Jane's and Daddy seldom overrode anything she approved.

"One hour, and that's it."

Just like the past few days, we ate supper in silence. After we ate, I helped clean up the kitchen and then went to Sarah Jane's with some art stuff as if I was going to draw something for her.

Sarah Jane made the call and I had to admit she was pretty cool. "Hello. This is Sarah Jane Allison. I am a friend of Lilly's from school and have a question about classes in the fall. May I speak to her?"

I could hear the maid say "I suppose it will be alright. Wait just a minute." Then I heard Lilly's sweet voice.

"Hello, Sarah Jane. Is something wrong?"

"Lilly, I know you are not supposed to talk to him, but I have Donno, uh Donald here with me. Can you talk to him without getting in trouble?"

"Yes, yes. I think I can. Grandfather isn't home and I don't believe Grandmother will listen in upstairs. Please let me speak to him."

I took a deep breath when Sarah Jane handed me the phone. "Hi Lilly. How are you? Are you okay?"

Lilly took a second or two to answer, "Oh Donald, I have been trying to find a way to talk to you in person. I didn't want to write you a letter about this."

"That's okay. I just wanted to wish you a happy birthday two weeks late and tell you I'm sorry about getting you in trouble. I can't wait to see you even if it's at school next month."

Lilly hesitated again. "I know you wouldn't do anything to hurt me and besides, I wanted to hear the band too. But, that's not what I needed to talk to you about."

I could hear sadness in her voice, something I had never heard before. "Why, what is it?"

"Donald, I'm, uh I'm going back home. My parents want me to come back to Israel."

I had not even considered something like that. "Why? Is it because of what we did? When do they want you to come back?" In the back of my mind, I knew she had come to Ashton at the beginning of second semester the last school year. Maybe, that was what she is talking about.

"No, it has nothing to do with you and me. My father wants me to complete high school in Israel so I can start at the University next spring. He has been thinking about it for a month." Lilly broke down and cried. "I have to leave next week." She started sobbing.

"Wait! No wait! You were sent here because it was dangerous over there. Why do they want you back? It isn't safe, is it?"

"Father says things have improved some, enough for me to come back. Oh, Donald, I don't want to go! I want to stay here. I mean I want to stay here with you!"

I was stunned and didn't know what to say until Lilly said, "I leave on Wednesday the 11th. Please try to see me before I go. Please!"

"I will. No matter what. I will see you."

Lilly hung up and I was still staring at the phone when Sarah Jane took it from me and put her arm around my shoulder. "Oh, Donno. I'm sorry! I'm really really sorry."

I told Mama about Lilly leaving and that I might not ever see her again. She put her arms around me and said she understood. Then she let me drive her car on the 11th because Daddy still wouldn't let me drive mine. I didn't care what Lilly's grandfather said or did, I just wanted to see her and say goodbye. I didn't know when they were leaving, so I went to her house at 8:00 in the morning. When I knocked on the door, I expected Mr. Goldstein to open it. Instead, it was the maid. "Sorry, young man, but they left yesterday to get an earlier flight out of New York."

After staring at the woman for a second or two, trying to comprehend what she had said, I dropped my head and turned to walk away.

"Wait a moment. Miss Goldstein, uh Lilly left something for you." The maid returned in a minute and handed me an envelope.

I opened it in the car.

Dear Donald, I am sorry I could not tell you goodbye in person. I didn't know we were leaving so early and Grandfather wouldn't let me call you. Please know that you have made the last months the most important in my life. It has only been an hour, but I have already started missing you. If I dance again, I will remember you as my very first special dance partner. You are a very talented artist and I expect to hear great things about you. I promise I will write and if you ever can come to Israel, please dance with me.

I truly love you, Lilly

At the bottom was a pencil drawing of a couple dancing, a bigger version of the drawing I put in her locket.

I cried.

I was supposed to go to work at 2:00, but I told Mama that I had a stomach ache and didn't feel like going. I'm sure she understood what was causing the stomach ache and told me to go lay down until supper and she would call the store and tell them I was sick. I asked her not to tell Daddy why I really was home and didn't go to work.

Daddy got at home at 6:00 and Mama had supper ready. Daddy and I still weren't talking much, so about the only conversation was Mama asking Daddy how his day had been and if he had called to make another doctor's appointment. I had been so wrapped up in my own problems, I hadn't noticed how much weight he had lost. Daddy had never been a big man, but had always pretty muscular. Now his face had become sunken and his skin had taken on an odd yellowish color.

"No, I didn't call. I got involved with a problem at work and didn't have time."

"Frank, you promised me that—"

"I know, I know. Just don't preach at me about it. I promised and I'll do it."

The look on Mama's face told me there was something serious to worry about. It gave me another reason not to have much of an appetite. Neither of us ate much that night.

After dinner, Daddy headed straight for the living room, turned on the news and laid down on the couch. I helped Mama with the dishes and then started toward the stairs to go back to my room. Then I heard Daddy cuss at the TV. "Look at those damn people, burning down their own neighborhood. I'll bet most of them have never had a job. All of them are on welfare. You can count on it."

I stopped in the living room and watched what was going on. There was film of burning buildings and people throwing things at a line of policemen. The newsman came on and said that it was a massive riot going on in a place called Watts near Los Angeles. It seems that a Black man had been arrested and hit in the face by police. Other people gathered around and fights broke out. The newsman said that the California National Guard was going to come to help police.

Daddy sat up and yelled at the TV, "They ought to call out the Marines from Thousand Palms or Camp Pendleton. They would put a stop to that shit in a damned hurry!"

I started to tell Daddy that "those people" and "those rich people who live across the river" were probably just like me, trying to figure out how to live in this world. Instead, I went on upstairs. What a screwed up time it was. Until school started back on the first of September, I was either at work at the A&P or in my room drawing, listening to music, nursing a broken heart and thinking about how I could get to Israel.

Chapter 34

Ever since the eighth grade, I had dreamed about being a senior in high school and how cool it would be to be one of the oldest, biggest and smartest guys in school, kind of like the life guards at the pool and Becky's boyfriends when she was in school. I never dreamed of being a star jock. I knew that wouldn't happen. I also knew I wouldn't be one of the super smart bookish types either. However, I believed I would do something special that would maybe get me into the popular crowd. When my artwork started drawing some attention in junior high, I thought that might do it. I was wrong. I had once thought my dancing ability might make people notice me the way I admired the god and goddess shaggers at the pavilion years before. I gave up on that pretty quickly.

When I started high school in the tenth grade, I was just another one of those middle of the pack, lower middle class West Ashton kids who would go virtually unnoticed by everyone other than a small group of similar kids. We weren't good enough to be considered outstanding examples of the excellence of the education system and we weren't bad enough to be singled out as the kind of trouble makers who become folk heroes. If it was like the past, most of us would graduate, go in the Army or the community college, get a job at the paper mill, have a family and drive five year old cars. I did think I was a pretty good artist and fair dancer and that not many others could do what I did — but that didn't make me rich, good looking, athletic, smart or drive a nice car. I was not going to be one of the guys who won "best or most" superlatives in the yearbook. I wasn't as smart or ambitious as Sarah Jane and wasn't as outgoing and gregarious as Rob and didn't have his white, straight teeth and cool car. Like Ricky Tilman, I was just sort of there.

Then Lilly appeared halfway through my junior year. I was still the same goofy kid as always, but just having her walk down the hall with me changed the way others saw me and what I thought about myself. If someone as beautiful, smart and talented as Lilly could actually like me, I must have something going for me. The thought of having a girlfriend like Lilly and of being a senior made me forget about smart groups, popular groups and yearbook superlatives. I was looking forward to September — until Lilly went away.

I had to take senior English, one more year of Spanish, and phys-ed. That left me room for two electives. They wouldn't let me sign up for two art classes, so in addition to art, I signed up for typing. English was okay. We started out reading a book written by a guy who grew up in Ashton. I kind of got into it because it was about him not getting along with his father and not knowing what he was going to do with his life. His mood closely matched mine. I managed to pass tests in Spanish but knew that if I ever went to Mexico I would starve to death because I didn't know the words for restaurant and couldn't even find a bathroom. Phys-ed was silly. We played badminton in the gym in our socks and I wasn't very good at it. Typing gave me an out with Daddy and I picked it up pretty fast. When I told Daddy that I was taking it, he said that at least it was something practical I might use in a job and not some pie-in-the-sky art crap. I didn't tell him I was taking advanced art too. Mama kept my secret.

With Lilly gone, I didn't have much interest in anything outside of school. It was funny, I concentrated more on my grades and they got better. At the same time, I started letting my hair grow longer and let my scraggly beard keep growing until the school assistant principal and the A&P manager both told me it was time to shave. If I wasn't working, I would usually be wearing beat-up jeans, a paint stained "Welcome to Myrtle Beach" sweat shirt, and worn out tennis shoes. There were no more Polo shirts, khakis or Weejuns for me. I think Daddy was too sick to care much about my appearance and Mama was too worried about Daddy to care.

The music I listened to changed too. The stuff I listened to got a little bit sadder and a little bit rebellious. Instead of all Motown and bubble gum from Herman's Hermits, Petula Clark, and Gary Lewis and The Playboys, I liked anything by Bob Dylan. I also liked "We Gotta Get Out of This Place" by The Animals, "My Generation" by The Who, and "The Carnival Is Over" by The Seekers. The only new Beatles song I liked was "Yesterday" and once I found myself singing along with Barry McGuire to "Eve of Destruction."

Sarah Jane said I was becoming too surly. I had to look that up. I might have been surly, but she still had me do more signs and other stuff for her election, which she won. It was the first time a girl had ever been elected president of the student body at Ashton High. After the election, Sarah Jane's mother threw a pizza party for the "Campaign Staff." I didn't go. I knew the other four or five people would be just as perky, ambitious and smart as Sarah Jane.

After the party, Sarah Jane brought me over a couple of pieces of pizza. Pizza was pretty new to West Ashton and she figured that I would like it. Because we didn't ride to school together anymore and hardly ever saw each other, she also used the pizza delivery as an excuse to tell me that she and Rob had broken up. When I asked her what happened, she said, "When he called me to ask about the election, he told me how happy he was for me and then, just like it was no big deal, he said he wanted to date other people at college and knew that I would understand."

I could tell Sarah Jane was fighting back tears and I sort of felt sorry for her. She and Rob had been going together for almost a year. And, I knew what heartbreak was like. "Well, you know I never really liked the guy. Seemed kind of phony to me. His teeth were too perfect too."

She tried to laugh at that but couldn't. "Donno, I think I loved him." Then she hugged me and I hugged back. We stood like that for a second or two until the perky, in charge Sarah Jane reappeared. "But, that's over now. Got too much to do to worry about him. Got to get my administration cooking and I need to start thinking about colleges for next year. In a week or two, I won't even remember the bum's face." We both laughed at that.

Sarah Jane turned to leave but stopped at the door. She looked at the picture of Lilly and me and nodded. "I know your heart is broken too. Don't let it change you too much and don't let the pain come between us. Things will get better. I'm sure you'll find someone else." Back to her perky voice again, she waved and announced, "Okay! Gotta go. Hope you like the pizza."

I turned the radio back up to catch the last part of "Hurts So Bad" by Little Anthony and The Imperials. "Sarah Jane, I don't want to find someone else. I'm not like you."

At the end of the past school year, Mr. Wertz told all of the juniors who were moving up to the advanced senior art class that we should fill up a sketch book over the summer and he would use them as part of our grades for the fall semester. After he saw mine, he brought me up to his desk during class to talk about it. "Mr. Emmerson, in addition to an obvious change in your appearance, the content of your summer sketch book took a distinctly different direction about half way through." He flipped through the pages and stopped at one in particular. "Beginning with this drawing, your work changed from light pencil strokes with a lot of almost cartoon action to heavy, dark lines and ominous shading. The faces of your human subjects are all dark and down cast."

I hadn't purposely changed the style of my drawings, but it wasn't hard to figure out why it happened. "Well, Mr. Wertz, there were a couple of things that sort of changed this summer. I guess I just didn't feel like drawing happy little pictures anymore."

Mr. Wertz looked toward the back of the room where Lilly and I sat together and nodded. "Yes, I suppose I understand one of the reasons for the change. However, as far as style, composition and emotion, I prefer the later drawings over the early ones. As I have told you before, you have a high level of technical skill but lack the story telling ability that makes for a true artist. Your drawings were wooden. The later drawings are superior in storytelling."

I looked at the sketch book and thought about what he was saying. I guess I did use my drawing to show how mad and sad I was about losing Lilly and the struggle I was going through with Daddy being sick and always on my back.

"Mr. Emmerson, artists, good ones that is, have a way of expressing emotion that most people don't possess. Artists have a soul that feels joy, pain, and grief. That soul transfers those feelings to the hands of sculptors and painters, to the voices of singers and to the brains of writers. True artists sacrifice a bit of their soul when they share their work with those of us who can't do what the artists can do. I believe you have that kind of soul even if you have done your best to keep it hidden."

That was the first time in my life that someone seemed to understand how I felt — how some things important to others was of no interest to me, and how I could feel so deeply about something that others thought was foolish.

Mr. Wertz went on to give me my assignment for the entire year. I was to pick a subject that I felt strongly about. It could be from a photograph or a poem, a book title or some other inspiration. He would approve the subject first and if approved, I would have to do pencil drawings in many compositions first. Once the composition was approved, I would be required to move on to more pencil drawings, then to charcoal, and then pen and ink. After all of those were critiqued, my final exam would be either a large water color or oil painting no smaller than 16x20 inches. I had to show him my subject for the assignment the next time the class met.

Over the weekend, I tried to decide on a subject for my art assignment. Mr. Wertz said he wanted to see emotion, so that meant it had to have people in it. That left out landscapes unless they had people big enough to see their faces. I looked through some magazines like National Geographic and Life, but didn't find anything that worked for me. I also thought about doing something that included me and Lilly. The only image I had of her was the one in the painting she did of us. Mr. Wertz had already seen that and I also thought how hard it might be to draw and paint her face for almost a whole year. I went down stairs to tell Mama about the assignment and ask her what she thought. As I walked through the living room, I passed Daddy asleep on the couch. He looked like he had shrunk and aged 30 years., he was only 41. I stopped and looked at him and then at the black and white picture of him and Mama on the mantle. That gave me an idea.

"Mama, I have to do some drawings and paintings for art and they have to have people in them. I like that picture of you and Daddy on the mantle, but it is sort of formal looking. Do you have any more pictures I can see?"

"Do you mean more recent pictures? Didn't you already do a picture of us at the beach?"

"No. not recent. Are there any more of you and him when he was in the Marines? Or maybe while you were teenagers?"

"You know your father was in the Marines when we met? He was 19 and I was 18, not much older than you are now."

"Yeah, way back then. That would be good."

Mama laughed, "Well, it hasn't been that long ago." She thought for a minute and said, "There are a couple of albums that have a few old pictures like that. They're up in the attic."

"Cool. Can I look at those?"

"That will be fine. But, try not to wake up Frank, and it would probably be a good idea not to let him know what you're doing."

I agreed with her and headed up to the attic. I found two photo albums back in a corner behind a doll house that must have been Becky's, some old dusty Venetian blinds and a box marked MOTHER'S THINGS. I figured those were some of Grandma's things that Mama just couldn't bear to get rid of. The albums were covered with dust too. I doubted anyone had seen them in a long time.

The first album I looked at had a lot of pictures of Mama holding Becky as a little baby and every one of Becky's school pictures from first grade to junior high. It also had a bunch of me as a baby and a few of me holding Friskie, the dog we had when I was six or seven. There were a lot of Christmas pictures of Becky and me opening packages. I noticed there weren't any pictures of Daddy. I figured he must have been the one taking the pictures. That album brought back a lot of memories but none of the pictures were what I was looking for.

The second album was obviously much older. There were faded pictures of who must have been my great grandfather and grandmother when they were young. There were some pictures of Mama when she was a baby up to high school age. One of them was her and another girl acting like they were dancing together, sort of like the shag. Mama had her head turned back a little and had a big smile. She looked like she was maybe 15 or 16. I wasn't sure what I was going to do with it, but I took that picture out of the album and laid it aside. Near the back of the book, I found another picture of Mama and Daddy posed like the one on the mantle. On the very last page, there was a small picture of Daddy, and I guess it was Uncle Al pretending they were boxing. Daddy was still in his uniform but his tie was undone and his hat was cocked sideways. His mouth was wide open and he looked like he was laughing. I took that one out of the album and put it next to the one of Mama dancing. The way Daddy was standing with his left arm extended toward Uncle Al, it was almost as if they were dancing. I folded the pictures back, leaving only Mama and Daddy showing. When I put them side by side, it looked like Mama and Daddy were dancing and I had my art project. I didn't know if Mama and Daddy ever danced together back then, but I was going to paint them as if they had.

I told Mama that I couldn't find anything I could use. I didn't want her to know what I was doing and wanted it to be a surprise if it turned out okay. Maybe even Daddy would like it. I did ask Mama about the time some of the pictures were taken. "There are a few pictures in one of the albums of you in high school, I guess. When was that?"

"I started high school in 1938 as a ninth grader. We didn't have junior highs back then. I graduated in 1942."

"Did you guys ever dance? I mean when you were in high school."

"Sure, we loved to dance. Your grandmother and grandfather weren't too keen on me dancing with boys, but we found a way to get together, especially after the war started."

"What was your favorite kind of music? Did you have radios back then?"

It was good to hear Mama laugh again. "Of course we had radios back then. That was our main entertainment. No TVs. Radio is where we heard all of the great bands. I loved Glenn Miller, Jimmy and Tommy Dorsey, Benny Goodman, there were lots of great big bands. Some of them came here and gave concerts in the auditorium."

"What was your favorite song?"

Mama frowned, "Why all of the questions, Donno? When did you start caring about the past?"

"I don't know. I guess because I was looking through all of those old pictures."

"Well, first off, they're not all that old. As far as songs go, I liked a Benny Goodman song called "Jersey Bounce." It was real peppy and fun for dancing."

"Did you and Daddy dance a lot?"

Mama looked toward the living room where Daddy was sleeping. "No, but almost. Your daddy had already been in combat when we met and he was very serious about things. I suppose the only times I remember coming close to dancing with him was when we first met."

"Where did you meet? And you almost danced?"

"USO club downtown. He was home on a 30 day leave before shipping out again. A bunch of my high school friends use to go to the USO club just to give the boys some-one to talk to."

"And Daddy asked you to dance?"

"Oh no. I asked him. He was sitting over in a corner by himself. He looked so alone in his dress blue uniform, I couldn't resist. But he turned me down. Said he couldn't dance. Didn't want to look like a fool. So, we just sat and talked instead." Mama paused for a second or two, then went on. "We met at the USO one more time and then went to the movies once. To make a long story short, we got married ten days before he went back overseas."

Mama started to go on until she heard Daddy stirring in the living room. "Maybe we'll talk again sometime, Donno. I love talking to you."

"I love talking to you too, Mama."

I did a few rough sketches in pencil trying to get the connection between Mama and Daddy the way I thought it ought to look if they were really dancing together. I got pret-ty close and decided, that along with the photographs, this idea was what I would show Mr. Wertz on Monday.

"Well, Mr. Emmerson, you have certainly chosen a challenging project. Do you remember the final piece, the one that will count for 75% of your grade, is supposed to be in color? Your subjects are black and white photos, so you will not have a starting guide on tone and tint or the colors."

"Yes sir. I know, but I can do it."

"Also, part of your assignment was to show real emo-tion in the face or faces in your painting. That means you must have at least some light on both faces. Your subjects are facing in different directions. I hope you have a plan to address that."

"Yes sir, I do."

"Lastly, your sketches show that you plan to have the subjects dancing. That means creating the illusion of movement on a static two dimensional surface. You will have to pay particular attention to the clothing, especially the woman's dress. It and the man's jacket must imply movement that is coordinated to their bodies under the clothing. Do you understand?"

"Yes sir, I uh, I'm pretty sure I can do it."

"Alright then, if you are sure. The next step is a pencil drawing with the compositions and background treatment you have chosen. Then on to pen and ink, charcoal or pastel drawings that finalize lighting and shadows before you start on the final painting. Have you decided on oil or water color?"

"I think oils."

"Alright then. That will be your project. You may work in class or at home on the preliminary work, but the final painting should be done here. You may work during class period and after school for one hour after regular class days. Do you understand?"

"Yes sir."

"Mr. Emmerson, I must ask, I assume the subjects are your parents and that they were the subjects of last year's final exam painting. Why did you choose them again?"

I started to give a long answer about how I liked the challenge and how the movement will make for a good composition. Instead I said, "Because my mother and father have never gotten to dance together before. And I am afraid it might be too late now"

Chapter 35

Just after Labor Day, I got my first letter from Lilly. She said she missed me and the fun we had together. She also said that she was glad to see her parents and old friends again and that it wasn't too hard to get back into the completely different lifestyle of kibbutz living. She talked about how American teenagers have it easier in some ways and how she imagined that I was excited about President Johnson passing the Civil Rights Act of 1965 in August. I was a little ashamed that I hadn't heard about it. Lilly thought that "California Girls" by The Beach Boys was her favorite new song. I hadn't heard the song more than twice on our radio station.

Lilly gave me her return address and I wrote her a four page letter that night. I told her about how much I missed her and that I thought about her every day. I told her about the senior art project, about Sarah Jane winning the election and about Daddy getting sicker. I told her I would write her every week and that I hoped she would write me just as often.

I wrote three more letters to Lilly before I got another one back from her at the end of September. It was a quick one page note that was mostly about how excited she was to teach her friends how to shag and how she had been named to help design and paint a mural on the school wall.

My next two letters to Lilly were like the earlier ones with me telling her how much I missed her and how much I looked forward to seeing her someday. I always signed them "Love, Donald."

My last letter from Lilly came around Halloween. She told me that there was a new boy living at the kibbutz who had grown up in Canada, but who had come back to Israel with his parents much like she had done. She said nothing about missing me or about wishing to see me again. She only said she would never forget the time we were "friends." She never used the word love in any of her letters.

I reread the letter several times, hoping to find some meaning other than good bye forever. I looked over at the pastel she had done of us and thought about how I was feeling much like I had when I saw Britney McMurry was pregnant, only much sadder. My dreams were crushed again. I don't think I ever really believed I would see Lilly again, but she had become lodged in my heart and my head so deeply that she would always remain there. I sulked for weeks after receiving that letter. I never wrote her back and now suspect that she was glad about that.

Chapter 36

I showed Mr. Wertz my next set of preliminary drawings of Mama and Daddy dancing and he brought up something I hadn't considered. "Mr. Emmerson, every painting must have a focal point. It is what draws the viewers' eyes and creates much of the story being told by the piece. In this sketch, I see two focal points. The first is the eye contact the two subjects are making. The other is where their hands are joined. You need to enhance one of those. I would suggest dealing with the hands. They are most central in your composition, but you have almost hidden them by the way you have them joined."

Mr. Wertz was right. I always had trouble drawing hands. I either made them too small or too large for the size of the person I was drawing. I found ways of compensating by having fingers balled up in a fist or hidden in a pocket or something. I liked the idea of having Mama and Daddy's hands almost touching as if they were about to dance spontaneously. Like Mr. Wertz said, that meant their hands would be one of the most important parts of the painting. I needed to practice drawing hands.

One Sunday afternoon in early November, I was stretched out on my bed sketching, working on hands. Daddy was asleep downstairs and Mama was gone somewhere. The radio was blasting "Get Off Of My Cloud" by The Stones and I was concentrating so hard, I didn't hear Sarah Jane knock on my door. She came on in anyway. Luckily, I was almost fully dressed in jeans, a sleeveless t-shirt and no shoes. "Whoa, Sarah Jane! You scared me. What are you doing here?"

"Well, I did knock, Donno. Maybe if you'd turn down the radio a little, you could hear me."

The Rolling Stones finished and The Yardbirds started in with "Still I'm Sad." I didn't turn down the radio.

Sarah Jane sat down cross legged on the floor. She was wearing a hooded sweatshirt, Bermuda shorts, and Keds. "They never play much Motown or shag music any more, you know?"

"That's okay with me." I swung my legs over the side of the bed and laid my open sketchbook down on the floor. "What are you doing over here?"

"Mom has gone to a church meeting and there's nothing on TV but football. I got bored."

Without asking, Sarah Jane picked up my sketchbook. "What are you working on? Oh, I see. You've got a thing for hands, huh?"

"Yeah, I'm a real hand freak. Actually, hands are a big part of my final project for art class. I've never been able to get them exactly right."

Sarah Jane never hesitated to criticize anything I did, especially my art work. She picked up my sketchbook and shook her head. "You make the fingers too stubby. Look at this one. It is obviously a woman's arm and wrist because they are slim and graceful, but then her hand is too wide and her fingers are like, I don't know, like little Vienna Sausages stuck on there."

"Jeez, Sarah Jane. You really know how to make a guy feel good, don't you? I mean, Vienna Sausages?"

"You know I have always been your most honest critic." Sarah Jane got up off the floor and sat beside me on the bed. She handed me the sketchbook and then laid her open hand across my thigh. "Here, look at my hand. I have long and skinny fingers. Draw my hand."

She was right, her hand was tiny and yet her fingers were long and slender. Her nails were long and the pale pink polish on them almost matched the color of her skin. I drew a few lines, paying attention to the way her fingers curled upward toward me and how the creases in her palm criss-crossed to form a pattern of light and dark. Sarah Jane had pulled the sleeve of her sweatshirt up to her elbow and I realized the hair on her arm was as red as the hair tied back in her ponytail.

Before I could finish my first sketch, Sarah Jane changed the position of her hand. She turned her palm down and her long fingers lightly touched the inside of my thigh. I looked down at her hand and back up at her face. Without warning, the radio got louder, my bedroom became very warm, and I began to sweat. Sarah Jane must have felt it too. Instead of her usual combination of a smirk and a smile, her eyes were open wide and there was a strange look on her face. We stared at each other for a second or two and I was faintly aware that she had not moved her hand from my thigh.

Without saying a word, we both leaned in and kissed a hungry searching kiss. I hardly noticed the loud "thud" when my sketchbook hit the floor. I was too busy pulling Sarah Jane down on the bed with me. She responded by throwing her left leg over my legs as we kissed again. Our hands went places they had never been before and neither of us resisted. The room was spinning, buttons were being unbuttoned and zippers were going down when through the sound of heavy breathing and Fontella Bass belting out "Rescue Me" on the radio, I heard the distinct sound of our back door being closed. Mama always came in through the back door.

I sat up and froze. "Oh crap! Oh Crap, Mama's home!"

"Oh God!" Sarah Jane jumped off the bed, pulled down her sweatshirt and tried to get her ponytail back in place. "What do we do?"

"Shut up a minute. Let me think."

Mama yelled from the bottom of the steps, "Donno, I'm home. Anybody call?"

"Uh, nobody called." Then I came up with a lie. "Sarah Jane is up here helping me with some homework. I figured it was okay since Daddy was here."

Sarah Jane yelled back, "Hey Mrs. E. I was just leaving."

Sarah Jane had previously walked into my bedroom unannounced and without permission dozens of times since we were little kids. I could only hope Mama wouldn't think that things were any different because Sarah Jane and I were 17.

Mama yelled again. "Don't rush off. Finish what you're doing."

Sarah Jane and I almost broke out laughing.

As she was about to leave my room, I stopped Sarah Jane. "I uh, I uh, I'm sorry. Not sure what happened. Are you okay?"

"I'm more than okay, Donno. Don't be sorry. I will talk to you later." She smiled and kissed me.

I heard Sarah Jane chat with Mama for a minute or two and speak to Daddy when she went out the front door. All I could think of was the few minutes we were entwined on my bed. *What did it mean? Were we both still getting over losing Lilly and Rob? Was it just an accident? Would it, could it happen again and not be interrupted?* Diana Ross and The Supremes sweetly answered my questions with "I Hear a Symphony" just before *Big WASH* switched over to Sunday evening gospel music.

Chapter 37

The week before I got out of school for the Christmas holiday, Daddy and Mama went down to Durham, North Carolina for three or four days to see a famous doctor at Duke Hospital. Daddy's part-time doctor at the paper mill and the old general practitioner he saw in town never could figure out what Daddy had and decided to send him to a specialist for more tests. We were having first semester final exams, so I couldn't go with them. I hate to admit it, but I was glad. Becky said she would call me every day. Sarah Jane's mother said she would feed me. Sarah Jane said she would make sure I got school on time and would check on me every evening. That's why I was glad I didn't have to go to Durham. For most of my life, the thought of spending time alone with Sarah Jane was nauseating. That all changed after that afternoon up in my bedroom.

As Mama and Daddy pulled out of the driveway, I felt a mixture of guilt and excitement. I had never been alone for more than a few hours during my whole life and I was looking forward to it. On the other hand, what if Mama and Daddy needed me? What if Daddy was really really sick? What if he died down in Durham and I wasn't there to tell him goodbye? I pushed that thought out of my mind. After all, Daddy was strong as an ox and he wasn't an old man. Besides, he survived the war. I figured that he had some kind of infection or something and the doctors in Durham would give him a new medicine that would fix everything. There was no way he could die.

Instead of thinking about Daddy being sick and maybe dying, I thought about how great it was going to be to go to bed when I wanted, to eat in front of the TV, to bring my sketchbook downstairs, and maybe have Sarah Jane visit a couple of times.

The first night I was home alone, Sarah Jane's mother had me over for dinner. I hung around there for a while and went back home about 8:00. I had forgotten to leave on any lights and the house was totally dark when I got there. I have to admit, going in alone and knowing that I would also be alone all night was a little spooky even for a 17-year-old. There were sounds, like creaks and moans that I had never heard before. I figured the best thing to do was go up to my room, turn on the radio good and loud and work on my art project. The radio blasting The Zombies, The Kinks, The McCoys, The Stones and occasionally The Temptations covered up any strange noises from downstairs.

All of the photographs I had of Daddy in uniform were black and white and he was in a sort of drab uniform. I wanted my painting to be colorful. I found color pictures of women in bright flowery dresses to use as models for Mama's dress, but I had a hard time finding a color picture of a World War II Marine in a fancy blue uniform with white hat, shiny brass buttons and red stripes down the pant legs. Finally, one day when I was in the school library supposedly working on an English term paper, I asked the library lady if there were any old magazines from World War II. She got all excited and told me of a wonderful collection of Life magazines covering 50 years or more. She said I was probably the only student who ever asked to see them. After going through a bunch of copies, I found an issue from 1941. Sure enough, there was a color picture of a marine in the fancy blue uniform and he had stripes on his arms that looked like the ones Daddy had on his arms in the black and white photo at home. I was pretty sure the library wouldn't let me check the magazine out and keep it until the end of the year. So, I checked to make sure no one was looking, and tore out the page I needed. I mixed that copy in with the other 100 or so copies and thanked the library lady. I figured if no one had asked to see the old Life magazines before me, no one would ever notice one page missing from a 1941 issue. I thought maybe I would come back some day and tape the picture back into the magazine.

After a few twirls of my color wheel, I decided that Mama's dress in the final painting would be bright yellow with orange blossoms. I thought that would be a good contrast to Daddy's dark blue uniform coat and light blue pants with red stripes down the side. I started a series of rough sketches using colored pencils to get a better idea of how the colors would work together. Mr. Wertz would grade those sketches as part of my first semester grade.

The next day, I drove to school by myself because I had to work at the A&P after school until 6:00. Sarah Jane, Ricky and I ate lunch together as usual. I told Sarah Jane I had started working on some color drawings. She said she would bring supper over to me around 6:30 or 7:00 and look at the drawings. I got excited, anticipating that we might end up in my bedroom and pick up from where Mama interrupted us.

After work, I came in the back door and forgot the front door was locked. When Sarah Jane brought supper at 7:00, I was surprised when she knocked on the door. She usually just walked on in. "Hey, come on in. Sorry the door was locked." I took the aluminum foil wrapped dishes and put them in the kitchen. "You want to come upstairs and look at the drawings I told you about?" I had straightened up my room, made my bed and turned on the radio in anticipation of Sarah Jane coming to my room.

"Uh, why don't you bring them down here for me to see? I can't stay long anyway."

I tried to hide the disappointment in my voice. "Oh, no problem. I'll show them to you later. I have to take them to school before the end of the week anyway."

"Well uh, I have to go. Are we going to ride together tomorrow?"

"Sure. I don't work tomorrow."

"Good. I'll see you then."

Then, surprising the heck out of me, she kissed me on the cheek and gave me a hug.

"Sorry I can't stay. Maybe another time."

"Uh, yeah. Good."

Sarah Jane stopped at the door. I hoped she had changed her mind about staying, but I was wrong. She said, "I've got to fill out the papers for taking the SAT test. You have to do that too. Don't forget. I'll see you in the morning. Oh, and Mom said you should come to our house tomorrow for dinner and you can help decorate our tree."

That was weird. *Had I thought too much about making out in my bedroom? Didn't it mean as much to Sarah Jane as it did to me?* I was confused by her attitude. I wasn't confused about her telling me that I needed to sign up for the college-board SAT test. That meant I had to think seriously about whether or not I would go to college.

Mama called long distance from Durham while I was eating my dinner. "Hey, Donno. Are you okay, Son?"

"I'm good, Mama. Eating some cold fried chicken and green beans that Sarah Jane brought over. How's Daddy. Have they figured out what's wrong yet?"

"Well, he's been through a lot of tests and has at least two more to go. They have really worn him out. We should get results the day after tomorrow."

That was not what I had hoped to hear and I could tell by the tone of Mama's voice that she was scared. "I'll bet they will find something they can fix. Don't you?"

"I hope so, baby. I truly hope so. Listen, I have to go. This is a pay phone in the hospital and others are waiting to use it. If everything goes well, we will be home day after tomorrow in the late afternoon." Before I could say goodbye, the line went dead.

I wasn't all that keen on going to Sarah Jane's for dinner. The dinner would be okay, but I wasn't in the mood for decorating their tree, but Sarah Jane and her mom insisted. They always had a big spruce tree they cut down themselves at a tree farm near Boone. Every ornament was special and they oohed and ahhed over each one. I checked the strings of lights to make sure they were all burning and put them on the tree. I did like the ones that bubbled and looked like a candle. After the lights, I just sat and watched.

After the tree was done, Sarah Jane's mother brought out fruit cake and eggnog. I hated fruit cake, but I ate it. Sarah Jane was her perky self and went on and on about how much she loved Christmas. Between bites of fruit cake, she looked at me and told me she had a great idea. "Why don't I come over to your house tomorrow with your supper and we can decorate your tree? That would be fun and it would be one less thing your mother would have to worry about. "

When Sarah Jane said she had a great idea, it usually meant a problem for me. This time, it wasn't so bad. Having our tree already decorated when they got home might brighten Mama and Daddy's moods and it meant Sarah Jane would be at my house again and for a longer time. I got a little excited until Sarah Jane asked her mother if she wanted to help. Luckily Mrs. Allison said she had a training meeting at the VA Hospital. She was going to volunteer to sit with wounded and sick soldiers coming back from the war in Vietnam.

The next day, right after work, I went straight up to the attic and brought down all of the boxes that were labeled "Christmas." There weren't many. There were a couple of boxes of ornaments and a thing for the front door that played "We wish you a merry Christmas" when you pulled a string on a plastic gold bell. Our Christmas tree was also up there. Several years before, Daddy said, "No more live trees in this house, damn it! They smell too much like all the wood coming into the paper mill." Grandma agreed and Mama didn't fight it. In spite of Becky and me not being happy, Daddy went out and bought a shiny aluminum tree anyway. It was stored in its original box, which I carried down to the living room after wiping off all of the dust.

I was assembling the tree (you stuck numbered branches in matching numbered holes in the broom stick trunk) when Sarah Jane came in with supper. She had fixed us a hamburger pizza using a Chef Boyardee Pizza kit. It was pretty good.

Because our tree was mostly metal, we couldn't put electric lights on it because it might short out and cause a fire. Instead of lights, the tree came with a small flood light that sat on the floor and was pointed at the tree. It had a revolving color wheel that went from red to green to blue and back to red as it shown on the tree.

It didn't take long to hang our few ornaments on the tree so the pizza was still warm when Sarah Jane and I sat on the couch, watching the tree change colors while we ate. I had turned on the TV before Sarah Jane came over and ironically, *A Charlie Brown Christmas* animated movie was on. Sarah Jane and I laughed out loud when Lucy told Charlie Brown that he had to go out and find "a big shiny aluminum Christmas tree" to use in their Christmas play. Our couch was pretty small and Sarah Jane and I sat close together, legs and shoulders touching.

Sarah Jane wiped tomato sauce from her lips and put her head on my shoulder. "You know, it is pretty cool. It almost looks like one of those psychedelic posters I have read articles about it in *Seventeen* magazine. Like Charlie Brown just said, it's not very Christmasy, but still pretty cool."

I had not read *Seventeen* magazine and I didn't know what psychedelic meant, but I was very aware of how close Sarah Jane was sitting and how she had not moved her head from my shoulder. When I bent down to kiss her forehead, she turned her face up to me and I kissed her on the lips. The taste of pizza didn't stop me. I kissed her again and she responded by lying back on one of the cushions Mama always had on the couch. Mama wouldn't be interrupting us this time. I bent down to kiss her again and Sarah Jane pulled me down on top of her. I couldn't hide my growing excitement and I was sure she could feel it when she arched her back to let me get closer.

I fumbled badly when I tried to unbutton the top of Sarah Jane's blouse and settled for feeling her breast through the fabric. She didn't stop me and that made me more excited. So, I reached down to the top of her jeans, hoping to have more success with that button.

Sarah Jane's body suddenly went rigid and she grabbed my hand. "Oh Donno, I can't! I just can't!"

"Uh what? Jeeze, you want me to stop now? Why?"

"I do love you and always have. God how I want to make love to you, but I just can't do it yet."

"Damn Sarah Jane, you're killing me." In pain, I sat up and tried to catch my breath.

"I'm sorry. I really am. I made a promise to myself that I wouldn't go all the way until I was 18. Please try to understand. I really want it to be you, but I just have to wait." She started sobbing.

I calculated how many months it would be before she turned 18 while I pulled her close and tried to be sincere when I told her that I understood and could wait. First it was Lilly who said I would be her first and now Sarah Jane. I was beginning to doubt it would ever happen, but then I thought *"Wait, did she just say she loved me and always has? What about Rob? What about all of the times she has treated me like an idiot? Why do I care? Could I possibly love her too? Have I always loved her?"*

Silently we sat, holding each other and watching the Charlie Brown show end with all of the characters singing "Hark the Herald Angles Sing" as my aluminum Christmas tree changed from red to green to blue and back to red again.

Chapter 38

Daddy died on January 16th, the day after I took the SAT test. It was Sunday and Mama had gone to church. She had been going to church a lot more after Daddy got sick. When she got home, she found Daddy unconscious on the couch and coughing up blood. I had my record player turned up pretty loud and didn't hear a thing until Mama screamed for me to come help her. She tried to wake Daddy up and told me to call an ambulance. She must have known something might happen because she had the number written on the hardware store calendar hanging in the kitchen.

Mama rode in the ambulance with Daddy and I followed in her car. All the way to the hospital, all I could think about was the argument Daddy and I had the day before. Even though he could barely breathe, he told me that he thought I was stupid to waste my time taking the SAT test and that the best thing I could do was join the Army or Marines after I graduated from high school. "That's where you'll get a real education, Donno. They'll teach you things you can use in the real world, not this silly art thing you're stuck on."

"My art isn't silly, Daddy. Besides, I haven't decided if I will go to college anyway. I'm taking the test just in case. Mr. Wertz thinks I'm pretty good and might even get a scholarship somewhere."

"So you're listening to some half-assed high school art teacher who I bet has never done a hard day's work in his life instead of listening to your father. Is that it?"

"He's a good man, Daddy! At least he's educated and appreciative of what I can do. You're neither. What has your hard work gotten you?" With the red lights from the ambulance flashing in my eyes as it pulled in front of the emergency room, oh God how I wished I had never said that to him.

The doctors in Durham said Daddy had lung cancer, probably caused by smoking two packs of Lucky Strikes a day and by working in a paper mill with all of the fumes he breathed there. They said if they removed all of one lung and part of another, they would give him a 25% chance of living another year or two, but only if he quit smoking and took oxygen from a tank 24 hours a day. Mama said Daddy told the doctors he would think about it and get back with them. Of course he never did.

Mama called Uncle Al and Becky from the hospital. Uncle Al got there just as the emergency room doctor told Mama and me that there was nothing they could do and that Daddy was gone. Uncle Al was the first of many to tell me that I was now the man of the house and responsible for taking care of Mama. Mama was the strong one and comforted Uncle Al when he broke down after they let us see Daddy's body. Becky and Eric got home that evening and Mama was the strong one who told Becky and me that she would be okay and there was no need to worry about her. Becky cried a lot and so did I.

The next few days were a blur of activity at our house: People brought food, a casket was picked out with the help of somber men at the funeral home, Daddy's burial suit came back from the cleaners and I got a new pair of black wingtip shoes. Becky and I went back to the funeral home so she could see Daddy for the last time. We both said how old and small Daddy looked in the casket. We hugged and cried again.

I hadn't known it, but Mama and Daddy had already planned a lot of things. He would be buried in a veteran's cemetery a few miles from Ashton and Daddy had said he wanted a military type funeral with an honor guard but only graveside services with no religious stuff. Mama agreed although she did ask her preacher to say a few things at the gravesite. She didn't tell Daddy that.

The funeral was on Friday, January 21 and it was cold and windy that day. The wind was blowing so hard that the canopy covering the grave shook and the flag on Daddy's casket had to be tied down. I don't remember much about the funeral except Becky, Mama and I all jumped when the honor guard fired their rifles. They fired seven times and we jumped each time. I also remember seeing Mama put her hand on the coffin as she clutched the folded flag a man in a Marine uniform gave her.

Mama, Becky, Eric and I rode in a big Cadillac back to our house. Uncle Al, Sarah Jane and her mother rode in Uncle Al's car right behind us. There were people already in our house when we got there. Some were neighbors, some were people who worked at the paper mill with Daddy and some were people from Mama's church. They spoke in whispers and looked at the floor when we came in the kitchen door. I was asked if I wanted something to eat or drink at least ten times before I was able to go upstairs to my room.

In a few minutes, Sarah Jane came in my room and sat on the bed next to me. The radio was playing "Five O'clock World" by an American band called The Vogues. She waited until the song was over before she spoke. "I like that song. You could almost shag to it."

"Yeah, I guess."

"Are you okay, Donno?"

"I'll be fine. Just needed to get away from all of those people downstairs."

"You know, Donno, he really loved you."

The next song on the radio was "I Can Never Go Home Anymore" by The Shangri-Las. Sarah Jane reached over and turned down the volume. "You know that, don't you?"

"Maybe, I guess—I just wish he said it every once in a while."

"How often did you say it to him?"

That question shocked me out of my self-pity for a second or two. Before I could answer, Becky and Mama came in my room and we started talking about memories from when we were kids.

Chapter 39

I started back to school the Monday after Daddy's funeral. I actually looked forward to going back. School was sort of a break from everything that had been going on at home. Of course, the only people who mentioned Daddy's death were Sarah Jane, Ricky and a couple of my teachers.

Mr. Wertz asked me to stay after class the first day back in art. "Mr. Emmerson, I am terribly sorry to hear of your father's passing. I also lost my father at an early age and I miss him until this day."

"Uh, thank you." I wondered how I would feel about my father when I was as old as Mr. Wertz.

"I realize that your senior project painting is of your mother and father when they were younger. If the subject of the painting is too painful for you, then you have my permission to change to something else."

I hadn't thought about the painting for a while and hadn't considered how it would make me feel until Mr. Wertz mentioned it. "I, uh I think I want to keep going on the project, if that's okay."

"Are you certain?"

"Yes sir, I believe so."

"If so, then I am going to give you an added challenge. I want the oil painting finished by Easter or no later than the end of spring break. That would be April 18th."

"I thought I had until the end of the school year."

"That's true. However, there are several student art competitions coming up before then and most of the fine art college programs make their admissions and scholarship decisions before then. I can submit some of your earlier work, but a well-crafted oil painting can sway decisions better than sketches, water colors and pastels. If you did reasonably well on your SAT scores, I think you can qualify for scholarships at some prestigious schools."

I could only imagine what my father would be saying if he heard all of this. *You'll never make a living with art. You need to grow up and take responsibility for your future. You ought to join the military.*

"Well, Mr. Emmerson. Do you accept the challenge?"

Mr. Wertz was forcing me to make a decision that went beyond agreeing to finish the painting early. If I did what he wanted, I was pretty much committing to the idea of going to college to study art. I had just seen my father being put in the ground and the last thing we talked about before he died was how much he hated the idea of me pursuing my art.

"You have talent, Mr. Emmerson, talent beyond that expected of a high school student. However, you need many more years of training before you can reach the potential of that talent. If you stop now, you will remain at this current level for a long long time and never reach your potential."

Damn it" I thought. *Do I need to decide my entire future right now? Will I have a chance to change my mind? Could Daddy have been right?*

"Donald, Mr. Emmerson, you can always take a different path in the future. But, your options are much greater when you have the training and experience higher education can provide. Think about that."

I had been thinking about that — thinking about it for a long time. "Alright, Mr. Wertz, I will finish the painting by April 18th."

I thought I would start on the painting immediately. I was wrong. Mr. Wertz said that I had to learn how to do the preliminary work of a painting first. He made me build my own wooden frame to stretch the canvas. I was able to use saws and tools in the school shop. I also had to learn how to stretch the canvas properly over the 24 by 36 inch frame using staples so it didn't have any wrinkles. Then I had to coat the canvas with thick white milky stuff called gesso. After it dried, I had to sand it smooth. Mr. Wertz said that was what the old masters made their apprentices do. The last thing I had to do before I could start putting paint on the canvas was to pick the colors I planned to use. Again, Mr. Wertz said I needed to learn the basics of painting. Modern oil paints came in all sorts of colors. There were three or four shades of blue, just as many reds and browns and there were even a couple of different flesh tones. I couldn't use any of them. I had to learn to get the colors I wanted by mixing basic red, yellow, and blue plus black and white. I was allowed to add a few basics like burnt umber and yellow ochre.

Finally, the first week of February, I could start. After sketching Mama and Daddy on the canvas in charcoal to make sure the composition and design matched my early drawings, I put the first brush on the canvas. When the buttery smooth mixture of burnt umber and cobalt blue paint flowed from my big pighair bristle brush across the canvas, I knew immediately that working in oil was what I wanted to do the rest of my life — if I could get my father's dying words out of my head. How could I love painting so much and still feel guilty about doing it?

That first day at the easel, I had planned to rough in the background. I wanted it to be slightly out of focus, like the background of a photograph when the main subject is close to the camera. I wanted the images of Mama and Daddy to standout as if they were dancing alone with no one very near. I lost track of time.

Around 5:00 p.m. Mr. Wertz stopped me. "That is all for today, Mr. Emmerson. Let me show you how to cover your painting so it doesn't get smeared. Be sure to clean your brushes and turn the bristles up to dry. By the way, you will need to be smoother with that under painting if you are going to have detailed images in the foreground. Van Gogh got away with thick layers of paint, but I'm not sure that is best for your painting."

I rushed to work at the A&P but my mind was on the painting. It would be two days before art class met again and I couldn't wait.

Chapter 40

As usual, Sarah Jane was the head of the French Club Valentine's Day Dance Committee. And just as usual, she roped me into helping with the decorations. This dance was different. First of all, I was a senior and this was one of the last big events of high school. Only prom and graduation were left. Secondly, being with Sarah Jane was not as big a pain in the butt as it had been for so many years. I sort of appreciated her energy and enthusiasm about things even when she was bossy and stubborn. For the dance, I did posters, banners and a big spaceship flying through a bright red heart to hang over the DJ. Everybody was into space travel. I kind of enjoyed helping Sarah Jane this time. It was only natural that I agreed to take her to the dance. I didn't even think about it being exactly one year since I brought Lilly to the same dance.

Of course, we never danced. She was too busy giving the DJ orders, refilling the punch bowl and handing out little boxes of candy hearts with silly sayings printed on them. I would have liked to shag when the DJ played "But It's Alright" by J.J. Jackson, but Sarah Jane was off doing something else, leaving me to man the punch bowl.

The closest we came to dancing was when "Devil With The Blue Dress" by Mitch Ryder and the Detroit Wheels played. Neither of us had heard it before and Sarah Jane started bouncing around to the fast beat and acting silly because she was wearing a short blue dress. About half way through the song, it changed to "Good Golly Miss Molly," a remake of an old song by Little Richard. We knew the words to that one and we sang along. Sarah Jane grabbed my hand and twirled me around. I almost stumbled into her arms and then she kissed me, a kiss that lasted a little longer than one of the nearby chaperones thought appropriate and we got a stern look.

That kiss led me to believe that Sarah Jane and I might spend some time up on The Mistletoe Overlook before going home. I was wrong. By the time we cleaned up the room, took down the decorations and rearranged the tables, we were tired and it was late. I was disappointed and thought all night about Sarah Jane dancing around in the short blue dress with her bright red hair falling down to her bare shoulders. Time up on Mistletoe Overlook would have to wait. She did give me a big kiss when I dropped her off at her house.

By the middle of March, the mood at home had improved. For the month and a half after Daddy died, Mama stayed at home, didn't touch any of Daddy's things and cried a lot. Almost every day she would hug me and say how much she missed Daddy and how much she loved me. To my surprise, about the time flowers started blooming in the yard and it looked like March was going to be warm and sunny, Mama gave all of Daddy's old clothes to the Salvation Army, sold his truck and got her hair all restyled with a little color change. Seeing Daddy's truck gone from the driveway made the changes that we were going through painful but real.

"Donno, I loved your daddy. He was the love of my life and I will miss him every minute I'm alive. But, I am alive and have to go on living. I'm only 40 for heaven's sake. You'll be graduating in a few months and going out on your own. So, I've gotten a job in the women's fashion department at Sears and it is something I've always wanted to do. What do you think about that?"

Mama's declaration was doubly shocking. First, it was because the changes she was making in her own life and second, it was because she had begun planning her future without me directly in it. She had already assumed that I would be leaving home and going somewhere after high school. She didn't know where and neither did I, but we both knew that we were in for huge changes. "Mama, I think it's dang cool. You go for it! You deserve to be happy and I think Daddy would approve."

Two big things happened the last week of March. I got my SAT scores and did pretty well, better than I expected. While the math score wasn't so hot, the English and writing score was high enough that Mr. Wertz felt sure I could qualify for art school scholarships if my painting turned out the way we both hoped. The biggest thing that happened came from Becky. She announced that she and Eric were going to have a baby in September and if it was a boy, they would name him Frank after Daddy. That news brought joy to the house, more than it had seen in years, even before Daddy got sick.

Time was running out on me. I only had three art classes before we broke for Easter on April 8th. Because he asked me to finish the painting early, Mr. Wertz said he would give up part of his break and open up the art room and allow me to work a couple of afternoons during spring break.

After Mr. Wertz made me scrape part of it off and start over, I finished the background and started on Mama and Daddy's figures. I wanted Mama's dress to be a flouncy floral thing with orange and yellow flowers that would contrast with Daddy's dark blue uniform coat.. I didn't want their images to be exact portraits like a photograph. I wanted them to be free and full of movement. I really liked Renoir's *Dance at Le Moulin de la Galette* and Monet's *Woman with a Parasol.* I liked the colors that Gauguin used on his paintings in Tahiti. I had seen them all in books Mr. Wertz had. I decided to put a flower in Mama's hair like Gauguin. I would wait until the very last thing to paint Mama and Daddy's faces. That turned out to be on the 18th, Mr. Wertz's deadline.

Chapter 41

With no one else at the school to bother, Mr. Wertz brought a record player to the art room and played classical music as I painted. I believe he was trying to give me some culture or something. He said his favorites were by a French guy named Debussy. He told me the names of the pieces before he played them. I would have preferred something by The Rolling Stones or The Kinks, but “Clair de Lune” and “La Mer” did put me in a kind of creative rhythm. I zoned out, concentrating on the painting.

I finished the detail of the dancers in the background and of Mama and Daddy’s bodies in the foreground. It was time for their faces. I had chosen the direction of the light so that both of their faces would be well lit and not covered by shadows. I wanted to make sure the expression on their faces was open and easy to see. Mama’s face was easy. Her flowing auburn hair created a frame for her soft flesh tone oval face with cerulean eyes, pink cheeks and bright red lips opened in a smile that showed her teeth.

Daddy’s face was harder. His skin had to be darker and his hair was almost black. The light had to bring out his sharp angular features that had to be strong and manly yet with a look of happiness. I struggled with it for an hour, scraping off paint and repainting. When I had Daddy’s face about the way I wanted, it came time for the final touch, the highlights in Mama’s and Daddy’s eyes. The highlights were tiny specs of white paint on the corneas of their eyes that were reflections of the nearest light had to add life to their faces. If I didn’t get it right, it would destroy the whole feeling of the painting. Mama’s was perfect. But I had to I redo Daddy’s twice. I used the tip of my smallest brush with just a minimum of titanium white paint to lightly touch the center of both eyes with a quivering hand.

I didn't realize Mr. Wertz was watching me until I heard him whisper, "Stop, Mr. Emmerson. It is finished." With Debussy playing softly in the background, Mr. Wertz slowly walked around the easel, looking at the painting from different angles. "Step away a few feet, Mr. Emmerson and get a different perspective."

Still holding my little brush, I stepped back and stood beside Mr.Wertz. There in front of me were the images of my mother and father — not photographic reproductions, but flowing spirits of contrasting colors, hands almost touching, bodies separate yet forming an integrated design, and faces full of youthful exuberance and hope. "I think it's pretty good, don't you Mr. Wertz?"

Mr. Wertz looked over at me and smiled. "Pretty good indeed, Mr. Emmerson. Pretty good indeed."

Chapter 42

Mama didn't see the painting until the day after Mother's Day at the award ceremony for the county wide student art competition. I won the senior division and was the overall winner for all divisions. Mr. Wertz found a simple but appropriate frame for the painting and I thought it really looked good when they unveiled it. Becky came home for Mother's Day and the ceremony. She, Mama and Sarah Jane gasped when they saw the painting. "Oh Donno, I can't believe it. It is the most beautiful painting I've ever seen! What a wonderful, wonderful Mother's Day present." Mama pulled me to her and cried. Becky and Sarah Jane put their arms around us and we all cried. Mama whispered, "Your Daddy would be so proud of you."

I turned and looked at the painting. I wondered if Mama was right. Would this painting have been enough to change Daddy's mind about me? *Would the painting be enough to convince him that my art talent was worth pursuing? Would he really have been proud of me like Mama said or would it have taken something else for him to say "Good job, Son?"* I looked at the eyes I gave him in the painting, wishing I could have looked into his real eyes one more time while he was living.

An Ashton Times Gazette reporter and photographer were at the award ceremony and they got a picture of me, Mama and Mr. Wertz looking at the painting. The paper ran a big article about me a couple of days later. The story mentioned that I had also won the scholastic art contest three times, including the one back in junior high. Luckily, this time, the painting didn't cause as much trouble as the one back then.

We didn't subscribe to the paper, but Mama bought several copies at the drug store and neighbors brought copies by. Our picture and story were at the bottom of the front page. I didn't look at any of the inside pages for a couple of days. When I did, there was a whole page with nothing but stories about Vietnam. One said that there were more than 180,000 American soldiers in Vietnam and 1966 was well on its way to being the deadliest year yet. Another story reported on a helicopter crash that killed all 20 people on board, most of them Americans. There was another story not directly related to the war. It talked about a big test thousands of college students were taking at 1,200 different schools to see if their grades were good enough to keep them from being drafted into the Army. I wouldn't turn 18 until July and hadn't even thought about the draft. I wondered if going to art school would also keep me out of the Army.

The Junior-Senior Prom was the last Saturday in May and was held in one of the downtown hotel ballrooms. I don't think I actually asked Sarah Jane to go with me. It just sort of happened. One day at school, she told me I needed to get a haircut and rent a tuxedo. That was okay with me.

For once, Sarah Jane was not in charge of a dance. The junior class was responsible for putting it on and seniors were guests. That drove Sarah Jane crazy and for once, I didn't have to do any art work for decorations. I made her promise not to criticize anything and just have a good time.

Ricky Stillman managed to get a date with a girl who had just transferred in from one of the county schools after Christmas. She was real quiet and shy. Ricky wasn't sure what to do with her alone so he pleaded with me to double date with Sarah Jane and me. I wasn't too thrilled about the idea until he told me that he had use of his grandfather's brand new Pontiac Grand Prix for the night. The rich kids from across the river rented limousines for prom. West Ashton kids usually ended up driving their mothers' station wagons. Riding in a big new Pontiac would be a step up. Sarah Jane agreed only because she knew that Ricky and his mousy date might never say a word and certainly wouldn't get up and dance.

Mama and I went next door to Sarah Jane's so both mothers could take pictures. When Sarah Jane came down the steps, Mama and I both said "Wow!" at the same time. I had expected her to wear a white dress full of ruffles and lace, looking sort of like a wedding dress. Instead, her dress was short, black and kind of tight. Her long red hair was piled on top of her head and not down on her shoulders. A single strand of white pearls around her slender neck was her only jewelry. I said "Wow!" a second time. I told her she looked like a short version of Ann-Margret who I had just seen on the news entertaining soldiers in Vietnam.

When I was in junior high, I thought Britney McMurray at the record store was the most beautiful girl in the world. Later on, I told Lilly that she looked like Natalie Wood when I picked her up to go to a dance. I thought Lilly was beautiful the very first time I met her. But neither Britney nor Lilly compared to the way Sarah Jane looked in her prom dress. She was breathtaking. How did that happen? How did my pest of a next door neighbor change from that short little kid with braces, glasses and a bitchy attitude to the striking young woman I was about to take to our Senior Prom? I must not have been paying attention.

When Sarah Jane and I climbed in the back seat of the Grand Prix, we were both shocked by Ricky and his date, Florence Ballard. They were two of the shyest and most socially awkward people either of us knew. You would not have known it the way they were dressed. Florence wore a low cut, bright red dress with big pink flowers down the front. Ricky's tux was bright yellow with a dark blue shirt with ruffles down the front and a lime green bowtie. Together, they looked like an explosion at a crayon factory. What shocked us even more was their dancing. They never sat down. Of course, they did a strange version of the "Twist" to every fast song no matter what it was. Sarah Jane and I had great fun watching them.

We really didn't dance much until the DJ announced a medley of Temptations songs.

"Alright, let's see if there are any beach music fans out there. Can we get some shaggers on the floor? Here's three in a row for your dancing pleasure." The first was "My Girl," which was a great song, but kind of hard to dance to. We got up and danced to the next two. "The Girl's Alright With Me" and "Beauty Is Only Skin Deep" had perfect shag beats. When we walked out on the floor, Sarah Jane asked me "It's been a long time since we shagged together. Do you remember how?"

"You kidding me? Just like riding a bike. You never forget how." I did have to count out the steps at first, "One and two, three and four, five-six. One and two, three and four, five-six." Sarah Jane and I must have looked pretty good because some of the kids near us applauded. We did fit together well. Sarah Jane kissed me on the cheek and held my hand walking back to our table. It all felt good — very good.

Once, when Florence and Sarah Jane went to the bathroom, Ricky moved over next to me and slapped me on the back. "Hey, dude, whaddya you think about my girl? She's somethin' else, isn't she?"

"Yeah, Ricky, you got that right. She's something for sure. You are too. Didn't know you could dance like that either."

"Gotta get my dancin' in now. Won't be able to soon."

"Why's that?"

Ricky slapped me on the back again, "Hadn't I told you? I head out to basic training right after graduation. I enlisted in the Army."

I was shocked. First, I had forgotten that Ricky was several months older than me and had already turned 18. Secondly, here was this goofy kid I'd known for 15 years dressed up like a big canary telling me he was volunteering to go to war.

"Ain't that cool? Pretty soon, my wardrobe will be all one color — olive green. So, my man, let's party hardy tonight!"

I was still in shock. "Uh, why, uh why the hell did you enlist? Are you crazy?"

"Why not? I'm not going to college, so I'd probably get drafted anyway. Besides, you know, it's kind of an adventure, going places I've never been before."

"Yeah, but there's a war going on, Ricky. People will be shooting at you. Have you thought of that?"

"It was good enough for my pop, and yours too. Can't be all that bad. Maybe you ought to think about it."

Florence and Sarah Jane came back to the table and Ricky suggested that we should leave early and cruise the strip. Just then, the DJ announced another song. "Here's a brand new one from those blue-eyed soul Righteous Brothers. Grab your sweetie and dance close to "Soul and Inspiration."

Sarah Jane loved the Righteous Brothers. "Come on Donno, one last dance and then we can go."

Ricky laughed and said, "Yep, one last dance for a long long time for me."

Sarah Jane pulled me to the dance floor and I held her close. "Donno, what did Ricky mean when he said this would be his last dance for a long time?"

"I'll tell you later. Let's just dance." I held her tighter.

As was the tradition after the prom, we cruised the strip up and back and the Grand Prix got some thumbs up and challenges to race a couple of times. We pulled into Buster's Burgers and joined the long line of cars waiting to make song requests to the Tower of Rhythm DJ. It looked like everybody else from the prom had the same idea. Ricky had a different idea. "Hey, I'll bet with all the kids in line down here, there is probably a parking spot up on the mountain."

Florence got all excited. "You mean the Mistletoe Overlook? Oh please, let's go. I've heard about it and never been there. Please Ricky, baby, let's go."

Sarah Jane laughed. "Sure, I'll go." She punched me in the ribs and said "I'll bet the view is really nice up there tonight, don't you, Donno?"

Ricky's news about joining the Army shook me out of the party mood. I don't know if it was because I couldn't imagine him fighting in a war or because it reminded me of Daddy telling me I should join up too. It also made me remember that I would be 18 in July and would have to make some decisions that I wasn't sure I was ready to make. "Yeah, I'm good with going up there, you know, to see the view." Sarah Jane snickered and punched me in the ribs again.

Ricky did find a parking spot on the mountain and in just a few minutes, the windows were fogged up and Ricky and Florence's heads disappeared. Without a whole lot of enthusiasm, I kissed Sarah Jane a couple of times. She must have figured out that something was bothering me and just put her head on my shoulder and we listened to all of the songs requested by the other kids from the prom. There were a lot of make-out songs requested like "Crying in the Chapel" by Elvis, "Unchained Melody" by The Righteous Brothers, " Hold Me, Thrill Me, Kiss Me" by Mel Carter and "A Lover's Concerto" by The Toys. Sarah Jane and I sang along with the radio while waiting for Florence and Ricky to come up for air and take us home.

The afternoon after the prom, Sarah Jane came over to my house to check on me. "You got awfully quiet last night and uh, weren't too affectionate up on the mountain. What happened?"

I told her what Ricky had said about enlisting and that he thought I ought to think about it too.

"You're not thinking about it, are you?"

"Well, I think about what Daddy said and I think about guys my age going to Vietnam. So, yeah, I started thinking about it a lot. I think about what I'm going to do after I turn 18 and get out of high school."

She took my face in her hands and whispered, "The only thing you should think about is going to art school and learning to be a great artist, even greater than you are right now." Then she gave me a quick kiss.

"Jeez! *What am I going to do?"*

Chapter 43

The week before graduation, Mama and I were invited to come to an awards ceremony at school. I figured that it had something to do with winning the art contest — no way it had anything to do with the rest of my classes. They didn't give out academic awards to kids with a low B average.

At the ceremony, all of the academic awards and scholarships won by seniors were announced. Sarah Jane and her mom were there too. Sarah Jane was the class valedictorian and one of the top three students academically. When she was called up on stage, it took about 10 minutes to read out all of the awards she won. She was also offered several college scholarships. The biggest one was a full ride to Radcliffe College, a fancy college for women in Massachusetts. I had never heard of it, but a lot of people in the crowd must have because there were a lot of "oohs" and "ahhs."

A kid sitting behind me leaned over and said, "Man, your girlfriend is a superstar."

I nodded and agreed, "Yeah, she is." Then two things hit me hard. It was the first time ever I admitted Sarah Jane was my girlfriend and, even more disturbing, if she accepted the scholarship to Radcliffe, she would be going to Massachusetts in the fall, probably a long way from wherever I was going after graduation.

I was still thinking about those things when Mr. Wertz walked out on the stage and said, "Would Donald Emmerson please join me here?" Mama had to poke me to get me going.

I stood beside Mr. Wertz while he started explaining what kind of process I had gone through for my senior painting project and how I had won the scholastic art contest for the whole county. I was still sort of day dreaming when I heard him say, "Mr. Emmerson has been offered a full scholarship to the prestigious Ringling College of Art and Design in Sarasota, Florida." All I understood was the word "Ringling" and wondered what the circus had to do with this. Then there was applause and more "oohs" and "ahhs" from the audience.

Mr. Wertz went on, "The Ringling College of Art and Design is very selective and only accepts students who display outstanding talent and potential. Their full scholarship awards are even more selective with only three offered per year." Mr. Wertz turned and extended his hand. "Congratulations, Donald. You deserve this."

In shock, I shook his hand and mumbled, "Uh, uh wow. This is uh cool."

I joined the earlier award winners who were standing at the back of the stage. Sarah Jane moved over to stand beside me and whispered, "I'm so proud of you and I can't imagine how proud your father would be right now." I couldn't imagine that either. I also couldn't imagine going to Florida, leaving Mama, being a thousand miles away from West Ashton and farther than that from Sarah Jane up in Massachusetts. Worst of all, I couldn't imagine how quickly I had to make some decisions that would probably affect the rest of my life. After the ceremony, Mr. Wertz told Mama and me that I had to accept the scholarship by the end of June. I think Mama knew how I was struggling with it all, especially with how Daddy felt about me studying art versus what he called my "call to duty". I hadn't even turned 18 yet.

Chapter 44

We graduated on Saturday, June 4th at the big auditorium downtown. All of the high schools in the county used that building for graduation, even the Black high school. The building was built in the ‘20s and wasn’t air conditioned. Our heavy black robes were miserably hot. The school superintendent was the first to speak and he droned on for what seem like an hour. Then the principal spoke and his speech was even longer. By the time Sarah Jane spoke as both the valedictorian and class president, the students were restless, chatting with people near them, fiddling with the tassels on their hats and using their printed programs as fans. A few even made spit-wads out of the paper and attacked people in rows ahead of them. I was tempted to join in the spit-wad battle, but I also wanted to hear what Sarah Jane had to say. She had not shared any of her speech with me. She got everyone’s attention, especially the principal and superintendent, when she opened with, “It’s hot as hell, I mean heck, isn’t it?” The graduates roared and so did their families.

Sarah Jane had the crowd with her then and she went on, “I know you want to get through this and celebrate with your families and friends. I won’t take too long.” The graduates roared again. “I’m not going to tell you that graduating from high school is a big step toward your futures. You know that. We’ve been working toward this moment for twelve years with the help of our families and of some wonderful teachers. I don’t want to talk about the future — I want to talk about this night. Many of us have known each other since first grade. When those of us from West Ashton and those from across the river got together three years ago, we made friendships that are just as strong as any that started in elementary school. Remember, we are all Ashton High Panthers!"

The graduates clapped and roared again.

"Please look down the rows where you are sitting and see the faces of those near you. Multiply that by all of the graduates in the class of 1966. Some of them will be life-long friends. Others you will never see again after tonight. Some of us have had our hearts broken several times in high school while some of us have found the loves of our lives in this group. "

My jaw dropped when she used the word "us" in that sentence.

"Some of us will stay here in our old hometown and never leave. Some will fight a war in a faraway place and never come home."

I thought of Ricky.

"Some of us will do wonderful things. Some of us will not succeed and will struggle with life. Some of us will remember our high school years fondly while some of us never felt connected and hated it. Some of us will come back for reunions while some of us want to stay as far away from Ashton as possible."

I looked around at the kids near me. I could tell they had heard what Sarah Jane was saying and it was affecting them deeply.

"I promised not to make a long speech, so let me close with this thought: we all know that after tonight, none of our lives will ever be the same as we all go in a thousand different directions. But tonight, this night of June 4, 1966, we are one family for one last time. I know this sounds really cheesy, but please do this. Look to the people beside you and the people in front and behind you, even if you can't remember their names, tell them that you love them. You may never have the chance again."

There was a second or two of awkward silence before the graduates actually did it, but we actually did what Sarah Jane asked. We stood and told the people around us that we loved them. There were tears, hugs, laughter and cheers. There were tears and hugs up in the family seats too.

I looked up on the stage as the principal and superintendent gave Sarah Jane a hug. When they turned her loose, she waved to me and mouthed the words "I love you." I threw her a kiss. I realized I loved her too and maybe always had. *How could a girl like that fall for a goof-ball like me?*

After Sarah Jane's speech, it was time to hand out diplomas. At other graduations I had attended, the popular kids and jocks got big cheers from the crowd when their names were read while the less popular and run-of-the- mill, everyday kids only got a smattering of cheers from their families only. On our graduation night, after Sarah Jane got us to appreciate each other no matter our social status, every kid got equally loud applause. It was a special night. It got a lot more special before it was over.

We sang the Alma Mater, heard the principal say, "Congratulations to the Ashton High School Class of 1966. You are now graduates." We shifted the tassels on our hats to the other side and clapped and cheered again. After we marched out of the auditorium, a lot of kids found their closest friends and promised, "I will never forget you, we'll be friends forever." Then the families found their students and there were more hugs, tears and lots of picture taking. Mama must have used a whole box of Polaroid film on me. After I hugged Mama for the last time, I worked my way through the crowd and found Sarah Jane surrounded by teachers, parents, and graduates, all of them congratulating her for all of her honors and for her speech. Her mother stood beside her beaming with pride. Sarah Jane finally saw me and gave me a big hug.

"That was some speech you made, kiddo. I actually listened to you for once."

"Did you hear me say that some of us have found the loves of our lives?"

"I did. Were you talking about yourself, uh, us?"

"I was talking about me. Do you feel the same?"

Sarah Jane looked up at me, waiting for an answer to a question I had not considered for the last 17 or so years. I then knew the answer —"Yes, I love you more than anything in the world and I guess I always have."

I bent down to kiss her but was interrupted by one of Sarah Jane's smart, rich-crowd kids grabbing her from behind. "SJ, are you coming to the party at the country club? There's going to be a band, and you know they're Black."

I had never heard Sarah Jane called "SJ" and that reminded me that she had a whole different group of friends other than just Ricky and me. I also hadn't heard anything about going to the country club for a party after graduation. Of course, typical for me, I hadn't thought of anything else to do that night either. I knew there were a bunch of kids leaving the next morning for Myrtle Beach, but I wasn't part of that group. I also wasn't part of the group that went to parties at the country club.

"I forgot to tell you about this party, Donno. I got the invitation a week ago. It said I could bring a date. Do you want to go? I don't want to go if you don't."

Sarah Jane's mother put her arm around my shoulder and said, "Go ahead, Donno. Have a good time. Your mom and I will turn in your caps and gowns. Just be sure you get our girl home safely."

I really didn't want to go, but I also didn't want to keep Sarah Jane from going. It was sort of her night. "Sure, why not. Maybe we can dance." I looked around the crowd to find Ricky to see what he was doing. I didn't find him. We hadn't talked about doing something together with him and Florence, so he was on his own.

"Oh, great! Let's do it. It will be fun and maybe I will give you a surprise later."

I knew where the country club was because I drove past the entrance to pick up Lily a couple of times, but I had never driven up to it. It looked like a castle surrounded by a golf course. I had to admit that I was impressed, especially when a young Black guy, not much older than me came up and told me he was the parking valet and he would take care of my car. I wondered what he thought when he parked my old station wagon between a shiny Cadillac and Lincoln Continental. I offered him a quarter tip and he laughed. The inside was just as impressive as the outside with big crystal chandeliers, shiny hardwood floors, old people dressed in fancy clothes and big landscape paintings in gold frames on the walls. I was inspecting one of the paintings when a stately Black man spoke to Sarah Jane. "Young Mr. Alexander's event is on the patio. Please follow me."

I followed Sarah Jane who was following the Black man. "So, Sarah Jane, who's Mr. Alexander anyway?"

"Oh, you know, Donno. He's the president of the French Club. I'm, or was, in his AP calculus class. He's the one throwing this party."

If Alexander took AP calculus, there was no wonder I didn't know him. That was not my normal social group.

We walked through a big ballroom and out to a patio on the edge of what looked like a putting green to me. There were maybe 30 or 40 kids already there. I recognized many of them from school, but would not consider any of them close friends. Sarah Jane and I were the only West Ashton kids as far as I could tell. Obviously, being from West Ashton didn't keep Sarah Jane from being in the group because at least half of them excitedly rushed to her, hugged her and congratulated her on her "awesome" speech.

I was surprised when a couple of kids congratulated me on the art awards and the scholarship. Even "young" Mr. Alexander spoke to me. "Hey, man, way cool on the art thing. I can't even draw a straight line. Glad I'm pretty good in math. That's the only way I could get into MIT. Thanks for bringing SJ to the party. She's super."

"Uh, sure. Thanks for letting me in." I had no idea what MIT was but it must have been pretty important if Alexander got in. I felt a little less self-conscience after he congratulated me. I figured I did have something to be proud about that night. When the band cranked up on their version of The Drifters' "Under the Board Walk," I knew I could hold my own.

Sarah Jane grabbed my hand and led me to the center of the tiny dance floor. "Okay, Donno, let's show these kids how West Ashton people shag. Just remember, one and two, three and four, five six."

I laughed and twirled her around in my arms. "Don't worry, I've got this."

There were a few other kids on the dance floor who knew how to shag and were pretty good, but none of them were as good as Sarah Jane and me that night. The band was out of Raleigh and was named Sonny Moon and the Rhythm Stars. They said they had just finished a two week gig at one of the Myrtle Beach clubs and their specialty was beach music. During a break, I asked the lead singer if they did "Sixty Minute Man." He laughed out loud.

"Hey man, you kiddin' me? We probably do that three or four times a night at the shag clubs. We'll give it a shot in the second set and see if any of the old folks take offense."

The old folks and chaperones either didn't understand the lyrics or didn't care, because the band played "Sixty Minute Man" and really emphasized the " rock 'em, roll 'em, all night long" line and no adult said a thing. Sarah Jane and I sang along with the band as we danced.

The chaperones also didn't care that Sarah Jane and I were a few weeks short of our 18th birthdays. The bar offered beer, wine and liquor and the Black bartender said he would give us whatever we wanted. I had a Pabst Blue Ribbon and Sarah Jane had champagne. I stopped at one, remembering how bad I felt down at the beach after too many PBRs.

About 11:00, the lead singer said they were going to do one more song and then take another break before coming out for their last set. Sarah Jane led me back out on to the dance floor and whispered, "Let's dance to this song and then I want to give you the surprise."

The song was "Any Day Now" by Chuck Jackson and we must have looked pretty good dancing to it because when it was over, the lead singer said, "Look at that smooth redhead and her long haired partner out there doing their thing." Several kids applauded.

I gave the valet parking guy my ticket and Sarah Jane gave him a dollar. He smiled at her and shook his head at me. After we pulled out of the parking lot and were almost to the bridge to West Ashton, I asked, "So, what's this big surprise you're talking about?"

Sarah Jane snuggled up close to me and said, "My mother left to go visit my aunt in Spartanburg right after graduation. I have the house to myself."

"Oh, okay. That's cool." That didn't seem like such a big surprise to me, but then it hit me. "Oh, uh, you mean uh, you mean…?"

"Yes, Donno. That's what I mean, if you want to."

I nearly drove off the road. "Of course I want to."

"Then I think you ought to stop at a gas station and buy something."

I looked at Sarah Jane wondering what she was talking about. "I've got plenty of gas, why should I stop at a …oh, you mean to buy…"

"That's right dummy. We don't want any little Donnos walking around now do we?"

I pulled into the cut rate Direct station on the other side of the bridge and started to go in, but had to stop and asked Sarah Jane, "Uh, can I borrow a quarter?"

I had been in Sarah Jane's room a bunch of times when we were little kids, but not so much in the last few years and not nearly as often as she had been in mine. There were still a lot of stuffed animals on the shelves, stars and moons on the bedspread and frilly curtains on the windows, but now there were also Beatles, Dave Clark Five and Ray Charles posters, college pennants, and a framed picture of her standing in front of her VW bug. The charcoal drawing I had done of her for her election poster was also framed and on one of her bedside tables. The other bedside table held a combination stereo, radio and clock. There was already a stack of 45s loaded on the record player.

Sarah Jane turned out the light and we quickly slipped out of our clothes, throwing them on the floor before pulling back the bedspread. “Are you sure you want to do this, Sarah Jane? I mean you said you wouldn’t until you turned 18.”

“I have wanted to do this since I was 14 I think. But, if you don’t want to, we can stop now.”

“Are you kidding? Stop now? No way. Come here!”

“No, wait. I want music.” She pushed the play button and the first 45 dropped on the turn table.

Giggling, embarrassed and awkward at first, we finally found each other and made love as Bobby Hatfield belted out “Unchained Melody.” It was better than I had been dreaming since I first learned the difference between boys and girls and what they could do together in bed.

Breathlessly, we clung to each other, tangled up in the sheets for 30 minutes and until the last notes of “You’ve Lost That Lovin Feeling” quit playing.

“Sarah Jane this has been the most wonderful night of my life, but I have to leave you. I’d rather stay like this all night, but I told Mama I’d be home by 1:30 or 2:00. After Daddy died, she worries about me a lot. She’s alone and I worry about her sometimes too.”

“I understand and thank you. It was beautiful and wonderful for me. I will remember it forever.”

“I love you Sarah Jane.”

“And I love you, Donald Emmerson, and probably always have.”

“Will I see you tomorrow?”

“Absolutely.”

When I got dressed, I realized I had left on my socks. We got a big laugh out of that.

Chapter 45

When I came in the back door, Mama was waiting for me in the dark living room. She must have been sleeping on the couch. I thought, *how could she possibly know what Sarah Jane and I did tonight?* "What is it, Mama? Why are you still awake? I told you I would be late."

Mama motioned for me to sit beside her. "There's been a terrible accident, Donno."

My first thought was that it couldn't be Sarah Jane, I had just left her. Next I thought of Becky and the baby. Becky was six months pregnant and having some troubles. That's why she hadn't come to my graduation. "Is it Becky, Mama? Has something happened to her?"

"No, honey. It's Ricky, Ricky Stillman. He was in a wreck leaving that night club out south of town. You know, that Maple Lodge or something like that. He's in critical condition at the hospital and the girl with him was killed."

"Oh God, Mama! What happened? I mean, do you know anything about it?"

"It was on the 11:00 news but didn't give any names. It said an 18-year-old who had just graduated from Ashton High School was involved in a one car collision. He hit a tree. The driver is in critical condition and his passenger, a 17-year-old Ashton girl was killed. The news said he might have been racing another car."

"Mama, I looked for him after graduation but didn't see him. That was before Sarah Jane asked me to go to a party with her."

"Donno, honey, his parents called here about 12:30 and told me it was Ricky on the news because they thought you were with him. Then, they didn't know how bad it was. You told me you were going to the party, but I was afraid you might have changed your mind and gone out with Ricky. I was so afraid you were with him."

I thought about what she said. "Maybe I should have been with him, Mama. This might not have happened."

"Oh, you can't blame yourself, honey. I just feel so sorry for his parents and the parents of that poor, poor girl."

I nearly forgot about Florence. Ricky really seemed to have fallen for her and now she was dead. "Mama, I'm going to the hospital. I've got to see him."

I started to wake up Sarah Jane and take her with me to the hospital. Then I thought of how happy she seemed when I left her. She would learn about Ricky and Florence soon enough.

The Ashton Memorial Hospital was the only hospital in the county and at 3:00 a.m. on a Sunday morning, the emergency room was like a war zone with all of the bar fights, heart attacks, stabbings and wrecks that happened on Saturday night. I held the door open for a middle age man who had his arm around a sobbing woman. The man was crying too. I wondered if they were Florence's parents — then again, the waiting room was packed and many people were crying.

Ricky's mother saw me before I saw her. "Donald, Donald Emmerson! Over here." She and Mr. Stillman got up from their chairs and engulfed me in a hug. We all cried. "Oh Donald, thank you for coming. Richard has considered you his best friend since you two were in grammar school."

I had never really thought about it, but I suppose Ricky had been my best friend since we were little kids. "How is he, Mrs. Stillman? Please tell me what happened."

Mrs. Stillman broke down and started sobbing loudly. Mr. Stillman answered my question. "He's really banged up, Donald. We know his right leg is broken in several places and he has several broken ribs." Mr. Stillman had to stop for a breath and to wipe the tears from his eyes. "The worst part is a head injury. He is in a coma so the doctors can't tell how much damage there is."

"Oh man, I'm so sorry. I can't believe it. Do you know what happened?"

"We don't know everything, but the Highway Patrol thinks Richard might have been racing someone he met at that night club. He had his uncle's car and it was way too fast for him. He really couldn't handle it."

"That was the car we took to prom."

"That's right. When he said he was going to drive it after graduation, we thought you might be going with him. We have always thought you were the level headed one and kept Richard out of trouble."

Damn, Why didn't I find him at graduation?." I'm sorry, Mr. Stillman. I should have been with him. If I had found him after graduation, I probably would have gone with him and Florence instead of where I went."

"We wish you had."

"Yes sir, me too. Tell me, what happened to Florence?"

"According to the police, neither one of them were wearing seatbelts. Florence was thrown out of the car when the passenger door flew open."

That reminded me of prom night when Florence scooted over close to Ricky rather than wearing a seatbelt.

Mrs. Stillman stopped crying for a second or two. "Did Richard say anything to you about marrying Florence after he got out of basic training? He was so excited about leaving for Fort Jackson in a few weeks and then coming home in October to get married before shipping out again."

"No Ma'am, he hadn't mentioned that. But I know he really liked her. He liked her a lot."

I couldn't imagine Ricky Stillman being married or being a soldier. He was just a goofy kid like me. "Mr. Stillman, may I see him? I mean, will they let me in the room?"

"I will take you to where he is, but get ready. He looks....well, he doesn't look like my son." Mr. Stillman left me at the entrance to an open bay where two nurses were working around a figure I didn't recognize in the bed. The only thing that looked familiar was the shock of sandy blond hair that always seemed to be standing straight up on the side of his head. Just like when I saw Daddy in the hospital, there were tubes running to both arms, wires attached to his chest and an oxygen mask over his nose and mouth. What little I could see of his face was bruised and swollen and his right leg was wrapped in a cast and suspended from a bar. Out loud, I said, "Jesus Ricky, what have you done to yourself? What have you done? I'm so sorry man."

One of the nurses turned to me and asked, "Are you a friend?"

"Best friend, I guess."

"He's lying here like this and a 17-year-old girl is down in the morgue because he was drinking and driving too fast. Don't make him a hero. This is the fourth fatal wreck involving teenagers since the middle of May. Don't let it happen to you. "

Ricky was still in a coma on the day of Florence's funeral. It was held in the chapel of a funeral home that had been on West Ashton's main street for a hundred years. Sarah Jane and I were surprised to see an open casket when we walked in the chapel. I didn't want to look at Florence, but Sarah Jane took me by the hand and we got in the line that led to Florence's parents and sister who were standing by the coffin.

"Mr. and Mrs. Ballard, we are, uh were friends of Florence from high school. We are so sorry about, uh about what happened." I didn't mention anything about Ricky.

"Thank you for coming. I am sure Flo would appreciate it. Doesn't she look beautiful?"

Sarah Jane and I couldn't help but look down. The face we saw looked nothing like the girl we remembered. We did remember her dress. It was the brightly colored floral design she had worn to prom. We both gasped and Sarah Jane grabbed my arm.

After the service, Sarah Jane and I sat in my car and watched the hearse and all of the other cars leave the funeral home for the cemetery. I didn't want to go to the graveside service. Even though there would be no flag on the coffin or an honor guard, I didn't care to see someone I knew lowered into ground like I had at Daddy's funeral.

"You know, if Ricky survives this, he's going to be in real trouble. More than likely charged with at least manslaughter."

Sarah Jane scooted over next to me and put her head on my shoulder. "Yes and even if he did recover enough to join, that charge will keep him out of the Army. At least he won't have to fight in that awful senseless war in Vietnam."

That was the first time I heard her make any kind of comment about the war, either bad or good. "Well, I think he felt it would be important. He told me he believed he could do something good in the Army, something he could never do coming back to West Ashton and working at the paper mill. Besides, isn't everybody's duty to fight? Look what our fathers did. They gave up everything to fight. Your father gave his life."

Sitting up straight, Sarah Jane cocked her head and looked at me. "Surely you aren't thinking about joining the Army, are you? You know Ricky doesn't have the same options you have. Other than maybe being killed in Vietnam, being in the Army was probably the best thing for him. You know that, don't you?"

"I don't know, Sarah Jane. Why is it right for Ricky and some of the other kids we know going to Vietnam while others like me and all of those kids at the country club get to do something else? You know Daddy thought being in the military would be the best thing for me too."

Sarah Jane scooted away from me and folded her arms. I had seen the look on her face before when she was about to issue an order. "Wars are ugly, useless things that destroy beauty in the world. You have the soul of an artist and the talent to go with it. Whether it came from God, or inherited from some ancestor or just pure luck, your purpose in this life is to create beauty. When people look at your art, there's no way they should think about making war. Don't you see what a waste it would be for you to join the Army?"

Damn, I thought. *My best friend wanted to go to the Army but probably never will. My father is dead, but I can still hear him telling me I need to join the Army. And now, my girlfriend, who I think I really love, tells me that I owe it to the world not to go to war. It's June 8th and I have to tell Ringling that I am accepting the scholarship by the end of the month. Damn, Damn!*

Chapter 46

In the middle of July, Sarah Jane and I celebrated our 18th birthdays together with our mothers at the Crystal Cafeteria just like we had when we turned 15. Later that night, Sarah Jane and I celebrated in a completely different way in the back seat of my car. We celebrated that way often. She worked downtown at Belk department store and I worked at the A&P and we met each other almost every night after work. Other than Ricky's wreck and the decision about my future I kept putting off, it was the best summer of my life.

About the middle of August, Ricky finally got out of the hospital. I visited him there a couple of times, but it was hard to talk to him because there were always nurses coming and going and I think he was doped up with pain medications. When I visited him at his house, he was in a wheelchair and had a hard time holding his head up and didn't make much sense when he talked. "You know what Donno? I'm lookin' forward to school starting. Florence says she is too. It'll be cool to be a senior with her being my girlfriend."

The doctors told Ricky's parents that he probably would never regain his memory and that his brain was so damaged that he was stuck in the time before the wreck.

"Yeah, Rick, it'll be cool. Something we have all been looking forward to." I tried a couple of times to get through to him and tell him that Sarah Jane and I would be going away soon and that he wouldn't be seeing us for a long time. That didn't register with him. He kept talking about how much he loved Florence and how he would marry her one day after he got out of basic training. He also talked about how he was going to be a hell of a soldier and "waste a bunch of gooks."

"No doubt, Ricky, No doubt. You're going to be a real hero for sure." I couldn't help thinking about the former Marine who, a couple of weeks before, had climbed a tower in Texas and shot 16 people.

At the end of August, it was time for Sarah Jane and me to leave West Ashton. I was set to leave on the 29th and she was going to catch a train to Massachusetts on the 30th. That gave us the day Saturday the 28th to be together. Sarah Jane had it all planned out as usual. First, we would go out to the veterans' cemetery and visit daddy's grave one last time. Then we would have a picnic lunch up on Mistletoe Overlook. I told her it was the first time I had been up there with a girl in the daytime. We ate Peter Pan peanut butter sandwiches, shared a bag of Cheetos and drank Cheerwine. We sat there looking down on the strip until *Big WASH* started broadcasting music at 2:00 and we turned the car radio up and listened to Bob Dylan, The Beatles, The Kinks and Peter Paul and Mary. There was no beach music played.

"You know what we need to do Donno? We need to dance before we leave."

"You mean here, on the asphalt? Besides, they're not going to play any dance tunes. It will be British stuff mostly."

"Then let's go to the pool. Today is the last day the pavilion will be open before Labor Day and school opens. You know there's still some shag songs on the juke box."

I had not been to the pavilion since the middle of summer the year before. When we walked up the steps, it was just as it had always been only with different people. Young kids stood around the wall watching the older kids trying to dance. The "Twist" was still the most popular and Chubby Checker was belting out "Let's Twist Again Like We Did Last Summer."

"I've got a couple of nickels. Let's see what we can find and show these young ones a thing or two."

"Here's one. Remember "Dance With Me" by The Drifters? We danced to that a long time ago."

"Of course I remember it." We both had on tennis shoes, but we kicked them off and danced in our socks.

After I put in my nickel and punched the number, Sarah Jane took my hand and led me to the center of the floor. "This is the last time we will dance together for a long time. You know that?"

"Let's not think about that. Let's just dance." I pulled her close and held her tight and we stood that way even after the song started.

"One and two, three and four, five six. Dance with me, Donno."

I released her from my arms and took her right hand in my left. In rhythm with the music, I pulled her past me and Sarah Jane spun twice before taking my hand again. With her hand still in mine, I twirled her around while spinning around the opposite direction myself. We glided across the old wood floor like we were on ice, small steps, barely lifting our feet off the floor, smooth and sexy. It was if The Drifters were singing just to us and we danced as we had never danced before, not knowing another soul was around. When the song ended, Sarah Jane fell into my arms and I pressed her head to my chest. "I love you, Sarah Jane and I'll miss you every day."

We stood there, holding each other, knowing that our lives would never be the same — wondering how time and distance would change us. We might have stayed that way longer except for the sound of applause from the kids who had made a circle around us. One 14-year-old boy looked at us and said, "Man that is cool. I want to learn how to dance like you guys."

Epilogue

In the early '70s, a new mall opened on the east side of town and downtown Ashton almost died. All of the big retail stores moved to the mall and the small businesses folded for lack of customers. Even the Crystal Cafeteria closed. West Ashton didn't change much until after the paper mill closed. The air smelled better but a lot of people lost their homes and businesses closed on Main Street. McMurray's Furniture Store hung on for a while but finally shut down in 1974.

The public schools started integrating in 1970 and that meant all of the city and county parks integrated as well. That was just too much for Mrs. Bronson and she retired, leaving the management of the pool and pavilion to a string of managers that kept changing. I drive by the pool on the way home and I am still shocked to see black children sitting on the side of the pool trying to warm up from the frigid water. I haven't been upstairs to the dance floor since that last time before I left town. I assume there is still a juke box and kids still dance, probably the "Twist."

I came back to West Ashton in 1973 after getting a degree in art education from the teachers' college up at Boone. The GI bill made that possible after a few months in a VA hospital. Things go full circle — I am now an art teacher at Ashton Middle School. There aren't any junior highs any longer. Kids from both sides of the river go to sixth through eighth grade at the same school. I have a few very talented students, but not many are serious about art. I also give private painting lessons on weekends and occasionally sell a few of my things at a local gallery. The painting of Mama and Daddy dancing is hanging over the fireplace at my house and I have never been able to get the same feeling and style in other paintings.

I am buying my old house from Mama. She has moved to the beach to be near Becky and her kids. Becky now has a little girl and a little boy. The boy is named Francis Donald. Becky and Eric promised me that he would not be called Franko or Donno.

Ricky Stillman never got any better and his parents eventually put him into a nursing home. I pick him up once a month and take him out on the strip for a ride. Sometimes we drive through McDonald's and get a milkshake. Buster's Burgers turned into a Mexican restaurant and the *Rockin' Tower of Rhythm* quit broadcasting when a new FM station started carrying popular music 24 hours a day. It plays a lot of disco music, but has an "oldies" show on Friday afternoons. Even though The Beatles broke up in 1969, their songs still play a lot.

The American Legion Hall in Ashton has a shag night with a DJ once a month and I try to go. Most of the people there are near my age and a lot are Vietnam era vets. We don't tell many war stories. The shrapnel in by right leg keeps me from doing of the fancy steps we used to do, but I still get out on the floor when I can find a partner. We dance to the old songs we danced to back in the '60s. Every now and then, a new song comes out with a shag beat. My favorite new song is "Boogie Nights" by K.C. and the Sunshine Band.

Sarah Jane and I exchange birthday cards every year. She's in DC working for a law firm that handles a lot of civil rights cases. Her mother still lives next door and tells me that Sarah Jane keeps talking about getting her North Carolina law license and coming back to Ashton with her new husband and to open an all-woman law practice. What would it be like to dance with her again? When I dance at the Legion Hall, I hear her voice in my head saying, "One and two, three and four, five six. One and two, three and four, five six."

The Dance Steps Playlist

"*The Duke of Earl*"
Gene Chandler

"*Playboy*"
The Marvelettes

"*The Theme From Dr. Kildare*
Richard Chamberlain

"*The Sounds of Silence*"
Simon and Garfunkel

"*How Sweet It Is (To Be Loved By You)*"
Marvin Gaye

"*It Will Stand*"
The Showmen

"*Downtown*"
Petula Clark

"*The Theme From Summer Place*"
Hugo Winterhalter

"*I'll Follow the Sun*"
The Beatles

"*Hey! Baby!*"
Bruce Channel

"*Moon River*"
Andy Williams

"*Moody River*"
Pat Boone

"I Can't Stop Loving You"
Ray Charles

"Wonderland By Night"
Bert Kaempfert

"All Shook Up"
Elvis Presley

"It's Now or Never"
Elvis Presley

"(Let Me Be Your) Teddy Bear"
Elvis Presley

"Twist and Shout"
The Beatles version

"Louie Louie"
The Kingsmen

"No Where to Run"
Martha and The Vandellas.

"Walk, Don't Run"
The Ventures

"People"
Barbra Streisand

"Peppermint Twist"
Joey Dee and The Starliters

"Stroll"
The Diamonds

"Let It Be Me"
Jerry Butler and Betty Everett

"Mr. Tambourine Man"
The Byrds

"Back In My Arms Again"
The Supremes

"Like a Rolling Stone"
Bob Dylan

"Nothing Can Stop Me"
Gene Chandler

"May I"
Maurice Williams and the Zodiacs

"(I Can't Get No) Satisfaction"
The Rolling Stones

"I Can't Help Myself"
The Four Tops

"Thank You John"
Willie Tee

"What Kind of Fool (Do You Think I Am)"
The Tams

"Ticket to Ride"
The Beatles

"Help Me Rhonda"
The Beach Boys

"Eight Days a Week"
The Beatles

"Still I'm Sad"
The Yardbirds

"Lonely Drifter"
The O'Jays

"Get Off Of My Cloud"
The Rolling Stones

"We Gotta Get Out of This Place"
The Animals

"My Generation"
The Who

"The Carnival is Over"
The Seekers

"Eve of Destruction"
Barry McGuire

"Yesterday"
The Beatles

"Hurt So Bad"
Little Anthony and The Imperials

"Jersey Bounce"
Benny Goodman

"Dance With Me"
The Drifters

"Love Potion Number 9"
The Searchers.

"Under the Boardwalk"
The Drifters

"Sixty Minute Man"
The Dominoes

"Stay"
Maurice Williams and The Zodiacs

"My Girl"
The Temptations

"Come and Get These Memories"
Martha and The Vandellas

"House of the Rising Sun"
The Animals

"Rescue Me"
Fontella Bass

"You Really Got Me"
The Kinks

" Hard Day's Night"
The Beatles

"California Girls"
The Beach Boys

"Surf City"
Jan and Dean

"The Way You Do The Things You Do"
The Temptations

"A Teenager In Love"
Dion and The Belmonts

"Blowing in the Wind"
Bob Dylan

"You've Lost That Lovin' Feelin"
The Righteous Brothers

"I Hear a Symphony"
The Supremes

"We Wish You a Merry Christmas"
Instrumental by the bells on the front door

"Hark the Herald Angles Sing"
from A Charley Brown Christmas

"Five O'clock World"
The Vogues

"I Can Never Go Home Anymore"
The Shangri-Las.

"But It's Alright"
J.J. Jackson

"Devil With Blue Dress On"
Mitch Ryder and t\The Detroit Wheels

"Good Golly Miss Molly"
Little Richard

"Clair de Lune" and "La Mer"
Debussy

"The Girl's Alright With Me"
The Temptations

"Beauty Is Only Skin Deep"
The Temptations

"Crying in the Chapel"
Elvis Presley

"Hold Me, Thrill Me, Kiss Me"
Mel Carter

"Unchained Melody"
The Righteous Brothers

"Soul and Inspiration"
The Righteous Brothers

"A Lovers' Concerto"
The Toys

"Any Day Now"
Chuck Jackson

"Boogie Shoes"
K.C. and the Sunshine Band

Author's Notes

Dance Steps is based on the town where I grew up. The character of Donno Emmerson is somewhat autobiographical and also a composite of several teenage boys with whom I grew up. Although the story was set in a small Southern town, it could just as easily have been set anywhere in America during the tumultuous early to late 1960s. Making the transition from childhood to adulthood has been difficult during any period of history, but in the decade of the '60s, kids faced huge cultural changes like the real threat of nuclear war during the Cuban missile crisis, the drama of the Kennedy assassinations, the societal changes of the civil rights movement and the national division caused by the war in Vietnam. Popular music changed just as dramatically. We went from big band music and early rock and roll in the late '50s to the emergence of black artists, The Beatles and the rest of the British invasion, anti-was protest songs and psychedelic sounds that glorified an exploding drug culture. The music of the '60s mimics the changes in the country during those 10 years. In my life, the music was an important part of growing up. In the book, I have referenced many different songs by many artists. I was careful to make sure that the songs were actually released during the timeframe of the story. There is a complete play list at the end of the epilog.

In the story, Donno wanted to learn to do the shag, a particularly southern dance that remains popular, especially among baby boomers who grew up in the South and one that I first saw at the pavilion above our neighborhood public pool. Donno managed to learn to shag but that was a minor challenge compared to the other things he faced. Would he follow his dream of being an artist or take the path his father demanded? Did he really want to be accepted to the popular group at school? Would he finally accept a girl who had been in his life since he was four years old?

I graduated from high school in 1965 and my world was much the same as Donno's. I made several close friends during that time. I am no longer close to some of them, but have reconnected with several others through reunions and I enjoy the fellowship and shared memories. We often discuss growing up in the '60s and occasionally speak of the classmates we lost in Vietnam. I am especially thankful for the reconnection with classmate, Jimmy Simmons. Jimmy is responsible for bringing a group of 1965 classmates together for monthly gatherings. A gifted writer, himself, Jimmy shares his short stories and poems with me and I share manuscripts with him. Ironically, Jimmy was a lifeguard at the municipal pool that is the model for the pool and pavilion in the book. His mother was the actual manager of the snack shop at the pool and loosely served as the model for Mrs. Bronson, the fictitious manager in the book.

I also want to thank friend and sometimes dance partner Jan Elinburg and friend Larry Harbin for reading unedited manuscripts of *Dance Steps* and advising me on the story. Both are baby boomers and Larry grew up going to the pool and pavilion like me.

Of course, I thank Tye Harris Joel for her expert editing and patience with her grammatically challenged father.

Author's Biography

Don Harris is a native North Carolinian and a graduate of Western Carolina University with a degree in creative writing. He lives in Asheville, NC. After a successful career in educational and non-profit fundraising and marketing, Don reconnected with his fiction writing passion. Since then he has published five novels and one children's book. They are: "A Dying Flame (out of print), "Lords of The Forest" (out of print), "Grandpa's Fish" (available through Amazon and W&B Publishers), "Family Cemetery" (available through Amazon and W&B Publishers), "Classmates" (available through Amazon and W&B Publishers), and "Mama's Quilt and Blizzard the White River Otter" (available through Warren Publishing).

Made in the USA
Columbia, SC
08 March 2023